The One That (Almost) Got Away

A Palm Harbor Novel

Kimberley O'Malley

This is a work of fiction. All names, characters, places, and events are a product of the author's very vivid imagination. Any resemblance to actual persons, events, or places is purely coincidental.

Published by Carolina Blue Publishing, LLC

ISBN: 978-1-946682-22-2

For all of us living in this crazy time, putting one foot in front of the other, daring to plan for a future and wondering what the new normal will be. And for the Class of 2020. Especially my beautiful daughter,
Jordan Anastasia Miller.

"Congratulations!
Today is your day.
You're off to Great Places!
You're off and away!"
— Dr. Seuss

Other Books by Kimberley O'Malley

Contemporary Romance- Windsor Falls Series

Coming Home

Taking Chances

Second Chances

Saving Quinn

Finding Kat

Coming Back

Cozy Mystery-Addie Foster Series

Death Comes in Threes

Dyeing for Change

Murder by Numbers

Angel of Death

Chapter One

"That which does not kill us, makes us stronger."
-Friedrich Nietzsche

Drumming her fingers on the steering wheel, Jamie Lawler bounced along in time with the music. While she loved the upbeat tempo of the song, there wasn't any point in lying to herself. Time to leave the car. She turned off the ignition and sized up the building in front of her. Nothing scary about the red brick nor the shiny glass doors. Jamie grabbed her phone and water bottle and left her car before whatever courage she'd mustered fled. The chill of the early March morning put some pep in her step.

Jamie strode into the gym, smile on her face. *Fake it 'til you make it.* She'd never been an athlete, unlike some of her friends. Unlike *him.* Heck, she wasn't even somewhat athletic. Jamie grimaced as she tripped over the metal strip in the doorway. Nope, not even remotely graceful. She'd always been an introvert, nose buried in a book while the real word melted away around her. Books allowed her to roam the planet, seeking adventures in far-flung locales. Books never broke her heart. Although many had made her cry. But those were good cries. Cathartic ones. Not like the endless tears she'd wasted over *him*.

She shook her head to clear such thoughts and approached the bank of treadmills. Standing before one, she looked it over, wondering if it would kill her. Bad enough she lacked in any type of physical grace, but the extra pounds she carried on her already curvy body didn't help the cause. Thus, the gym. New year, new ideas. Twenty-twenty would be a new beginning. Over a few too many champagne cocktails with her best friend, Sam, on New Year's Eve, Jamie had broken her ban on resolutions and vowed to change a few things about her life. She awoke the next day on Sam's couch with a headache she was sure meant an aneurysm. When she didn't die from it, ten ounces of orange juice and a few over-the-counter painkillers later, her idea to change the way she lived started to take form. There would be healthier eating habits. And the gym membership she'd signed up for online under the influence the night before.

But that had been two months ago. Already, she'd fallen behind in her grand scheme to remake herself and show Chad a thing or two. Jamie glanced around the chilly room. She spied people here and there, a few using various machines, a couple guys lifting weights in the back corner. Busy but everyone seemed preoccupied with their own routines. No one to witness her upcoming humiliation. Coming in at a not-quite-human hour helped. The place was probably packed at other times. She stepped up onto the closest treadmill and stared at the control panel. It might as well be a cockpit. All she wanted to do was walk, slowly, maybe work up to a fast walk. She wasn't ready for anything tougher.

Jamie reached out, still unsure, and played with the settings. The beast roared to life, rolling at an alarming speed, and taking her with it. She grabbed the siderails, holding on for dear life as a few choice words ripped from her mouth. She let go with one hand long enough to stab at the speed, lowering it to an acceptable number. One that might not kill her.

Congratulating herself for not falling off, or dying, she slid earbuds in and cranked up her 'happy list.' She'd downloaded high-energy songs to motivate her the night before. She might not have made it here the first week of January, but she was here now. Today was a new day. Today was day one of her 'show Chad what he'd missed' plan. So what if she had gotten up way earlier than she cared to? She blew out a heavy breath. She hoped Chad would notice.

Thoughts of her long-ago crush spurred her determination. That and the save the date card announcing her fifteenth high school reunion now living on her fridge. Front and center, held in place by a colorful parrot magnet from her trip to Hawaii last summer with Sam. The dreaded invite arrived in her mail before Christmas and sat unopened on her kitchen counter for a few days until curiosity got the better of her. She'd ripped it open, looked at the May date and decided on the spot to attend. She'd skipped the previous ones. Always too busy with work, or so she told herself. Although working for an accounting firm kept her busy, she could have arranged her schedule around the past reunions. But she'd chosen not to. Until now. And she wasn't sure why, other than a faint curiosity to see people she'd spent four long years with. And to see Chad, who had fueled her teenage dreams of love and everything that came along with them. Or hadn't in her case.

She upped the speed and incline on the machine and grabbed the handles again to keep from falling off. If only she wasn't the clumsiest person on the planet. She walked as quickly as she could manage, desperate to not trip over her own feet. She pictured Chad, all blond-haired and blue-eyed and over six feet tall. At least that's how he always looked in her mind. And her dreams. She hadn't actually seen him in over fifteen years. Not since she'd left her small Pennsylvania hometown and never looked back.

Memories of her childhood, including the painfully awkward teenage years, raced through her head like a video she couldn't stop. Never going to prom. Always watching Chad from afar, hoping for a day she'd gather the courage to approach him. Talk to him. At least about something other than the math she'd tutored him in for four years. But the day had never materialized. Until now. Now, she had a second chance.

Spurred on by thoughts of him, she upped the speed again, breaking into a fast walk on the treadmill. This time, she was going to her high school reunion. In past years, she'd always recycled the invitations immediately, not even opening them. Not this time. This time, she was going. And, damn it, she was going to walk in there looking good. She grimaced as she caught sight of herself in the floor-to-ceiling mirrors. Or at least better than she looked at the moment. She had just under nine weeks. Sixty-three days, give or take. Fifteen hundred hours or so. Math had always been her thing.

Less than nine weeks to shed some weight and tone up seemed reasonable to her. She wouldn't ever be another Angelina Jolie. Or a Mandy Simpkins, eternal love of Chad. At least back in high school. But turning a head or two would be nice. Jamie looked into the mirror, studying the rows of machines behind her. She needed to add something to her workout. Something involving those evil-looking machines. She'd read it somewhere. Of course, she had. That's what she did.

Soon after her impulsive joining of the gym, an email had

arrived, offering a free, introductory offer for a private personal training session. She'd refused, of course. There was no way she could learn how to work the other machines while some buff guy named Chuck hovered over her, secretly judging her. Or worse, some Barbie type with perfect skin and a waist the size of Jamie's pinky. Nope, she'd figure this out herself. At least that's what she told herself each time she thought about finally getting to the gym. So far, she'd managed the treadmill, and it hadn't killed her. At least not yet. Getting out of bed tomorrow morning might prove difficult.

The thirty-minute timer she'd set dinged on the machine as the treadmill slowed for her 'cool down' phase. She slowed her pace and mentally pumped a fist in the air. She'd survived the treadmill. Maybe she'd try something different. She glanced at her phone. Plenty of time before she needed to drive home and shower for work. Maybe, just maybe.

Knowing she'd talk herself out of it, Jamie hit stop on the machine. After wiping it down and using hand sanitizer, she gathered her courage and approached a row of machines. Surely one of them was right for a beginner like her. She walked slowly, eyeing each. "Now, which one of you will cause me the least amount of pain. Or damage," she mused aloud.

"They don't bite, you know," drawled a man's voice from behind her.

Jamie yelped, clutching her chest as she whirled in his direction. "I didn't think anyone could hear me." Her heart slammed in her chest and not only from fear. The man looked like sex on a stick.

"I just walked in and saw you there, talking to them. They're not great conversationalists." He nodded his head toward the silent machines. "Thought I'd help." He didn't bother to conceal his smile, causing a set of adorable dimples to appear. He stuck out a hand. "I'm Griff, well Griffin, but folks call me Griff."

She wiped one sweaty hand on her yoga pants before taking his. "Jamie. Nice to meet you. And I know they don't bite. I'm trying to figure out which one will hurt the least." She pulled her hand from his grasp, realizing she'd waited a bit long to do so and marveled at the immediate sense of loss.

A deep, male chuckle erupted from him. Griff cocked his dark head as if trying to figure her out. "Why will any of them hurt you?"

Jamie averted her gaze, cursing her loose tongue and the heat creeping into her cheeks. She pushed thoughts of his delicious laugh to the shadowy recess of her overheated brain. "Uh, I tend to not be the most graceful person in the room." She waved a hand in the direction of the machines. "And this seems like asking for trouble. But the treadmill isn't enough."

"You're right. Are you new? I've never seen you in here before."

She glanced around the gym. He seemed nice enough. Didn't look like a serial killer. But then neither did Ted Bundy. "I am. This is my first day, in case you couldn't tell."

"You know the gym offers a free intro lesson to learn the machines. Maybe you should consider it."

Jamie shook her head, ponytail flying. "I turned it down. The last thing I need is some guy who lives in a gym trying to help me." She glanced at him quickly, realizing she may have insulted him. "I mean nothing personal, but I couldn't handle some musclebound guy named Bruno laughing at me. No thanks. I need to get going. Can't be late for work." She started to turn away from him.

"I could help you. Maybe give you a few pointers."

She glanced at him over her shoulder.

"If you wanted," he added.

Griff smiled, but she didn't get the feeling he was laughing at her. Or worse, judging her. Indecision warred within her. Pride won out. She shook her head.

"Thanks, but I'm a lost cause. And I really have to get to work." Small lie. She had plenty of time. But he didn't need to know. She waved and bolted for the exit.

Jamie didn't stop until she stood before her car.

"Uh, Jamie," Griff called, jogging from the front door to stand beside her.

Under the parking lot lights, shades of copper and red shown in his dark hair. *Don't think about that!* Turning to him, Jamie mustered up a small smile. "I know you want to help me. And I really do appreciate it." One thing she loved about her adopted hometown, hundreds of miles south of where she grew up, was the lovely manners most folks seemed to have ingrained in them.

He grinned, those cute dimples once again popping out and turning her brain to mush. Not to mention her knees. One hand extended toward her, a familiar looking key chain dangling from his fingers. "I think you forgot something."

She didn't say anything at first, giving the earth time to open up and swallow her whole. When that didn't happen, darn Mother Earth, she stammered a thank you and turned back to her car. A quick escape would be the next best thing.

But before she could flee, Griff offered, "I'm here most mornings. Think about it. I'd be happy to help you."

Jamie nodded and escaped into the relative safety of her car. At least there, she wouldn't be able to make a fool of herself. And do something crazy like agree to this. She started the engine and headed home, passing a few fast food places and a local favorite, A Hole in One Donuts. At least *her* favorite.

Everyone was a bit golf crazy around here. But if she was serious about change, and impressing Chad, then donuts were off the menu. The corners of her mouth dipped at the thought, but she applauded herself for the conviction. There was a protein shake in her immediate future.

Chapter Two

"Hell isn't merely paved with good intentions; it's walled and roofed with them."

-Aldous Huxley

Griff stood still, watching until her car pulled out of sight. He wondered if Jamie would return tomorrow. January tended to bring a flood of people with good intentions, courtesy of their resolutions. Most stayed the course, but only for a few weeks or so, never to be seen again. He hoped she wasn't one of those. She'd made him laugh, something there was too little of in his life. Maybe since she waited until March to join, Jamie would be one of those who meant it and stuck around. Shaking his head at such foolishness, he turned and walked back into Getting It Done, the gym he'd opened eighteen months ago with his life-long friend, Jack Whittaker.

The dream had taken longer than either man liked. They'd both worked for years, he serving in the military and Jack working as a personal trainer, scraping together enough money to finally open it. The bank might own it, and would for years to come, but Getting It Done was theirs.

He held the door for a petite, blonde woman, gesturing for

her to proceed him. He ensured his smile was the perfect mix of courtesy and attention, nothing to encourage her.

She threw him her practiced, megawatt smile, adding in a view of her perfectly sculpted cleavage. Damn, he must have smiled too much.

"Morning, sugar," Darla cooed, dragging one perfectly-manicured, blood-red nail down his arm.

No more smiling! Griff made his face as bland as possible, not wanting to give the over-dyed, overdone blonde even a hint of encouragement. "Morning, Darla. Here a bit early for Jack's class, aren't you?" And immediately wanted to kick himself. He'd given the appearance he knew her schedule.

"You know I'd rather sweat, or whatever, with you, honey. If only you didn't insist on teaching classes for those, uh, amateurs."

Her tone alone was enough to raise his blood pressure. But her intimation almost blew his good intentions out of the water. Those 'amateurs' she'd referred to were his favorite members; a lively group of seventy and above women and men who took his low-impact classes in an effort to ward off arthritis and other ailments of aging. Keeping his face and tone neutral, Griff turned to her.

"At Getting It Done, we include everyone. We're not one of those gyms catering only to the more advanced folks. Have a great workout, Darla."

He strode ahead, making a beeline for his office, tucked away in the back corner. Their office, really, as he and Jack had decided to share one rather than sacrifice valuable real estate for two. Once safely on the other side of the closed door, he tossed his keys on the desk and dropped into the faux leather desk chair. And tried to not scream. That woman, that type of woman really, made his blood boil. And not in the way intended.

Their shared vision for Getting It Done was a place for everyone to work out, get healthier. He abhorred the gyms which promoted a meat market attitude, or worse yet, steroid usage. Their clientele, for the most part, consisted of people wanting a safe and non-judgmental environment to work out in. To get or stay healthy in. Of course, there would always be the Darlas of the world. She probably wasn't a bad person, but she wasn't their target audience either. And her crack about his geriatric clients didn't endear her to him.

He leaned back in the chair and closed his eyes for a moment. An image of Jamie popped into his mind. She was exactly the kind of person he'd had in mind. She had seemed more than a little unsure of herself, standing there staring at the machines. A small smile curled his lips. Poor woman had no idea he'd come up behind her when she spoke to the machines. The blush creeping across her cheeks had intrigued him. He didn't know many women who blushed. Her small, curvy body appealed to him on another level. Not that he'd go there. Mixing business with pleasure was a no-no.

His eyes popped open at the sound of the door opening. His partner and friend, Jack, strode into the room, usual evil grin on his face.

"What did you do to ruffle Darla's feathers so early this morning?"

Griff groaned, dropping his head into his hands. "Oh, no. What did she say to you?" Jack's chuckle brought up Griff's head. "What?"

"Well, there might have been something about your attitude. To be honest, I didn't really listen. Darla is a drama queen with a capital D." He took a drink of his smoothie. "Why? What did you do this time? Other than ignoring her rather blatant come on?"

"She made a crack about my geris. I didn't appreciate it."

Jack's long, low whistle made up his reply.

"You know how I feel about it."

"I do indeed. I also know how she feels about you," he smirked.

"Funny," Griff muttered. "Did she complain about my behavior? I tried to be as neutral as possible, even when I wanted to thump her for her nasty attitude."

Jack smothered a laugh. "She did mention you could be a bit more, uh, 'friendly' I believe is the word she used. But then again, I think she enjoys the challenge."

"Never going to happen. If I even so much as smiled too much in her direction, I'd have to beat her off with a stick. No thanks. I will continue to be professional, treat her like any other member. But that's all."

"And that's all I would ever ask of you. I knew, before she ever approached me with her complaint per se, you'd never do anything to place our business in any jeopardy. After all, we have too much riding on this."

"Exactly!" Griff shrugged his shoulders, rolling his head on his neck to loosen some of the tightness the run in with Darla had caused.

"How was your workout this morning?"

The thought of earlier, and his brief interlude with Jamie, brought a genuine smile to his face.

Jack stared at him. "Must have been a great one."

"Oh, I didn't get mine in yet. I got distracted." He tried for a neutral tone, hoping to keep Jack from pursuing it."

"Okay, what aren't you telling me?" One of Jack's raven black brows met his hairline.

So much for that thought! He really should have known

better. "Nothing," he protested. "I had just warmed up when I stopped to help a new client. Or at least I tried to."

"And?"

"And nothing. Jamie, the new client, declined my help before rabbiting out the door." He filled in the rest, running into Darla in the parking lot and immediately retreating to their office.

"Jamie, huh? Tell me everything."

"I just did, Jack. She's a new client, first-timer by the looks of it. I came upon her talking to the machines." He stopped at the look of shock on Jack's very expressive face. "Not in the bad, she should be on medications way. I think she was trying to figure out how to use the machines. Or rather, which one to use."

"Ah, a virgin, then?" Jack's grin added layers to his choice of words.

"Yes, she had a look, sort of a deer in the headlights one. She looked like she thought the machines might reach out and bite her." He laughed. "In fact, she actually said it out loud."

"Think she'll come back?'

Griff shrugged, not wanting to give away his hope. "We'll see." Then he brought up some equipment they'd been discussing buying for the gym, successfully distracting Jack from this train of thought as he'd hoped. The last thing he needed was his best friend knowing how intriguing he'd found her.

*****

Across town, Jamie sat in her office, email forgotten as she glanced out the windows. Having an office facing the beach might be a lovely perk, but on days like this it sure made concentrating more difficult. *Not that she needed another reason to lose focus.* Thoughts of the ridiculously hot guy in the gym this morning brought a bit of heat to her face. She reached for her cold water bottle, yet another resolution, and swiped it across her heated cheeks before taking a sip.

She purposefully swiveled away from the gorgeous late morning scene, dragging her eyes back to this morning's email from her boss. Charles, who'd founded Smith & Smith Accounting with his brother, Lawrence, more than thirty years ago had sent a company-wide missive asking for creative ideas from his employees to "breathe some life into the place."

Jamie made a face at the screen and minimized her email. Rake in more money is what he really meant. As if they didn't have enough already. Lawrence, she liked and admired. The older man had taken her under his wing when she started her internship here so many years ago. He'd been the one to offer her a full-time position after her college graduation. Charles, not so much. She avoided him like the plague. Avoidance was something she excelled at.

She'd taken the internship based more on its location than the company itself. Jamie and her family had never seen eye to eye on, well, anything. Leaving Pennsylvania, not to mention everything and everyone she knew in the world, was the first big step in coming out of her shell. She grinned, still having trouble believing she'd gathered the nerve to take such a leap. Not to mention accepting the full-time position Lawrence had offered at the end of her internship. She still shuddered at the memory of packing all of her belongings into her car and driving away from everything she'd ever known.

But she'd done it. And never looked back.

"Earth to Jamie," called Sam from the doorway to her office.

"Oh, I didn't see you there."

"Obviously," drawled the vivacious Southern Belle who happened to be her best friend in the world. "What's got you so focused?"

"Nothing really. Musing about how I ended up here."

Sam entered the office, closing the door behind her. "I thought maybe you were reading the dragon's latest email." She shook her head, long, riotous red curls tossing back and forth, and slid into a chair in front of Jamie's desk. "Like he doesn't already have enough money!"

"Shush," corrected Jamie. She lowered her voice to a whisper. "Don't call him that here in the office." She glanced around, not entirely sure there weren't hidden cameras. Or at least microphones.

"Oh, honey, the dragon knows how we all feel about him. I'm also quite sure he knows we call him the dragon. Bet he likes it."

She laughed at her own joke while Jamie stared at her.

"How do you do it? How do you go through life so fearlessly?"

"What's he going to do, fire me? Let him. I'm good at what I do. I could find another job like that." She snapped her fingers, bright red nails flashing in the light. "And so are you."

"True, we are."

"Exactly! The only difference between us is I believe it, and you don't. Which never ceases to amaze me."

"Not to mention about six inches and more pounds than I care to admit." She grabbed her water, even though she craved a caramel latte. What she didn't need were the billions of calories that came along with it.

Sam shook her head. "What you need is a new attitude, girl. You are beautiful. And smart. And funny. When you forget to hide behind your big brain."

"As if you're slacking in the brain department," Jamie protested, trying so hard to not squirm under the weight of the compliments. Sam had always been her biggest cheerleader, ever since the day they met, right here at Smith & Smith.

"I know how smart I am. Only I don't use it as a shield to keep out the rest of humanity." She stuck out her tongue in typical Sam fashion. "Hey, I almost forgot to ask. Did you make it to the gym this morning?"

"I did," replied Jamie, waiting for the onslaught of questions.

She didn't have to wait long.

"Good girl! I knew you would, one of these days. How'd it go? Are you going again tomorrow? Maybe I'll join with you."

Jamie didn't answer right away, wondering how to politely decline. She loved Sam, but her friend was one of those naturally beautiful and graceful women. Next to her, Jamie always felt a bit, well, less.

"What?" Sam demanded. "What aren't you telling me? Was it awful? Did you hurt yourself?"

"No, nothing like that. There was a moment where I almost flew off the treadmill. Almost being the operative word." She glared at the suppressed laughter coming out of Sam.

"I'm not laughing," protested Sam, who then lost it completely, bent over laughing. A moment later, under a little better control, she tried again. "Okay, I might have been laughing."

"Might have been?" She handed Sam a tissue from her drawer. "Your mascara is running from all the not laughing you were doing."

Sam dabbed at her eyes, shoulders still quaking. "In my defense, that's quite the image you put in my head. I can just see you, clinging to the railings for dear life."

Jamie shrugged "True. Luckily, I left before the hot stranger could help me. Can you imagine how much worse it could have been?" She instantly realized her mistake.

Sam scooted to the edge of her chair. "Um, hot stranger? Do tell."

Chapter Three

"The best defense is a good offense."
-Mao Zedong

"His name is Griff, and he was ridiculously hot, like panty-melting hot, but I will never see him again, so it doesn't matter." There. Better to get it out in the open than to let Sam ferret out this information as she inevitably would. And then bang her over the head with it. "And it doesn't matter, because I cancelled my membership." She crossed her fingers under the desk against the small, white lie she told.

"No, you didn't, Jamie." She pointed a finger at her, shaking it. "Your eyes shift when you lie. Honestly, you're so terrible at it, I'm not sure why you try. Now, tell me more about this Griff."

"What more is there than panty-melting?"

"Please tell me you weren't wearing your dreaded yoga pants?" She paused the length of one heartbeat before pouncing. "You were! How many times do I have to tell you only wear those at home. Alone. With the curtains drawn. Better yet, toss them! Remember the show where they came in with a huge trash can and rifle through someone's closet?"

Jamie merely nodded, afraid to speak once Sam got on a roll.

"Good. Guess who I am in this scenario."

"Probably not the person getting their entire wardrobe trashed." Jamie opened her desk drawer out of habit, reaching for a Snickers that no longer lived there. She was a stress eater. But what woman wasn't? She grabbed the miniscule bag of almonds instead, ripping open the top and putting half the bag in her mouth.

"You're right, I am the one doing the trashing. By the way, that woman was fabulous! Loved her hair. Anyway, do you know why I am saying this to you?"

"Because you love me?"

"That's right! And because someday, I want to be Auntie Sam. And before you go telling me technically, we aren't sisters, you know we are."

"Are you done?"

"For now."

"Okay. First, of course my children, if I ever have any, would call you Auntie Sam. I expect the same."

Sam nodded while drinking from her water bottle.

"And second, I was not wearing yoga pants."

"Oh thank the star!" Then her eyes narrowed. "Do not tell me."

"Tell you what?" Jamie squeaked, ruining her air of innocence.

"No, Jamie, just no. Please tell me you were not wearing..." She threw a hand over her eyes, dramatic to the end. "Sweatpants!"

"In my defense, I went before dawn. To a gym."

"Not sure there's a defense for wearing sweatpants in public."

"I went to a gym to work out. Should I have worn Dior? Or maybe Marc Jacobs?"

"Do not use those names in vain," Sam quipped. "As if you've ever worn Dior."

Jamie glanced down at her perfectly acceptable shirt and pants then smoothed a hand on the scarf around her neck. "I'm wearing a well-known designer right now." She stopped just short of stating, 'So there' and sticking out her tongue. She and Sam were thick as thieves, but polar opposites when it came to fashion.

"Please. You're claiming Vera Bradley?'

Jamie sat a bit straighter, holding in a laugh. "I am indeed. Like the good Southern woman I am becoming."

"Saying 'y'all' doesn't make you a 'good Southern woman' by the way. Neither does wearing Vera Bradley. I hear they sell it north of the Mason Dixon as well," Sam smirked. "And you don't even like sweet tea!" Her gasp told Jamie everything she needed to know about how she felt about it.

"I don't drink any kind of tea, as you well know. And that stuff could put you in a diabetic coma."

"Hm, true, but don't think for a moment you've thrown me off the scent. Tell me more about Griff."

"Honestly, I didn't leave out anything. He witnessed me talking to myself."

"You didn't!"

"I did, but then again before any hour decent human beings are awake, so the gym wasn't packed. And I didn't actually talk to myself. I spoke to the row of machines."

Sam doubled over, howling. When she gathered herself, she wiped her eyes. "And somehow that's better?"

Jamie thought about it for a second. "At least he didn't run in the opposite direction."

"Tell me what he did do. And say. Word for word."

"Don't you have work to do?" A chime announced another incoming email. Jamie glanced down to see it was from her biggest client. March meant work had gone from busy to crazy for her.

Sam gave her a glare, the one she used to fend off guys hitting on her she wished weren't. Like men with comb overs. Or worse, man-buns. "Of course I have work. I'm an accountant, and it's March." She stood, smoothing out imaginary wrinkles in her dress. As if one would dare to appear. "You're not off the hook. Tacos and margaritas for dinner?"

Jamie groaned but agreed, watching Sam's retreating, and perfect, form. "Wonder how many hours on the treadmill that will cost me?" she mused to the empty office.

*****

The next morning, Jamie jumped out of bed right before her obscenely early alarm was about to blare. Then sank back down into the welcoming fluffiness of her down comforter when every muscle she owned, and many she had no prior knowledge of, protested. For a moment, she considered surrendering to her bed, after all it called to her. Instead, she hauled her butt up again and reached for some sweats. Sam could protest all she wanted, but March meant chilly temps at this hour. Even in South Carolina. And there was no way she was wearing tight leggings as Sam had pleaded over nachos. Her well-known love of Mexican food was one of the reasons she wouldn't be wearing skin-tight leggings to the gym. Maybe twenty-five pounds from now. Maybe not.

Stopping to pet Fiona, her old, mostly deaf, and blind cat,

she cooed a few words of love in her ear before hustling to the door. With one last glance at her ratty sweats and ancient Pink Floyd concert t-shirt, Jamie left the house before the persuasive calling of her bed won.

Fifteen minutes later, she pulled into a spot right in front of the door of Getting It Done. Yes, she should probably park further away for the cardio, but it was dark and chilly. She'd stay an extra minute on the treadmill. Gathering her earbuds and resolve, Jamie left the warm car and hurried to the door. Once inside, she noticed a pair of younger guys in the back corner. They seemed harmless enough, ignoring her entrance, and she made her way to the treadmill. Better to start within her comfort zone. If she actually had one.

Taking care to hold on with one hand, Jamie started the beast and programmed in a slow but slightly better than turtle pace of three miles per hour. You had to start somewhere. After a few minutes, she upped the speed to a more respectable, or less embarrassing, three point four, and kicked up the incline a bit as well. She hit her playlist and tried to lose herself in the rhythm of the machine.

Which worked great until a deep voice called 'good morning' from her right. Turning her head to acknowledge the intruder threw her off balance, making her lunge for the side rails.

"Sorry," came a less than sincere acknowledgment.

The accompanying laughter made her straighten her posture. Sure enough, there stood Griff, feet spread apart, each balanced on the side rails looking way too good for having rolled out of bed. He wore his hair short but just long enough to look mussed. She didn't allow herself to even think about how good he smelled, a mix of something woodsy and pure male scent.

And then she realized she was staring at him. "Morning," she muttered, turning her gaze from his. "If you could even call it that."

A low chuckle rumbled from him, making her grip the rails tighter to stop from flying off the back of the machine.

"Not much of a morning person, I take it."

She didn't dare look at him again. "When morning starts at a decent time, sure."

"Then why come in this early?"

"Less witnesses."

He didn't laugh this time. "Should I ask?"

Jamie blew out a breath and upped the speed on her treadmill while she thought about how to answer him. She opted for brutal honesty. "Look, you seem like a nice enough guy, all fit and whatever. Obviously, you know your way around a gym. I, on the other hand, do not. Nor do I possess even the slightest bit of grace or coordination. But, I'm here anyway. I'm here to get into a better shape and live a little healthier. I don't think it's too much to ask to do it without a lot of your type watching." She glanced his way, offering a small smile to cut the edge to her words and waited for the anger or hurt.

But Griff leaned in ever so slightly closer and grinned. "You think I'm fit?" he asked.

"That was your take-away message?"

"Yep."

She stared straight ahead, avoiding making eye contact. His eyes probably twinkled. Instead, she bumped up both the speed and incline, needing to concentrate on something, anything, other than the warm, male body only inches from her. Now at three point eight, faster than she had tried yet, she struggled to keep up, breaking into a light jog. Being only five-three didn't give her long enough legs, she grumbled to herself.

"You might want to pace yourself," Griff suggested from the neighboring machine.

"I'm fine," she bit out between gritted teeth. Jamie tried to not notice the graceful way he ran on the treadmill. Griff seemed to be one of those born with the ability to walk and not trip over nothing. Lucky him! She snuck a peek at his numbers. *Six!* Good Lord, she'd be dead on the floor at that pace.

Jamie concentrated on not dying. She wanted to take another peek at him but resisted. No use seeing the alarm on his face at her ragged breathing. Clearly, three point eight was a bit much. She stuck it out for another minute before dropping the speed to a more reasonable three. And tried to not die. Her breath came in gasps, searing her lungs as it did. Her poor heart galloped like that of a hummingbird, threatening to explode. She wouldn't think about the sweat dripping down her face and other places. Nothing she could do about it.

"I know you don't want advice, and I promise I'll shut up after this. You might want to think about building up your speed instead of pushing yourself too hard right away. That's how injuries happen."

Her mouth dropped open. How could he speak in full sentences while running? Was he a robot? Marathoner? "I'll try to remember," she sniped before instantly regretting it. "Sorry," she wheezed. "Dying apparently doesn't bring out my good side."

He waved a hand, as if to brush off her concern. "No worries."

Once she could breathe again, Jamie pushed up the speed a bit and concentrated on each step. Every muscle in her body hurt, but she couldn't stop the smile from spreading across her face. She was doing this. Two days in a row might not be a big deal to others, but it was two more than she had ever accomplished.

They continued on, side by side, in total silence unless she counted her labored breathing, for the rest of her thirty-one minutes. Jamie almost cried when the machine slowed to the cool down phase. She let her arms fall to her sides, no longer needing the death grip on the machine for balance and watched as the seconds ticked along. She checked out the rows of machines in the mirror, trying to decide which to start with.

"I'd pick something that targets your upper body, since you've already given your legs a workout today," advised Griff.

Great! Now he reads minds.

"Do you ever break a sweat?" she blurted out before covering her mouth with her hands. "Disregard that question, please," she mumbled from behind her hands.

He chuckled, apparently not in the least offended. "Of course I do. Once I get into my workout, there will be more sweat than you can imagine."

"Into your workout? You just ran for almost thirty minutes." Jamie tried hard to not imagine him covered in sweat. Both of them covered in sweat, together. She shook her head as the heat creeped into her face. As if…

"Because I am a gentleman, I won't ask what thoughts are racing through your mind to cause that kind of blush."

Did he just wink at her? Do not think about them sweaty together again. Oh, she'd done it again, deepening the heat in her face until she feared she might combust. "Oh, it's nothing. I'm overheated from the workout," she managed.

"I'd be happy to help you with that," he offered.

Chapter Four

"Kindness makes a fellow feel good, whether it's being given to him or by him."

-Frank A. Clark

Griff hopped down off the treadmill and made his way to the refrigerated case where they kept water and sports drinks for customer purchase. Grabbing two waters, he headed back. "Here you go," he said, holding out one bottle toward her. "Hydration is important."

Jamie took it from him with an odd expression on her face. She hesitated before twisting off the cap and downing almost half of it.

"Careful," he warned. "You don't want that coming back up."

She grimaced before replacing the lid. "How much do I owe you?"

Griff shook his head. "Don't worry about it. I know the owner." He pointed to the first row of machines. "Why don't I give you some tips to get you started?"

She chewed on her bottom lip, and he felt it all the way to his toes.

"I'm sure you have your own routine to get to. I'll figure something out."

She didn't yet know he owned the gym. For some reason, he let her go on thinking that. "It's no problem. I'll show you a couple for your arms and upper body then go do my thing." His thing was to always come in and do his own workout, showering in their private locker room before starting his day. Without waiting for an answer, he led the way to the corner, looking over his shoulder to ensure she followed.

Griff stopped at the pulley station. "The most important thing about working out is to do it correctly, including your position and how much weight you use. That way you drastically cut your chances of injury."

Jamie gulped. "Staying home on my couch also cuts my chance of injury." She eyed the machine as though it were a cobra, poised to strike. "There's no way I can do this without injury."

"Sure you can. There are seventy-year-old ladies in here every day using this." He tapped the machine. "You'll be fine." He tried not to wince at his words. He just compared her to a septuagenarian. *Great going!* "Uh, what I meant to say was…" but he stopped at her raised hand.

Giggles bubbled from her. "I take no offense, as I am sure there are many much older folks who do better in here than I do. So far today, I've managed thirty-one minutes on the treadmill without being tossed off the back of it."

He laughed along with her and chalked it up in her favor. A woman who didn't take herself all that seriously was a plus in his book. Not that she needed more points. Not that he was counting. Not that he would date a client.

"And thirty minutes on the treadmill, two days in a row mind you, is probably more than you did last week. Am I right?"

She ducked her head for a moment before making eye contact. Griff sucked in a breath. To call her eyes brown would be an understatement. They were the color of a fine whiskey with golden flecks in them. He could lose himself staring into those eyes. Which is why he pulled his gaze away. *Remember, she's a client.*

Jamie stood a little straighter, taller. "You're right. Last week my only exercise was lifting Fiona."

Griff tilted his head. "You lost me."

"Of course, because it's not like I bring my cat to the gym with me. Fiona is my rather old, almost blind, and mostly deaf cat. She's also very fluffy, which is a sweeter way of saying she's fat."

"Ah, that makes more sense. I was trying to picture you carrying around someone, maybe a co-worker."

"I don't think I can lift any of my coworkers, as they're all full-sized adults." She lifted one arm in a classic muscle pose. "See, not much there."

"We can change that. Or I mean you can change that. Although I don't advise going around lifting co-workers. That might invoke some sort of sexual harassment suit."

"Can't have that." Jamie eyed the machine. "I guess if you have a minute, you could show me how to not end up strangled in this thing."

"Of course." He moved to the back of it where the weights sat. "Since you've never used it before, I'd start with maybe twenty-five pounds. It doesn't sound like a lot, but you'll feel it." He adjusted the weight and then guided her to stand at the end of the bench. "Now take a seat here, facing the machine."

Jamie did as he asked, her expression letting him know she had her doubts. When she was seated, she glanced up at him.

"Great. Now keep your back straight and plant your feet." He waited until she did before reaching up for the bar, pulling it down toward them with one hand. "Now, grab the bar with both hands, keeping yours centered on the black grips. Griff pulled the bar lower until it was in her grasp. "Now, I'm going to let go. You'll be fine. I promise.

Jamie bit her lip. "I'm trusting you. If anything happens to me, you've just inherited one overweight cat."

"I've got you. I promise." He let go and waited until she seemed comfortable. "Okay?"

With her hands straight above her head gripping the cross bar, Jamie nodded. "Got it."

"Okay, you're doing great. Now, draw the bar down in front of you until it reaches your chest. Then hold it for a moment before letting it go back up again."

He watched as she pulled it down to her chest, trying hard to not actually look at her chest. He wanted to, but he also didn't want to be a perv.

"Look, I'm doing it," she cried.

He was about to congratulate her when she started back up. Way too quickly. She gave a strangled yelp as she lost her grip on the bar, and it crashed into the top.

"I might have forgotten to mention releasing in a slow, controlled manner," he offered. "Sorry about that."

"Tell me I'm not the first person to make that mistake. I don't even care if you lie to me." She started to stand, but he placed a hand on each shoulder.

"You're not the first, nor the last, and that's not a lie. You may have made the cutest sound doing it, though." He pulled the bar back down until she could grip it, encouraging her to try again.

"If by cute, you mean the sound of a turkey being strangled, sure." She slowly allowed the bar to drift upwards before pulling it down adjacent to her chest again.

"And you've heard a turkey being strangled? Where are you from that they regularly strangle turkeys? Surely not from around here. This is a turkey-strangling-free zone." He took a step back, watching as she performed several reps while they continued their inane conversation.

"I'm from Philadelphia. Well, I'm from a small town outside of Philadelphia you've never heard of but close enough. And, no, we don't strangle turkeys. And Benjamin Franklin never proposed a turkey for the national symbol. That's a myth."

"I never said he did," Griff joked.

"Sorry, I babble when I'm nervous."

Grigg let that one go, resisting asking why she was nervous. He watched her do a few more reps, counting in his head until she reached ten. "Remember to breathe. Philadelphia, huh? That explains the outrageous accent."

"You think I have an accent? That's funny coming from you."

He grabbed the bar, stopping her from doing an eleventh rep. "Congratulations, Jamie. You just completed your first set of ten. Now breathe normally for a moment and then do two more sets of ten, with a break in between."

She twisted her upper body to look up at him. "Wow! And I didn't kill myself. Or anyone else. I worry about that, you know."

Griff glanced around the mostly empty gym. "Good thing you come at an off hour then. Now, I want two more sets of ten. I'm going to go do my thing."

He moved down the row of machines picking a leg press.

After adjusting the weight and seat, he sat down and started, keeping his mind everywhere but where it wanted to stray.

*****

Jamie watched him go, pride with herself and a sense of loss warring in her mind. He'd stood so close behind her; she felt the heat radiating from his body. *Not why you're here, Jamie!* She stood to grab the crossbar and sat back down, starting her second set of reps. Pride won. Second set! She remembered to breathe as he had instructed. He was a great instructor, explaining things in a way she could understand and without making her feel stupid or clumsy. Not that she didn't always feel clumsy.

She finished her second set and sat back on the bench to rest for a moment. Turning her head to the side, she spied Griff a few machines over, pushing against a metal plate with his sneaker covered feet and gaped at the amount of weight he'd chosen. Although she couldn't make out the exact number from her perch, the sheer number of bars above the peg boggled her mind. Not to mention the insane definition in his calves. Not that she was looking.

After taking a swig of her stolen water, she had to remember to pay someone for that, Jamie completed her third set of ten. By the end, her arms felt like wet linguine, but her heart soared. She'd done it! She'd actually made it through three sets of ten reps on a machine that she wasn't even sure of the name.

Jaime stood, backing up away from the bench. Her foot caught on the base, and she started to stumble backwards, arms pinwheeling like a cartoon character. She would surely have landed in a pile of humiliation if a set of strong arms didn't reach out in the nick of time.

"Whoa now, I've got you."

Of course it had to be him. Her skin tingled everywhere they touched. She tamped down the feeling, concentrating on getting back on her feet and pulling down her shirt that had ridden up, revealing way too much blinding white skin. "Sorry," she mumbled as she turned away from him.

"I'm not. At least I'm not sorry I was here to break your fall. Are you okay? Hurt anything?"

"Only my pride. Nothing a pint of ice cream can't fix. I have to go." She walked away, head down, determined to not trip over anything this time. Go home. Get a shower. Go to work. Work made sense. The endless numbers made sense. Being here, trying to be something she wasn't did not. "Thank you," she all but yelled over her shoulder before leaving the building.

She reached her car, sanctuary really, and paused to take a breath. Then the sound of the door opening shattered her relief.

"This is becoming a thing, me chasing you out into the parking lot." He stopped a few feet away as though afraid to come closer. Her fault. "I wanted to make sure you're okay."

Jamie looked up at him, grateful for the shadowy light. Between her overheated cheeks and wild hairs escaping her ponytail, she must really look a fright. "I'm sorry for being rude back there."

"You were rude? To me? Must have missed it." He took a step closer and cocked his head. "Tell me what's really wrong," he asked in a gentle voice.

A harsh laugh escaped her. "Where would I start? I'm as graceful as a herd of hippos. Seriously, I trip over nothing on a regular basis. I'm awkward. And, I'm fat. What else would you like to hear?"

"Not everyone can be a ballerina. Or an athlete. Most people are just themselves, with good and bad days. I think you're funny. In a good way. And you're certainly not fat."

"Okay, let's say I'm too short for my weight. It's still the same bottom line or number on the scale. And numbers don't lie. They're all I can believe in."

He took another big step closer until he stood within reach. Then Griff placed a finger under her chin, lifting it, until her gaze met his. "Is that why you joined? To lose weight?"

"Yes. Isn't that why everyone joins a gym?" She put everything she had into not squirming and to holding eye contact.

"No. People have many reasons. Losing weight is up there but not the only reason. Tell me. What else are you hoping to get out of this?"

Jamie stared at him a second, seeing nothing but sincerity in his green eyes. She huffed out a quick breath. "There's this guy. I know it's stupid since the last time I saw him was fifteen years ago."

She blurted out the whole sad story of joining the gym to impress him at the reunion. For a moment, just the quick passing of a heartbeat, she swore something dimmed in his eyes. But the flash of whatever it might have been passed.

"Chad, huh? All right. I can work with that. See you tomorrow. Same time, same place." Without another word, Griff turned away and disappeared back into the gym.

Jamie stood there for a moment, shivering as the chilly early morning breeze met her sweaty skin. She wasn't sure what had just happened, but she couldn't wait to find out.

Chapter Five

"Dating is a numbers game. What we try to promise is good first dates."

-Sam Yagan

"Well, Fiona, what do you think?"

The gorgeous tuxedo feline in question blinked and rolled over to lick her lady parts.

Great! Now she was on her way to being the crazy cat lady. She might only have one at the moment, but surely more were on her way if she was sitting here, alone, talking to her cat as though expecting a response.

Instead of telling Sam about her encounter with Griff at work today, like a normal woman would do, she chose to tell Fiona. Sam would ask too many questions. Questions Jamie lacked an answer for nor had any desire to delve beneath the surface to find. Fiona asked none.

And now Sam was on one of her many dates. One of her many first dates. Inevitably, the guy in question was either too tall or too short, too quiet or she couldn't get in a word edgewise. Sam had 'high standards' as she liked to say. But then, when you were gorgeous, witty, and intelligent, Jamie guessed you could set your standards as high as you wanted.

In her defense, Sam had gone on some strange dates. One man, in his thirties, still lived with his mom and had her sit a few tables away during dinner to get her opinion of Sam. Then there was the guy who had Googled her and told her, on their first date, why they were meant to be together forever. Based on their respective astrological signs. Jamie had laughed herself silly over that one.

But at least her best friend had bad dates to laugh over. Jamie lacked these things because she never dated. Okay, rarely dated. The last guy had tried to guess her pants size and offered to take her shopping where he took his grandmother. *Grandmother!*

And while Sam might have unrealistic standards, Jamie, on the other hand, only wished for a guy she could talk with. Someone who made her laugh. Someone who 'got her.' Was that asking too much? Someone like…no. She was absolutely not going to say someone like Griff. But she said the words out loud, and they felt right. He was funny and kind. He didn't judge her or make fun of her feeble attempts at the gym.

He even followed her outside this morning to make sure she was okay. Not something every guy would do. And he did so after her rude attitude. Griff had earned major brownie points for that. Not that she kept score.

She grabbed a water bottle, her millionth in the day in an effort to drink less soda and opened her work laptop. It might not be April fifteenth yet, but things were ramping up. Soon she'd be spending upwards of eighty-plus hours per week in the mad rush to finish on time. She dreaded this time of the year but knew what to expect. That's why she took a long, extended vacation in May or June. Or she usually did. This year, she was headed back to Pennsylvania. Maybe she'd go somewhere after being there for a bit. She kept visits to her family brief.

A few hours later, her cell phone buzzed, announcing an incoming text. Jamie took a sip of water before checking the message. Good thing she had swallowed first.

"Another one bites the dust."

She picked up the phone, dashing off a quick reply. Then hit accept when it rang instantly.

"How bad could it have been?" she asked and settled back, waiting for the drama. She loved Sam, but her friend tended to dramatize her dating stories for 'added flavor' as she put it.

"No need for embellishment this time, I'm afraid. Are you sitting down?"

"I'm ready, not even sipping my water. Go ahead."

"You might rethink your beverage choice. In fact, I'm walking into my house now and considering having a glass or four of wine." A huge sigh sounded across the distance. "I'll start with the fact that he was late. And you know how we feel about that."

Jamie nodded even though Sam couldn't see her. "Agreed. How late?"

"Thirty minutes!"

"Not punishable by death but not a point in his favor either," Jamie replied.

"Funny. If only that was his worst fault. Then he ordered for me, without even asking first. Can you imagine? And as if that weren't bad enough, he did so in terrible Italian. I could have done better."

Giggles bubbled up and out of Jamie. "No! He didn't! What a pompous ass!"

"Yep! The poor waiter winced with every mispronounced word. I'm afraid his face might be stuck like that." The sound of liquid pouring confirmed Sam's wine declaration. "So far, we have late and pretentious. Did I mention narcissistic? There was a mirror hung next to our table, and the jerk preened all night, turning this way and that to catch a glimpse of himself." Another sigh followed by the sound of wine being swallowed.

"Ouch! And you wonder why I don't date? I don't have to. You're going through all the losers for me."

"Oh, I'm not done."

"Oh boy. My turn for a drink."

"Before I'd even taken two bites, he hinted the evening would end in sex. Or at least in 'his happiness.'"

The giggles swelled to outright laughter. "Shut the front door." Tears rolled down Jamie's face as she fought for control. "You're making that up."

"I wish. I'm not that creative."

"What did he say, exactly, to make you think that?"

"He said, and I quote, 'Your place or mine' with a leering smirk on his too handsome face. You know I don't care for pretty boys." More sounds of swallowing wine followed. "The man used more hair product than me."

"He didn't! And I know."

"He did! And when I declined in so many words, he told me I could at least 'end the night on a happy note for him.' Can you believe? I was pissed; I didn't finish my dinner. And now I'm hungry!"

Indignation had raised Sam's voice to a pitch dogs could probably hear for miles.

"Your story was funny until then. What a pig! Does he kiss his momma with that mouth?"

"Don't know, don't care. But he won't be kissing me with it." The sound of another gulp of wine sounded in her ear. "But I saved the best for last."

"What could be worse?"

"He stuck me with the bill!"

"No!"

"Yes! He walked out once he heard there wouldn't be 'dessert.'"

"He might have just leaped over mommy issues guy for worst date ever."

"You think?"

"I do. I'm sorry, Sam."

"Yeah, me, too. I don't understand, Jamie. I'm hot with a brain and well-developed sense of humor. What's wrong with me?"

"That's the wrong question. You should be asking what's wrong with *them*."

"And that's why, along with a laundry list of other reasons, you're my very best friend in the world."

"Ditto. And Sam, do me a favor."

"Anything, honey."

"Remember this bozo next time you ask me why I'm not dating."

"Fair enough. You get a two-week moratorium on me grilling you."

"Whew! Thanks!" she replied, tongue firmly in cheek.

"But that doesn't include the cutie from the gym. Nice try."

Jamie grimaced and sighed. "You mean Griff?"

"Is there another cutie at the gym I don't know about?"

"Good point. I'll consider myself warned. Why don't I pick you up? I haven't had dinner yet."

"I'll be ready when you get here."

Jamie disconnected before her friend could press the matter. She'd gotten away with not mentioning today's incident which ended with her in his arms, even briefly, because the dragon had insisted on a two-hour 'planning meeting' which really meant badgering senior staff into coming up with more money-making ideas. That put them all even further behind than they already found themselves. But Sam wouldn't be put off forever.

*****

Across Palm Harbor, Griff and Jack snagged a corner high top at Dusty's, their favorite bar. Jack went off to grab them two IPAs, leaving Griff to sit and think about his encounter with Jamie this morning. Not that he'd been thinking about much else since. The short brunette took up way too much of his day. There was something about her. She was different from a lot of women who belonged to their gym. She wasn't there to meet a man. She wasn't spending her time showing off a bare midriff. What he'd seen, or rather felt, was lightly rounded. A real woman's shape.

He had no idea how long Jack stood there, waving one icy bottle in front of his face before he noticed him. "Oh, sorry. Lost in thought I guess." He accepted the cold beer. "Thanks. Next round on me."

"Let me guess, you were thinking of mystery woman again."

"She has a name."

"You *were* thinking of Jamie again. I knew it."

"How do you know I wasn't thinking about the business or the Braves' chances this year? Or even the meaning of life?" He took a sip of the cold brew while he waited for the inevitable scoffing.

"Because, at the risk of sounding like a girl, you had a

dreamy, far-off look on your face. That only means one thing: a woman. And the Braves will do what they'll do. No use worrying if they'll go far again only to blow it in the post season. Who gives up ten runs in the first inning? And as for life, you're way too practical to worry about crap like that. That leaves Jamie, or Mystery Woman, as I like to call her. Tell me. You know you want to."

"Why are we friends again? You're a pain in the ass."

Instead of being insulted, Jack threw back his head and roared. Then he took a swig of his beer. "We've been friends since the start of school, as you know. And now we're business partners, so you're stuck with me."

Griff let out a fake sigh. "You're right." And he wouldn't have it any other way. The two were closer than brothers could ever be. And because of that, Jack always seemed to know what Griff was thinking. Like now. Which annoyed him. His feelings, or whatever they were, for Jamie were too new to dissect. Hell, he didn't even know what he thought about her.

"As always," Jack cackled, before signaling a passing waitress.

Stella, one of their favorites for her sass and other attributes, slid to a stop at their table. "Evening, gentlemen, and I use the term loosely. What can I get you?" She kicked one hip out to the side, drawing their attention to her tight jeans, as she probably planned. "Let me guess. An order of wings, Crazy Spicy for Jack and mozzarella sticks for the guy with the hang dog look on his face."

"See, she noticed it, too," Jack chortled, way too happily at his best friend's expense.

Griff straightened and plastered a fake smile on his face. "I do not have a hang dog look, whatever that might be."

Stella laughed, "Now you're trying too hard. Be right

back." She walked away, tossing, "If it's a woman, I'd be glad to make you forget her," over her slim shoulder.

"Now there's an idea," Jack agreed, watching the waitress's curvy hips sway across the room.

"You know Stella is kidding. It's all part of the sexy banter she keeps up with the regulars. Besides," he tossed his head in the direction of the bar owner, Dusty, a man towering close to seven feet tall and tipping the scales at three hundred, "Dusty would chew me up and spit me out."

The words still hung in the air when they turned to watch Dusty track Stella's progress across the bar. The perky waitress picked up what looked like a pitcher of his world-famous margaritas before heading back into the crowd.

"True," Jack decided. "Mountain Man would wipe the floors with you. And me just for being your friend." He pointed a finger at Griff while taking another sip of his beer. "I'm still waiting to hear about Jamie."

"There's nothing to tell."

Jack crossed his arms and raised one brow.

"Fine, there is something to tell. But there shouldn't be."

"Because she's married? Or lacks a sense of humor? I know how important that one is to you."

"She's not married. And then there's the guy she's going to see for the first time in fifteen years this May. Probably not married then." Griff took a long pull of his beer. "She's also ridiculously funny. Without even trying."

"Single and funny? Great! Oh, I get it, she's a client, and you're above all that."

"*We're* above all that. Remember when we agreed to it before the ink dried on the lease?"

"Yes, Dad, I remember. And I agree, in theory…"

"You either agree or you don't. There's no 'in theory.'"

"There is if you're sitting in a crowded bar filled with attractive women mooning over someone from the gym."

"Agreed," smirked Stella before setting their appetizers in front of them. She glanced around the rapidly filling room. "If no one here's catching your eye, you've got it bad. Another round, gentlemen?"

"You're a goddess, Stella, and yes. Oh, and put it on his tab. The round that is."

"Got it, Jack. Back in a flash." She winked and turned toward the bar.

"Now, where were we? Oh right, you were telling me why you can't date a client." He rested his chin on his hand. "I'm all ears."

Sensing defeat, Griff took another drink and started. "Okay, here's the thing. She's sweet and easy to talk to, very funny without even trying. Adorable in her clumsiness and self-consciousness. Jamie isn't like the other women, or a lot of them, who come to Getting it Done. She's there to better herself, but she has no idea how sexy she already is." He cleared his throat. "She makes me laugh."

"Ah, she's the antithesis of Sheila. Good for Jamie."

"This has nothing to do with Sheila." He shuddered even saying her name. His ex-girlfriend didn't bear remembering.

"Good. Because that woman messed with your mind before leaving town with what's his face."

"You know his name. Dan. You can say it. She left for greener pastures with Dan." Dan, their former friend, was one of their college roommates. He'd come from an old-monied Charleston family, which translated into a better bet in Sheila's eyes, much better than a struggling new business owner.

"He deserves her. Wonder what Mommy Dearest thinks of her about to be daughter-in-law."

The One That (Almost) Got Away

"They deserve each other. And I'm sure Dan's mother is not thrilled. She barely tolerated us, and we weren't marrying into the illustrious Chambers family."

"You've got that right! I'll never forget the look on her face the time good old Dan brought us home for spring break. You'd have thought we were a couple of serial killers." Jack shook his head.

"Serial killers would have been fine as long as they had good breeding. We were just a couple of no-name middle-class kids from somewhere other than Charleston," Griff added before draining the last of his beer. "It doesn't matter. In the long run, Dan did me a favor. Sheila wasn't a good match for me."

"She was a looker, though."

"I'll grant you that."

"Don't forget built like a…"

"We get the idea."

"Are you guys talking about Sheila? I would have tapped that. If I batted for that team." Stella deposited their beers, taking the empties with her. "Of course, beyond that, the girl was a bitch and totally wrong for you."

"See, what did I tell you?" Jack grabbed another wing and the water Stella left for him.

"I didn't love Sheila. We had a good time together, that's all. Not that I agree with how she ended it, mind you."

Griff glanced at two women coming through the door. The first was a tall woman with flaming red hair. But she wasn't what caught his eye. Jamie stood next to her; face animated with whatever she was saying to the other woman. The redhead laughed aloud. Jamie looked around the room, probably for an empty table. He knew the second she caught sight of him, her eyes widening a bit.

"We're about to have company," Griff remarked before sliding off his seat and making his way across the crowded bar.

Chapter Six

"Of all the gin joints in all the towns in all the world, she walks into mine."

-Rick Blaine, *Casablanca*

Jamie stepped into the crowded bar, smiling at the rustic interior. She and Sam had never come here before. She couldn't really say what drew them tonight, other than wanting a new place to try. Some coworkers had mentioned a large range of beers on tap.

She halted her perusal when the tiny hairs on the back of her neck stood at attention. Despite the multitude of people in the bar, Jamie saw only one. Griff. Making his way toward her with a confident stride and a smile on his face. A funny little flutter started in her chest, making its way down to her belly. But before she had time to wonder at it, he drew even with them.

"Jamie, what a surprise!"

The husky tone of his greeting set the butterflies loose in her stomach and brought Sam's head snapping around.

"Hello, Griff. It's a surprise to me, too. I thought maybe you never left the gym." *Stop talking!*

"So, you're Griff. How interesting to meet you. I'm Sam," her friend all but purred, holding out a hand for him to shake.

Jamie stood back and watched yet another man fall to her friend's charms. In three, two, one...

He shook her outstretched hand. "How do you know Jamie?" Griff turned and beamed at Jamie, furthering the zings running along her nerve endings. "Did she tell you she's conquered her fear of gym equipment?"

Jamie didn't know what to think. Normally, one look at Sam's flaming red hair or never ending legs left men drooling. Or worse. They certainly didn't inspire giving Jamie a second look.

"My friend has been oddly silent on the whole bettering herself phase. Feel free to fill me in."

"No can do," answered Griff, shaking his head. "What happens at the gym, stays at the gym. However, I would love to hear more about Jamie, since she refuses to tell me anything about herself." He pointed to where Jack stood next to their high-top table. "Why don't you ladies join us?"

Without waiting for their answer, Griff turned and made his way back through the crowd, leaving Jamie to scramble to keep up. Sam followed behind her, laughing in Jamie's ear.

"I do believe you may have forgotten to mention just how adorable this man is." She leaned around Jamie, taking in Griff's tight jeans-encased butt. "Not to mention smoking hot."

Jamie whipped her head around. "Will you shush? He's not deaf." She lowered her voice to a whisper. "And I did mention panty-melting."

"Oh, you worry too much. He can't hear me over this din."

Jamie chose to not reply, practically jogging to catch up with him. She loved Sam, really, she did, but some days, she could also strangle her friend.

"Jack, this is Jamie and her friend Sam. Ladies, this is Jack, my oldest friend in the world."

The other man came around the corner of the table, making a beeline for Sam. Of course. But standing next to Griff, Jamie found she didn't mind at all.

"By oldest friend, Griff here is referring to the fact that we met the first day of kindergarten."

He may have addressed both women, but Jamie nearly laughed aloud at his laser focus on Sam.

"What Jack failed to mention is that he and I fought over who got to sit next to Daisey Thompson in the reading circle that day. I may have bloodied his nose a bit."

"True, but I did get the girl," Jack added.

"Who promptly jilted him the next day for Tommy Jackson." He turned to Jamie, grinning at her. "Tommy's mother packed enough cookies for both of them. Hard to top that." He winked at Jamie, holding out a chair for her. "Please, have a seat."

Not to be outdone, Jack pulled out a chair for Sam, who graced him with her brightest megawatt smile. Jamie held back a laugh as Jack fell further under Sam's spell.

Griff held out one hand as Jamie climbed up onto the chair. "Thanks," she murmured, trying to catch her breath around him.

"Of course. Have you ladies been here before?"

"I've never seen them," called a gorgeous waitress, approaching their table. "Hi, ladies, I'm Stella. Welcome to Dusty's. What can I get you?"

"I'll have a white wine, please," Sam answered.

"I'll have your favorite on tap. Surprise me," Jamie added.

Stella grinned. "I like this one, Griff. She's a keeper. Coming right up. Appetizers are on the menu on the table. Be right back."

"Beer drinker, huh? Never would have guessed it." Griff reached for his own bottle and took a drink.

"Why is that? Because I'm a woman?" She heard it a lot, but Jamie had never really cared for the taste of wine. Another of her many faults in her mother's eyes.

Griff tilted his head, considering her. Or maybe how to answer. "Well, when you put it like that, I'm not sure I want to answer."

"My friend here has been known to put his foot in it more than once," Jack joked.

Sam looked through her lashes at him. "And what are you known for, Jack?"

Her sultry tone made Jamie want to laugh. Poor Jack had no idea what was about to hit him. The slightly glazed look in his eyes confirmed it. She held her laughter as he leaned forward, intent in answering the siren's call.

"Well, Griff and I have a… Ouch!" He turned to his friend, who wore a suspiciously bland look on his face.

"Did you just kick him under the table?" Jamie asked Griff.

"Why would I do that?" He grabbed a mozzarella stick, dipped it in sauce and shoved the whole thing in his mouth.

"I notice you didn't answer the question," she replied.

Griff, intent on not choking, merely shrugged his shoulders and pointed to his overstuffed mouth.

Sam, amusement shining in her bright eyes, turned her attention back to Jack. "You were saying?"

"I'm, uh, a personal trainer at Getting it Done. Have you heard of it?"

"Isn't that the gym you joined, Jamie?"

Jamie nodded, eyes narrowed. "You're a trainer there,

Jack?"

"I am indeed." He turned his attention back to Sam. "Have you been in? You look like you might know your way around a gym."

Sam's light laughter drifted across the table. "I'll take that as a compliment, sir. I've not been to your establishment." She batted her lashes at him. Actually batted her lashes. "Doesn't mean I won't be."

"I'd be happy to give you a tour. Anytime."

Jamie resisted rolling her eyes. "Well, I love it. Although I haven't seen you there yet."

"In my defense, you've only been in two days so far," Jack smirked. "And I don't crawl out of bed that early."

A soft thud, sounding very much like someone being kicked, again, under the table caught Jamie's attention. She looked at both men. Jack gave a tight smile. Griff merely laughed.

"And how do you know my gym habits?" Jamie asked

Jack grinned fully this time. "Oh, Griff must have mentioned it. He told me all about your first day, something about talking to machines. Hopefully, it got better from there."

Sam threw back her head and laughed. "You told Jack about that?"

Griff ducked his head. "In a moment of weakness." He turned to Jamie. "You told Sam? "

"Well, she is my best friend," Jamie grumbled.

"Well, Jack is my best friend," he countered.

"Isn't this cozy?" Sam commented.

Jamie felt the heat creep across her face and thanked the universe for the darkened interior. "In my defense, I am a klutz. There, I said it. My name is Jamie, and I am a klutz."

Of course, as happened with her, the music chose that very

moment to switch songs, leaving a brief, but obvious, pause.

"Oh, honey, admitting it is half the battle. Or so I hear." Stella dropped off a beer for Jamie and white wine for Sam. "Now, can I get you ladies something to eat?"

Jamie, eyeing the nachos listed, ordered hummus and veggies. She sighed, not thinking about all the gooey cheese she passed up.

"I'll have an order of the wings please," Sam ordered. "And make them spicy."

Of course she'd order the wings. Sam's deplorable diet, and size nothing clothing, equaled a mystery. Lorelai Gilmore move over.

"I found it cute, how you talk to the machines," Griff announced.

Would this ever end? "I wasn't talking to the machines." Jamie glanced around the table. All eyes on her. Great! "Fine. If you must know, I was working out which would be least likely to cause my death. There, I said it. None of you coordinated people get it. I trip over my own feet. And sometimes, if I'm lucky, over nothing at all. Which means taking on a hulking bit of metal was brave." Suddenly parched, Jamie lunged for her frosty beer, gulping down a third of it.

"Agreed. Which is why I gave her some pointers the next day," Griff added, throwing a grin her way.

"Whatever you did worked, Griff. She's planning on a third day in a row tomorrow." Sam saluted Jamie with her wine glass.

"And will you be joining her?" asked Jack.

Sam shuddered. "At that hour? Are you crazy? Some of us value our beauty sleep."

"I'll be there," Griff volunteered.

Jamie peered around her glass at him. "Do you always go

before work? As hard as it is getting up so early, not sure I could drag myself in after a long day in the office."

"Especially since those days are about to get a lot longer," Sam groused. She grabbed a wing as Stella placed a plate on the table, holding it up to punctuate her words. "Soon, Jamie won't be able to drag her butt out of bed that early."

"Don't remind me." She glanced at the two men, both with raised eyebrows and let out a sigh. "Sam and I are both accountants."

"Brains and beauty," Jack said, eyes for Sam only.

Griff leaned in, murmuring, "That's one more thing I know about you now."

That and the stuff I blurted about my high school reunion. But she kept that to herself, merely nodding. She hadn't seen him since then and had no idea how he'd feel about her pathetic revelation.

"What else would you like you know? I'm pretty boring."

"Anything you want to tell me." He leaned in as though there was nothing he'd rather hear. Jamie glanced across the table to where Jack hung on Sam's every word. Jamie played with the edge of her napkin, not familiar with undivided male attention.

"I'm a dog person but currently a cat allows me to share my home with her since I work long hours, and it wouldn't be fair to a puppy. I don't discuss religion or politics ever but believe ice cream should be its own food group and will argue that to the death. I love the idea of the ocean more than getting into it." She finished with a sip of her beer. "Your turn."

"Challenge accepted. I was born right here in Palm Harbor. After college and more than a few years in the military, I moved back. Most of my family lives within thirty minutes of here. I'm definitely a dog person, as cats are evil, but I don't have one either. I work way too much. The Braves break my heart every year, but someday when they don't, I can hold my head up and say I've always been a fan." He leaned in until mere inches separated them. "And I love a girl who drinks beer."

Jamie sat back in her chair, giving herself a bit of space and a chance to breathe. "Never been much of a wine fan, much to my sister's chagrin."

"And mine," added Sam. She grinned at Jamie. "Just kidding. She knows I don't care what she drinks."

"Tell me more about this wine-drinking sister," Griff demanded.

Where to start in the complicated relationships between sisters… "Some other time, like when you have a day and a half. And maybe some Tequila. Do you talk about your military experience? I know some who don't care to, and I wouldn't want to overstep."

"Not a lot to tell. I was in high school when 9/11 happened." He sat back, waited a moment. "'Happened' as if it was an ordinary event. Anyway, I wanted to enlist right after graduating, but my mother made me promise I would get my degree first. Uncle Sam paid for my business degree, and I gave him a decade of my life." He took a sip of his beer. "I saw some things. I did some things. Things I wouldn't want to discuss with you. Believe me, you'd thank me when you sleep tonight. The longer I'm out, the easier it's gotten. But I was lucky, luckier than most. I came home whole, both physically and mentally."

"Thank you," she murmured before scooping some hummus on a slice of red bell pepper.

"For?"

Jamie shrugged her shoulders. "Telling me. For not brushing me off."

"Oh, of course. Can you tell me about the high school guy?"

"Chad?"

"Is there another?"

Jamie gulped. *Where to start?*

Chapter Seven

"Beauty, more than bitterness, makes the heart break."
-Sarah Teasdale

"What are you kids chatting about?"

Thank goodness for Sam and her fabulous timing! "Uh, Griff and I were just getting to know each other a bit." She waved a hand toward Sam and Jack. "And you guys?"

"Sam was bewitching me. Ruining me for any other woman. Ever."

Jamie looked at Jack and wondered where that comment fell on the scale of utter crap and sincerity. Judging by the look on his face, possibly closer to the latter. But then, she'd seen that look before on men's faces. At least when they looked at Sam.

Sam laughed, running one perfect nail down Jack's well-muscled arm. "You should be so lucky," she murmured.

Jamie glanced down at her phone, laying face up on the table. "I have to go." She turned to Sam. "We have to go. Butt crack of dawn comes early."

Sam made a face. The kind of face that told Jamie everything she needed to know about her thoughts on Jamie's announcement.

"I'd be happy to drive Sam home," offered Jack, still sporting that lovesick puppy look.

Since he hadn't ordered for her or suggested oral sex, she guessed Sam might give him a chance.

"If you're sure," asked Sam, southern drawl very thick. Scarlett would be proud.

"Oh, I'm sure," Jack confirmed.

"Well, okay then." Jamie handed some money to Sam. "Here's for my part. See you in the morning." She hugged her friend before waving to the table. "See you, guys."

Griff slid off his chair. "Wait up. I'll walk you out."

"Thanks, but I'm fine."

"Come on, take pity on me. I just became the third wheel."

She glanced back at her friend and his, chatting with their heads close as though the only humans left on earth-or at least in the bar-and felt sorry for him. "Okay, that would be nice."

"You can never be too careful, you know," added Griff.

"Because Palm Harbor is a hotbed of crime?" she joked.

"Well, 'hotbed' might prove a stretch, but a pretty woman out alone can never be too careful."

She glanced at him, seeing nothing but sincerity in his eyes and smiled to herself.

Griff held the door, and Jamie welcomed the chilly night air. "Whew. I had no idea how hot it was in there until we stepped outside."

"So tell me. Is Sam going to break my friend's heart?" Griff stopped beside her car.

"I think the better question is if he'll break Sam's," countered Jamie. She dug in her purse for her keys.

"I know he comes off as a bit of a player, but Jack has a heart of gold. And I have to say, I've never seen him fall this hard. Or this fast."

"That's Sam for you. The funny thing is, she doesn't even try."

"Try?"

"You know, she doesn't have to try to make men fall for her. It just happens."

"And how about you?" Griff took one step closer, warming the air around them.

Jamie laughed. What else could she do? "You got me. Real man-killer. You should see the line of men left in my wake." She laughed harder, making it difficult to find her keys. "Every day, I swear I'm going to empty out half of the junk in my purse so that finding my keys doesn't become a marathon."

Griff shook his head. "My sisters, and my mom, say the same thing, but they never do. I don't even want to know what y'all carry in there. Some things are better left unknown."

"A ha," she cried, holding up her keys. "Sorry. I consider it a moral victory every time I find them. Mind you, if I had walked out here alone, I would have grabbed them before leaving the bar. Self-defense one oh one."

"Good to know. I'd hate to have to lecture you on personal security. Although we do offer those classes at the gym. Uh, I mean I hear they offer them. I think Jack mentioned it."

"I'll keep it in mind." She muffled a yawn with the back of her hand.

"I'll try to not take that personally," Griff said with a grin.

"Don't. It's the hour."

"Yes, nine o'clock is very late."

"Well it is when I've been up since four thirty." She opened her door with the remote and threw her purse on the passenger seat. "I'm going now. See you."

"Tomorrow, Jamie. I'll see you tomorrow," he reminded her.

Her heart did a funny little flip in her chest. "Yes, I'll see you tomorrow." She got in her car and drove away before she could do something stupid like kiss his socks off right there in the bar parking lot.

*****

Griff stood there, grinning, and watched her drive away, yet again. *This was becoming a habit.* And he didn't mind in the least. Whistling a happy little tune under his breath, Griff made his way to his own car. No point in going back inside. Nothing sucked more than being the third wheel.

On the drive home, he tapped the wheel along with an old Garth hit. Why didn't he want Jamie to know that he and Jack owned the gym? Nothing to be ashamed of there. And he wasn't. But he also didn't want her thinking that he hit on every woman he came across in the gym. But lying didn't sit right either, even if it was only by omission.

He stopped at a red light and considered his options. Better to tell her now before too many days passed. On the other hand, what was the danger of letting her think he showed up before work like she did for a bit longer? Right?

He turned onto his street when the light changed. Her knowing wasn't the real obstacle in all this. His rule of never dating clients was. And since he was the owner, and she was the client, there didn't seem a way around that. And then there was Chad, who had unwittingly brought her into his life. His mouth turned down as he pulled into his driveway. Figures that the first woman to make him laugh in ages would have to be a client of the gym.

Chapter Eight

"I think heartbreak is something you learn to live with as opposed to learn to forget."
-Kate Winslet

Jamie had barely turned off her car before she sprang from it into the cool, early morning air. Although she wasn't sure how she would get shampoo out of her hair later and prayed today she could focus on something other than her arms, she hurried toward the door. Not letting herself think about her eagerness to see Griff, she pulled open the door. The usual few people, some now looking vaguely familiar, scattered around the gym. But no one over six feet tall with dark hair and the ability to kick her heart into high gear. Oh well.

Shoulders sagging the slightest bit, Jamie made her way to the treadmills. Now that she wasn't as afraid of them, she jumped onto the nearest and set off at a nice clip. She thought about the busy day ahead and not about a certain someone. She also wasn't thinking about the fun she'd had with him last night, getting to know each other at Dusty's. And she certainly had not dreamed about him last night.

"Good morning," came a soft, husky voice from her right

elbow.

He really had to stop that!

Jamie grabbed a siderail to anchor herself. "What are you, a ninja?" she hissed at him. And then burst out laughing. "Sorry, I didn't sleep as much as I would have liked."

"No worries, and I am sorry. I thought you'd have seen me coming." He motioned with one hand toward the wall of ceiling-to-floor mirrors.

"Oh, I keep my eyes closed."

"You do? Why?"

"Thought maybe I might be less likely to fall off."

"Hmmm. And does it work?"

"Until some guy scared the stuffing out of me, as my dead grandmother would say."

"I'm sorry for your loss."

She turned to look at him. "Thank you, but I might be more inclined to believe you if not for the twinkle in your eyes."

"You were looking at my eyes, huh? And who did you think put the twinkle there?"

"I wouldn't know," she huffed before upping the speed and incline on her machine. "Do you think my friend and yours hit it off last night?" She tried to breathe through her nose as if having a conversation while walking on a treadmill was an everyday thing for her.

"They looked like they were when I left."

"And how much later was that? I didn't hear from Sam again last night, so I'll have to grill her later."

"I never went back in," Griff answered, not sounding the least bit winded even though he was running. *Damn him...*

"Oh," she grunted in response, focusing on the sharp pain in her ribs. Would she ever work up to running? And talking? Surely not.

"You never told me about Chad."

"Uh," she mumbled, desperate to not fall off the bloody machine. *That* was the last thing she expected out of his mouth. "Not much to tell."

"Really? I would have thought he was important if you're changing yourself for him." He glanced her way, green eyes meeting brown. "Especially when there was nothing wrong with you in the first place."

She blamed the sudden jump in her pulse on her increased pace. "You wouldn't understand."

"Try me."

"Have you ever wanted someone to notice that you're alive? That you're more than meets the eye?" *No, probably not, as the Griffs and Chads of the world weren't invisible.*

He never broke stride, continued pounding on the machine next to her for so long, that Jamie was convinced he hadn't heard her. And then he hit the emergency stop button on his treadmill, turning to her.

"Do you think you're the only one who's ever wanted someone they couldn't have? The only one who's been dumped?"

He grabbed the towel draped over the center of the machine and wiped some sweat off his face, and she found herself jealous of a piece of cotton. *Get a grip!*

"Of course not, Griff. That's not what I meant. But, surely, you have no idea."

"Of what? What can't I possibly understand?"

"What's it like to be invisible," she all but whispered. Jamie turned back to face the wall of mirrors, choosing to concentrate on her feet moving on the machine rather than the hurt in his voice.

"I see you, Jamie. I see a woman who's full of life and not

afraid to take chances."

"Ha! If that's what you see, then you might want to visit an eye doctor. I'm afraid of everything."

Griff leaned over, hitting her stop button. He waited until she turned to face him. "If you're afraid of change, then why are you here?"

"Fifteen years, Griff. I haven't gone to any of my high school reunions in fifteen years."

"And? Tell me why not."

"Because I wanted to be different, better, when I did." She blew out a big breath and pushed sweaty hair from her eyes.

"What's wrong with you? Really? Because you're not a stick figure? Because you have curves? Real women do."

"Oh." Brilliant come-back, but what did you say to that? Especially when all she could think of was catching a lone drop of sweat running down his neck with her tongue.

"Was Chad the one who told you that you weren't good enough?"

"No, Chad never thought of me outside of my ability to help him pass math. He needed to in order to play football."

"Then who?"

Jamie climbed down from the treadmill and sat on the edge of it. "I'm the *other* daughter. You know, the one who wasn't popular and didn't cheer."

"Ah, and what is this paragon's name?"

"Melissa. She was older, funnier, bubblier. You get it." Jamie stopped, wondering just how pathetic she sounded. "Look, you're making too much of this reunion. I visit my family every year in May, after I survive another tax season. This year happens to coincide with my high school reunion. No big deal."

"The one you feel the need to change yourself for?"

"What is this? Therapy?" Jamie asked with her tongue firmly implanted in cheek. But his impassive face stayed the same. *And now I sound like a total bitch.*

"Sorry. Didn't mean to pry," Griff replied in a flat tone.

She stood with hands planted on her hips. "Look, this is all coming out wrong. And you're reading too much into it. I am going to visit my family and for my reunion. And at said reunion I will be seeing a bunch of people I haven't seen in fifteen years. Nothing more, nothing less. So, sue me if I want to look better than this." She stopped in front of him, waving a hand up and down her body.

"You haven't told me why."

"Why, what?"

"Why now? Why, after skipping the first few, are you choosing to go now?"

And all the fight left her. Jamie slumped back onto the machine. "I don't know. Normally, I get the thing in the mail and toss it in the recycle bin. This time, I didn't. This time, I stuck it on the fridge under a parrot magnet and ignored it for a few days." She laughed, but it sounded harsh even to her own ears. "By ignore, of course I mean I stared at it, read it a hundred times, and then gave in and emailed my R.S.V.P." Another loud laugh, bordering on a snort, ripped from her. "And here's the best part. Apparently, I'm bringing a plus one. Not that I have one, mind you. Isn't that hysterical?"

"I'll be your plus one," Griff offered.

If Jamie hadn't been holding one of the railings, she would have fallen over. "What? Why? You don't even know me."

"I know you a little. And I'd really like to meet this Chad guy. When is it?"

"What?"

"The reunion, silly."

"Oh. It's the first weekend of May. Which is a really pretty time in Philadelphia, actually. Which is also very much beside the point."

"Perfect."

"How is that perfect?"

"May gives us a few months to get to know each other better. I mean, after all, shouldn't your plus one know something other than the fact that you're an accountant from Pennsylvania?"

"Uh, I guess. What did you want to know?"

"Let's start with something tricky, like your last name."

Jamie stood up, wiping her very sweaty palm on her sweats before sticking it out in front of her. "Hi, I'm Jamie Lawler. Nice to meet you."

Griff enclosed hers in his much larger, pleasantly calloused one. "Hello, Jamie Lawler. I'm Griffin Layne. But you can call me Griff. Nice to meet you as well." He winked at her. "There, that wasn't so hard, was it?"

Jamie realized she was still holding his hand and pulled hers back, instantly regretting the loss of his. "No, Griff, not at all. But now I have to do something else before I go home to get ready for work. And it cannot involve the use of my upper arms, because I can hardly move them today."

Griff tipped back his head and roared with laughter. The sound curled all the way down to her toes.

"And you say Melissa is funnier than you? She must be a professional comedian. Let's do some leg work today, shall we? There are a few machines I know for a fact haven't eaten a human in months."

"Ha ha, very funny. You people have no idea how much you take for granted."

"What does that mean? 'You people?' What kind of people

am I?"

She ducked her head, wishing, as always, that the earth would open up and swallow her. "The kind of people who walk into gyms like they own the place."

Jamie slammed into Griff's back when he stopped abruptly.

"Own the place?"

"You know, like you and Jack. And Sam for that matter. Naturally graceful types who run around without tripping. Ever. I wake up with bruises that I have no memory of acquiring. That's how graceful I'm not."

"Oh. Well, I promise to be gentle."

"Uh, okay," she choked in reply.

"Follow me," he commanded before leading her back to the area they'd used yesterday.

She followed along, nerves picking up when he stopped in front of the leg press machine he'd used yesterday morning.

"Hop on. I'll show you how to adjust everything."

Jamie stood there, arms hanging at her side. "You're kidding, right?"

"No, why would I?"

"This is the one you used yesterday. I saw you." *Watched you and drooled over your amazing legs.* She chose to not mention that part.

"Don't worry, I cleaned it," he joked.

Jamie crossed her arms over her chest. "That's not what I meant, as you know. It's just, uh, too…well, something."

"Jamie, I don't expect you to use the same amount of weights I did."

"Oh, okay then I guess." Jamie looked at the stacked weights behind the footrest. "How do I know where to start? That looks like a lot of weight." She pointed to the bottom of the stack.

"Well, that is a lot of weight. And nowhere near what you're ready to tackle."

"Whew. How do I know?"

"By trying out different weights. You want it to challenge you without injuring you."

She glanced again at the weights. "Maybe thirty pounds?"

Griff laughed and slid the pin under seventy-five. "Try this on for size." After adjusting the seat for her height, he hopped onto the machine next to her. "Now square your feet against the base like this."

He demonstrated, and she tried to follow his lead, sitting with her knees pretty much in her chest. "Comfy."

Griff laughed. "Okay, tough guy, now push, slow and steady. You want to move smoothly, no jerking, to protect yourself."

"Smooth without jerking. Got it, here goes nothing."

Griff gave her a thumbs up and started his own set.

Jamie tried to keep her eye on her own machine and off his amazing legs. She pushed against the metal plate, a groan escaping her. But as she continued, it became easier. She watched him bring his back down, pause, then push up again, in a long, smooth, controlled movement. *How did he make it look so easy?* She brought hers back down, knees collapsing into her.

"Little more control," he offered in encouragement, never missing a beat.

"More control, smooth, no jerking," she muttered half under her breath. How was she supposed to remember all that? She started her second rep, the mantra playing over and over in her mind.

"Tell me what you liked about this Chad guy. Start with one thing."

*****

Griff mentally kicked himself before the words ever left his mouth. *This should be good.*

"Wow, where would I start? He had the thickest blonde hair. And the sun always seemed to glint off it, picking out a thousand different shades. You know, the kind of blonde women pay top dollar for."

"Let me guess. He had stunning blue eyes to match." Next, he'd be growing an ovary. Sheesh! Jack would revoke his man card if he could hear this conversation.

Jamie turned her head toward him, grinning. "Did you Google him? Yes, he had the most amazing blue eyes. Clear, sky blue, and they crinkled when he laughed. Not that he laughed around me a lot. He didn't find math amusing."

"Does anyone?"

"Maybe not amusing, but I do find a certain comfort in math. It makes sense to me. It's predictable."

She let the weight return down easier this time, he noted. "Good job, Jamie! Do another eight then rest for a minute before you start a second set. Then rest and do a third."

"Yes, sir," she called with a snappy little salute.

He grinned at her attitude and then dropped his eyes to take in her shapely calves. Today was the first day she wore anything other than full-length sweats. *Eyes straight ahead!* Gawking at her bare legs wasn't helping his resolve to keep her firmly in the client zone. He had to remember his vow to never get involved with a client. He'd worked too hard for this. They both had.

"Tell me your plan to get this Chad, once and for all."

Chapter Nine

"I had nothing to offer anyone except my own confusion."
-Jack Kerouac

"Are you planning to drink that or just stare meaningfully at it for another hour?"

Jamie started at Sam's voice. She glanced up at her friend and then down at her coffee. She took a sip, wincing at the now cold brew. Setting it down on her desk, she quipped, "Staring wins I guess."

"Where were you just now? I passed by fifteen minutes ago, and you held the same exact position. Earth to Jamie."

"Lost in thought?" *Way to state the obvious...* She hoped Sam would take it at surface value.

"Nice try. What happened this morning? I'm guessing it had something to do with a certain guy at a certain gym?"

Her soft laugh floated across the space between them. She loved Sam; felt closer to her than to her own sister. But Sam was a piranha when it came to matters of the heart. She could sniff one drop of blood in the river.

"Come on, you know you want to tell me," she crooned from the doorway of Jamie's office.

"I'm sure this is something we all want to hear, Ms. Lawler. Please, do tell." The unpleasant voice of Charles Smith grounded Jamie.

"Yes, sir. Uh, I mean no, sir. Sam was trying to wiggle out my great grandmother's top-secret recipe for New England Clam Chowder. Hailed from Boston, Granny Lawler did. But that recipe never leaves the Lawler family." She turned to Sam. "Sorry, no can do."

Charles's perpetual frown deepened, turning him even closer to the human embodiment of a bulldog. "Fascinating, I'm sure. However, this is a place of business, ladies. Please keep your hen talk to your own time." With that, the squat, rotund man turned away from her doorway.

Sam made a goofy face and fled to her own office, leaving Jamie alone with her riotous thoughts. She'd left the gym this morning not knowing which end was up. First, Griff goes out of his way, once again, to help her learn a new machine without maiming herself. Then while she's still basking in the glow of his praise, he commits to helping her nab Chad at the reunion. *Men!* Was it any wonder she didn't date much? If someone like Sam, sleek and uber-confident, still hated dating, what hope was there for her?

An email alert from her laptop pulled her from the fog of her thoughts about Griff. Yet another 'team-building' missive from the dragon. This subject line read, 'Reminder of proper use of work time.' Subtle.

Not for the first time, not even for the thousandth, Jamie allowed herself to dream of leaving this place. As much as she loved and respected Lawrence, she equally loathed his brother, Charles. A few months ago, over one too many adult beverages necessitating an Uber home, she and Sam doodled ideas for their own firm on a series of cocktail napkins. Each round of fruity cocktails inspired more elaborate logos and names for their mythical firm. But at the center of it all was a burning desire for both to escape the dragon.

Jamie pulled her purse out of a lower drawer and dug inside the cavernous center. There, at the very bottom, tucked into a clean plastic zipped bag, sat those cocktail napkins. She closed her hand around the bag, drawing support from their very existence.

For over a year now, Jamie had felt a growing restlessness with her career. She loved what she did but hated her job. She slaved her life away for a man who only valued the bottom line. Jamie held no foolish notions about loyalty at Smith & Smith. She excelled at what she did, her clients sang her praises. But the dragon wouldn't bat an eye if she left tomorrow. He'd replace her with someone fresh out of college at half the cost to him. Lawrence would miss her, but that wasn't a reason to stay. And she secretly believed Lawrence would cheer on her escape from his brother.

Sam had met her Margarita-born vision of starting their own firm with a rousing cheer and another round. The two had toiled over ideas of how to venture out on their own. They were both smart, well-educated women who could whip up a sound business plan in the space of a weekend. By the end of the night, they were cruising the web, searching for a small office space.

But the harsh light of day had brought more than a pounding headache for her. Waking up on Sam's sofa, Jamie remembered all the reasons why venturing out on their own wasn't such a great idea. Like the need to eat and have a roof over her head. And so the cocktail napkins stayed in the shadowy recesses of her oversized Vera Bradley.

And yet, the idea of starting something new, taking a leap, niggled at the back of her brain like a sapling reaching for the sun. Before she could stop herself, Jamie grabbed her phone and sent a cryptic message to Sam.

"Operation Phoenix must see the light of day!"

They'd named their partnership that, giggling over something rising from the ashes left behind by the dragon. Sam had squealed with delight, having bestowed the moniker on Charles.

"This requires lunch offsite. High noon! La Hacienda. Be there or be square!"

A giggle escaped Jamie's lips before she threw a hand over her mouth. La Hacienda was only their favorite Mexican place and the site of the too many margaritas and coming up with The Plan. She tapped off a quick consent and tucked her phone into a drawer. The dragon didn't like anyone to waste his precious money on social media or a personal life.

*****

"Let me get this straight. You offered to help Jamie, the woman who has obviously captured your attention, to win her lost love. Am I missing anything?"

For not the first time today, Griff resisted the urge to lower his forehead to his desk. Hard. He sighed instead. "Did I mention I offered to be her plus one for the reunion in May? In Philadelphia?"

A long, hardy laugh ripped from Jack's throat. When he finally stopped long enough to breathe and wipe his eyes, he stared at Griff. "Not only are you keeping her squarely in the client zone, you've boxed yourself nicely into the friend zone. Anything else to add?"

"No, that about covers it." He took a long drink of water, feeling spent after an hour with his senior group. Might be due to the sleep he wasn't getting. No need to tell Jack *that*.

"Since you asked, Sam and I had a very cool time last night."

He hadn't asked.

"I didn't ask because I knew, judging by your goofy grin this morning, you'd tell me. Any advancement in your plan to leave the friend zone?"

Jack's smile dimmed. "No, not yet. She's fabulous, Griff; smart, funny, sexy as hell. We talked. For hours. When's the last time that happened with a woman?"

"First of never?" guessed Griff.

"Right again. Give the man a cigar!" Jack crowed, getting up to slap Griff on the back. He dropped back down into his chair, goofy grin still in place.

"Let me get this straight. You sat and talked for hours and that's why you're so happy? Should I check for a fever or maybe a head injury?" Griff asked.

"No need. I feel great. Eventually, I'll wear her down with my charm. Sam told me all about growing up in a very dysfunctional family and how Jamie is her family now. Did you know they want to quit and open their own firm?"

Griff clenched his jaws. "How would I? Up until last night, I didn't even know she was an accountant." He rubbed his jaw, unclenching it.

"They don't like their boss, at least one of them. Apparently, he's a money-grubbing old coot. They have this whole scheme."

Jack went on to tell him about something called Operation Phoenix. He listened with half an ear while he thought about the situation. It seemed as though Jamie was out to change more than just her looks. Which he still thought didn't need changing.

He sat back in his chair, kicking his heels up on the corner of his desk. How to get Jamie to see herself as he did?

*****

On Monday morning, Jamie sat in her car outside Getting it Done, and stared at the rain coming down half-heartedly. *It's raining just enough to be annoying,* she thought. Not a fan of the rain and its inconveniences, she wondered as always why it couldn't rain when she was sleeping. Or while she sat in her office. But dragging her butt out of bed on this chilly, wet not quite morning should at least earn her a medal. Or a donut.

She'd officially been on this bettering herself kick for a week. Seven days. One hundred sixty-eight hours. She stopped at minutes and seconds, although she could as she was a math nerd.

And today was the day. Scale day. Jamie shook her head. She didn't own one and would have to use the professional looking one she'd spied near the locker rooms. She really should have weighed herself last week, she mused, heading inside the gym. Surely, she'd lost weight after working out (almost) every day for a whole week. Jamie had skipped the weekend, preferring to go for a long walk along the deserted beaches to being inside. But then again, there'd been lunch at their favorite Mexican place and drinks after work on Friday.

Dashing inside out of the mist, she spotted the usuals minus Griff. Not that she was looking for him. She made a beeline for the scale, glad he wasn't here for once. The last thing she needed was a witness. Emptying her pockets, she said a quick prayer to the universe before stepping up. Then jumped off and kicked off her shoes. Those had to be worth a pound or two at least. Maybe even each?

"That lip balm can't weigh more than a few ounces," Griff mentioned from his position leaning against a wall. He stayed where he was, well out of range of being able to read the numbers. Unless he had eagle eyes. "Surely your sweatshirt weighs more."

"Oh, good idea." Jamie jumped back off and ripped off her sweatshirt, exposing several inches of skin in the process. She pulled her t-shirt down, looking at her remaining clothing.

"If you want to remove something else, don't let me stop you," he advised.

"No, I think I'm good, thanks." She stepped back up on the scale, slower now that she had an audience. Jamie adjusted the bars, sliding one further to the right than she'd hoped. "Drat," she muttered.

"Sounds like something Charlie Brown would say after missing the football." He took a few steps toward her.

Jamie slammed the weights back to the left and jumped down from the scale. Then felt like an idiot.

"I wasn't going to look," he admonished in a gentle voice.

"I know," she muttered. She looked up at Griff, now only a few feet away. "Please don't tell me it's just a number. I know that." She dropped her eyes to the ground. "It just wasn't the number I wanted to see." Because one week at the gym didn't melt away twenty pounds. Or thirty.

"Don't become obsessed with the number. It's not healthy and won't help your long-term goals. Other than dazzling some guy named Charlie, what are your goals?"

"This isn't only about *Chad*." *Okay, a lot of it was, but that would sound pathetic right?*

"Good. Then what else is this about?" He stepped in closer, lowering his voice. "Anything to do with Operation Phoenix?"

She whirled on him then. "What? How do you know about that?" She thought for a second. "Oh, Sam, right?"

"Via Jack, yes."

"You probably think it's a pipedream, huh?"

Griff shook his head. "No, I think it's amazing. If you're not happy with something, then change it. Or at least work on changing it." He reached out and squeezed her shoulder.

"Oh, thanks." Other than Sam, Jamie didn't have a lot of people in her corner. "Sorry. I shouldn't have snapped."

Griff laughed, leading her away from the scale by the elbow. "Come on, Tiger. Let's go hit the treadmill."

She let him lead her. "How is it you're here this early every morning?"

"Like you, I enjoy the relative peace of very early mornings here."

"You ask a lot of questions, but you don't give a lot away about yourself." She grinned at him. "I've noticed."

"Have you now? Come on then, ask." He sprang up on the treadmill next to her in that disgustingly athletic way of his. "I'm an open book."

She watched as he loped into a faster pace than she could ever hope to achieve. At least not without flying off the back. She opened her mouth to ask him what he did for a living when he turned to face her.

"Hey, speaking of questions, I have one. What's going on between your friend and mine? I've barely heard from Jack all weekend. Think they ran off to Vegas and eloped?"

Despite her sloth-like pace, his query almost made her faceplant. "Vegas?" she yelped. Grabbing the rail like a lifeline, Jamie got her feet back under her. "Absolutely not."

His laugh echoed through her belly, all the way to her sneaker-clad feet. "No, I doubt they went to Vegas. I was joking.

They do seem taken with each other, though. Don't you think?"

Jamie thought about that. Did Griff know Sam refused to date his friend?

"I'm not sure."

"Okay, what does that mean? What aren't you telling me?" He swiped a small towel across his face.

"What? Nothing. I mean I'm not not telling you anything." She crossed her fingers of the hand furthest from him, hoping he didn't notice.

"And yet there's something in your voice. A tone. And then there's your face," he added.

"What's wrong with my face?" She stretched her neck, turning her head this way and that in the ever-present wall of mirrors.

"Nothing, Jamie. It's the expression you're wearing. The one that tells me you shouldn't play poker. Unless of course its strip poker, and it's just you and I."

He grinned as she grabbed for the side rail once again. "Kidding," he said, holding up both hands as though in surrender.

Jamie would have thrown something at his handsome face if anything were within reach. She was an excellent poker player, one benefit of being a math nerd. That could be interesting.

"What's the grin for? Thinking about my offer?" he joked.

"I am not," she stated. She turned off the treadmill and turned toward him, waiting for him to do the same.

Griff must have noted the seriousness of her face because he did the same.

"The thing about Sam is that she's sort of a serial first dater." She wished she could bite her tongue right in half after blurting out the information.

Chapter Ten

"Thank God for the potholes on memory lane."
-Randy Newman

"Is the FBI aware?" Griff joked, grinning. He probably shouldn't joke, but he couldn't help it.

"Okay, I deserved that." She bit her lip, making Griff want to soothe it with his own.

"Whatever it is, Jack is a big boy. And he's not exactly a virgin. He can handle himself."

"Of course, he can. I didn't mean to imply he couldn't. It's just that Sam doesn't really spend a lot of time with any one man."

He watched in wonder as the cutest blush spread across her cheeks. Not being stupid, he didn't point it out.

"Ugh, I'm making this sound so much worse than it is." She blew out a breath, blowing damp tendrils from her eyes. "Sam doesn't believe in happy ever after. Says that isn't meant for her. She has a lot of first dates. A lot. And every once in a while, a second date. And that's about it."

"And you're worried about my friend, Jack? How cute are you?"

The blush deepened as she shrugged her shoulders. "I'm trying to tell you that I saw the besotted look on his face. I've seen it before. Sam never means to hurt anyone, and in her defense, she is ridiculously gorgeous. Men just can't help themselves."

"Still, Jack is a big boy."

"Consider yourself warned," she muttered before wiping down the treadmill with a bit more force than needed.

"You and Sam are best friends, huh?"

That got her attention. Jamie turned back to him.

"Since the first day of our internships, summer before senior year of college." She smiled, maybe at the memory. "I was nervous. I tripped getting out of my car in the parking lot if you can imagine. And I know you can because you've seen what I'm capable of. Anyway, I sort of landed in a heap at her feet."

"That's one way to make a first impression," joked Griff.

"You think? Anyway, this girl reaches down a hand to help me up. 'I'm Sam. That was quite the entrance.'" Jamie shook her head. "I knew right then we'd be friends. She helped me gather my purse and keys, and in we walked to Smith & Smith as if nothing ever happened." She laughed. "As if my knees weren't bleeding from hitting the pavement."

Griff burst out laughing. "I'm sorry. It's not really funny."

She joined in with him. "Yes, it really is. If I didn't laugh, I'd have cried. And who needs that?"

"Interesting perspective."

Jamie glanced at her phone. "I don't have a ton of time this morning. The dragon, uh, I mean Mr. Smith, called an early meeting." Her lips pressed together, telling Griff how she felt about that. "I'm going to go do some arm work."

Griff watched her wipe down her machine before walking

away, heading to the free weights area. He'd showed her some reps she could do last week with those. It was nice of her to worry about Jack, but his friend seemed to know what he was doing. Seemed...

He chose a yoga mat and spread it out, deciding to do some planks. He still didn't know anything else about the mysterious Chad and worried the other man had grown into some sort of mythical figure in her mind after fifteen years. What was it about him that drew her to him? Was it purely physical? Seemed kind of shallow for Jamie. Not that he knew her well yet.

Griff thought back to his own high school experience as his arms started to burn with the effort of holding his position. A few girls stood out, but no one that caught his imagination this far out. Too much time, and experiences, had passed. Maybe this Chad was 'the one that got away.' He grunted both at the thought and exertion the position required. He glanced down at the time on his phone. One more minute to go before he could collapse to the mat. Time for happier thoughts.

*****

Jamie watched Griff from beneath lowered lashes. Even at this distance, she didn't want him to catch her watching him. Okay, ogling might be a better description. She had no idea what he was doing, but it looked painful. Her arms hurt just watching him. She curled the five-pound weights in her hands, alternating arms as Griff had taught her.

She wondered what he thought as he held his body taut in the position. Taut didn't cover it! Even from across the room, she could see the muscles in his arms bulging. His toes planted on the mat, taking a lot of his weight. She winced thinking about how much that had to hurt. Hopefully, he wouldn't get any bright ideas about her trying that. Whatever *that* might be.

Jamie dragged her eyes from his physique and turned her thoughts to Chad. That's who she should focus on. She tried to picture him in her head. The problem with that was she hadn't seen him in fifteen years. What did he look like today? Was he still big and strong? Or had his muscles turned to fat after years of no longer playing football? Not that she should judge…

Beyond the obvious physical appeal, Chad had made her feel special when they spent time together. Like she was the only girl in the world. Jamie had treasured the hours they'd spent tucked away in the shadowy library corners. Twice a week, sometimes three times if he had an exam, she spent an hour with him, going over his math homework or helping him learn new ways to look at math problems.

She sat there on the large fitness ball, remembering long ago afternoons spent with him. One in particular burst into her memory.

"Jamie, you're not going to believe this!" Chad tossed his bookbag on the floor and opened the zipper to root inside. He pulled out a piece of paper, holding it up for her to see.

She glanced up, her heart thundering in her chest at his nearness. A huge B in blood red ink graced the upper right corner of the page.

"Chad, that's amazing!"

Before she understood what was happening, Chad lifted her from the chair, spinning her around in his arms. She closed her eyes, reveling in the feel of his body pressed to hers.

"A 'B,' Jamie. Can you imagine? I've never gotten a 'B' on a math test in my whole life. And I owe it all to you."

He squeezed her tight before placing her back on her feet.

She felt his absence to her bones. "I'm so proud of you, Chad."

She sat down when her shaking legs threatened to give out beneath her. "I knew you could do it."

He dropped into the chair opposite her, his long legs brushing hers under the table. "We did it, Jamie. We did it. I could never have done it without you."

"Oh, I don't know about that," she breathed, heat flooding her cheeks under his praise.

"Well, I do." He glanced at the crumpled paper again, almost as if making sure it still said 'B.' "Coach is never gonna believe this."

She pulled out a pencil from her bag, hiding her smile from him.
"Jamie?"

She blinked before looking straight at Griff's crotch.

"Eyes up here," he scolded with more than a hint of humor.

Jamie jerked her head up, throwing off the precarious balance she held on the ball. Before she could catch herself, the ball slid from under her. As though in slow motion, she dropped the weights, and pinwheeled her arms trying to right herself. *No such luck.* She landed in a heap on the floor at Griff's feet.

He lurched forward to help, grabbing her by the upper arms to lift her back to her feet. "Are you okay? Did you hurt yourself?"

She resisted rubbing her butt, which had taken the brunt of her fall. "Only my pride. Nothing new there."

She glanced at the purple hand weights, now lying on the floor at his feet. "Oh, no. Did they land on your feet?"

"Nah, I'm fine. Besides, they're only a few pounds. How much damage could they do?"

"I'd have at least broken a toe."

Griff held her upper arms. "Nah, I've got you," he murmured.

A shy smile lit her face, kicking up his heart rate. "My rescuer."

He released her slowly, almost as if he didn't want to. "You don't need rescuing, Jamie. Maybe a little direction now and then."

"In my defense, you did startle me, thus setting in motion that absurd cascade of events."

He nodded. "But in my defense, I did call your name several times. Where were you just now?"

"Oh, lost in thought, I guess. It happens."

"I see. Thinking anything in particular? Or anyone?"

"Nothing special. Thinking about the reunion."

"Oh. You never did tell me about Chuck."

"Chad, as you know, and there's nothing to really tell. He. Uh, we…" She glanced at the phone in her hand. "Sorry, I really have to go. Glad I didn't break your foot," she added as she turned and all but fled.

*****

"No worries," he called out to her retreating back. Griff watched her leave, something he was getting a little too good at.

"You know, you could just ask her out. Screw the rules."

Griff whirled, unaware he had an audience, and glanced down into the face of Harriet Newman.

"I didn't know you were there, Miss Harriet."

"Of course not, dearie, you were too busy pining after that young lady. I'm telling you, kiddo, life is short. Like me." She broke off cackling at her own joke.

"Miss Harriet, you know the rules. No mixing business with pleasure."

"I know, Griff. That's what you say every time one of those old biddies hits on you in class."

Not laughing took every bit of his will-power. Besides being his favorite of the geriatric set, Miss Harriet also held the distinction of being the oldest at the ripe old age of eighty-three.

"Now, Miss Harriett, you know you're the only woman for me," he crooned, continuing their running joke. She'd shown up on the very day Getting it Done opened. Marched right up to Griff telling him she needed to stay young. Miss Harriett was a force of nature, and Griff didn't know what to think at first. But she kept showing up, bringing more and more of her friends from the senior center. This prompted his creating the 'Move It So You Don't Lose It' class. The name was all Miss Harriett, but he loved it. The twice weekly class focused on low-impact cardio workouts for the sixty-five and up crowd. Much to his surprise, it was an instant hit.

The old lady winked at him. Winked! "And you have a special place in my heart, dear, but that young woman has you by another part of the anatomy if I'm not wrong." She winked again. "And I'm never wrong."

She wasn't wrong, not that he was giving the old hellion that bit of information.

"Jamie is a new member. I'm helping her out, teaching her how to use the machines safely. That's all."

"Then you're more stupid than you look," she muttered before making her way to the female locker room.

Griff shook his head, wondering at the wisdom of her words, as he headed to his office. He met Jack at the doorway to it, coming in from the front door. The other man's grin stretched from ear to ear.

"Did I just see Ms. Harriett schooling you, Griff?" Jack threw back his head and roared with laughter.

Griff unlocked their office door. "You did indeed. She gave me some advice on my love life, what there is of it."

"Did that advice include getting one by any chance?"

"You know it did. What else does she ever say to me?" He blew out a breath and dropped into his chair. "If you must know, she saw me talking with Jamie and had a few things to say about that. But she knows my rule." He directed a stare at his best friend. "As do you."

Jack held up his hands. "I get it. I do. And I agree it's a great rule to have."

"But?" Griff asked. "Sounds like there's a but coming."

Jack laughed. "Ah, you know me well."

"Well enough to know you won't shut up until you've had your say. Out with it."

"Touché. Normally, I'd agree with you. *But* there's something about Jamie. I know you like her, and she's not that woman coming to the gym for a hook-up. And she's not Sheila."

"Both true, but she's still a client. And I'm still the owner. Or half owner in this case." He took a sip from his water bottle. "And let's not forget the specter of Chad the almighty hanging over us."

Jack made a face. "Chad lives in Pennsylvania for Pete's sake. You have home court advantage."

Griff scowled at him. "Did you roll your eyes at me?"

"Yes, and I'd do it again. You're being a ninny."

"Look, just because you're over the moon about Sam doesn't mean I have to go down that path as well. My life is fine, thank you very much." But he knew the words were hollow as soon as they left his mouth. As would Jack.

He expected some snarky answer, but his friend's face fell at the mention of Jamie's friend.

"I am completely over the moon about Sam, freely admitting that one. But she keeps shooting me down when I ask for a 'real' date." His normally chipper friend sighed. And you're right about the second part also. I do want you to be as happy." He held up one finger when Griff would have interrupted. "I'm only saying this because I see your face when you're around her. Jamie makes you happy. And you deserve that. Especially after Sheila the shark."

"Well, none of it matters. Jamie's a client. You and I own the place. End of discussion." He swiveled to his computer, turning it on. Maybe Jack would take the hint.

Maybe not.

"All I'm saying is she makes you laugh. And happy. That's not nothing. Okay, you know what I mean. Life is short."

"Funny, that's what Miss Harriett just said to me. The part about life being short."

"See? I'm not wrong. Miss Harriett knows a thing or two about life. She and her cronies could teach you something." He ducked as Griff threw a towel at his head. "Okay, I give up. For now. And only because I have a client in exactly one minute. But I'm not letting this go."

Griff lowered his head into his hands and groaned. "Just what I need."

"You're welcome," Jack called as he left their office.

Griff knew Jack was right, at least about getting out there again. He hadn't really dated anyone since Sheila. But it wasn't because he was broken-hearted. The only thing she'd hurt was his pride. And even though he'd only known Jamie for a few days, he had a funny feeling she could do a lot more damage than Sheila ever could.

Chapter Eleven

"Greed is so destructive. It destroys everything."
-Eartha Kitt

Jamie clutched her pen so hard under the table, she feared she might snap it in two. The dragon had droned on for the past forty-five minutes, mostly about their need to bring more clients, in other words money, into the firm. Which translated into another vacation home for him for sure. How many vacation homes did one man need?

She avoided eye contact with Sam, who sat across the conference table from her. A deliberate choice on Sam's part. Not looking directly at Sam was Jamie's choice. Nothing good could come from that. Sam was evil that way. Even now, her phone, thankfully set to silent, glowed with incoming texts from her friend. She let go of the pen long enough to flip it over. No need to read something that would only make her burst out in laughter in the otherwise silent room. The dragon was the only one who'd spoken since the meeting started.

And yet she was dying to read whatever Sam had sent her. *Think of something else. Anything else.* An image of Griff holding the plank position (yes, she'd Googled it) popped into her head.

Definitely not funny. But also, not work appropriate as she squirmed in her seat a bit.

"Am I boring you, Miss Lawler? Is there somewhere you'd rather be?"

"*Yes!*" she screamed in her head.

"Miss Lawler?"

Jamie realized she hadn't answered him, as all eyes turned toward her. "No, sir."

"That's what I thought. Do try to pay attention then," snapped the older man.

"Yes, sir," she replied in the smallest voice possible. For the rest of the meeting, what felt

like hours rather than ten minutes, Jamie kept her face blank and eyes straight ahead, staring at a

point over Jim Murray's shoulder. If he thought she was staring at him, so be it. Worth the risk.

Mr. Smith ended the meeting, finally, by imploring them to 'go out and grab new business by the horns.' She snickered under her breath.

Sam grabbed her by the elbow, whisking her from the room. When they were a safe distance away, she doubled over laughing.

Jamie stood there, watching her, and felt her own lips twitch. "It's not funny," she said with no conviction in her tone.

"It kind of is," wheezed her friend, trying for control.

Jamie shoved Sam into her office, closing the door behind her. "I can't take it anymore. Not one more pep talk about bringing in more money for that greedy man."

"Agreed. You know what we have to do."

Jamie walked around her desk and collapsed into her chair. "We aren't ready yet, Sam."

"You mean you're not ready, Jamie. I've been ready since

that night in the restaurant when we dreamed up Operation Phoenix."

Jamie nodded and grabbed the small stress ball she kept in her drawer. She squeezed it while gnawing on her lower lip. "You're right. I'm the problem."

Sam sank into one of the visitor chairs in front of the desk. "Ah, honey, I didn't mean it like that."

"I know, but you're not wrong. I'm the one trapped in the rut. I'm the one afraid of change. Not that life here is wonderful."

"You're not wrong there." Sam leaned forward in her seat. "Look, I'm not saying this will be easy. Because it won't. There's a lot to be said for the security of a regular paycheck. But this is the time to do it, Jamie, before either of us marries and has kids."

"No danger for me. I'd have to have a date first," Jamie replied.

A knock on the office door proceeded Mr. Smith entering the office. "Ladies, I trust this is an impromptu strategy meeting of some sort."

His gruff tone left no doubt about his feelings finding Sam in Jamie's office. Jamie stood, searching for something to say to explain the situation, when Sam turned her head toward him.

"It's my fault, sir. I have cramps you can't even imagine. I mean, I don't know how I haven't exsanguinated this month. The amount of blood just this morning alone." She stopped for a moment, maybe to take in the crimson color of his face. "And I ran out of tampons. Luckily, Jamie has some."

"Oh, uh, very well then." He backed away from the women as if having a menstrual cycle might be contagious.

Jamie bit her lips, hard, to keep from laughing at the sight of his retreating form. Poor man couldn't get out the door fast enough.

"You're evil," she admonished her friend without any heat in her voice.

"Tell me something we don't know already." She glanced at her perfect nails as if bored before getting up. "We have to move forward with Operation Phoenix, sooner rather than later. That's all I'm saying." She gave a small wave of her fingers on her way out the door.

She's not wrong.

Jamie swiveled her chair to look at the ocean. The churning, grey waves matched her mood. She'd been unhappy at Smith & Smith for a long time; years really. But inertia and fear of the unknown were powerful motivators.

Ideally, they would build a client load before leaving the safety net of a full-time job, but it wasn't a possibility. Ever since that drunken conversation, Jamie had squirreled away whatever money she could. Her current splurges had been limited to her gym membership and Netflix subscription, with the occasional night out with Sam tossed in. She drove an older model car and lived in a modest home.

Jamie turned back to her desk and clicked her mouse to wake up her computer. Lord knows she had a lot to do today and well into the evening. Sitting here, daydreaming, wouldn't get that done. Then she picked up her phone. The latest text from Sam, sent during the ridiculous meeting, was a GIF of a phoenix rising from flames. She smiled at her friend's enthusiasm. Then a small frisson of excitement wound through her belly. *Why couldn't they start planning for Operation Phoenix? What did they really have to lose?*

Before she could stop herself, Jamie tapped in the words *'let's do this.'* She crossed her fingers before hitting send. The she placed her phone in her top drawer and started her day, singing a happy tune under her breath.

*****

"Great, ladies, keep it up," Griff encouraged the morning group of senior citizens. Generally, he had a few men in this group but not this morning. "Okay, that's terrific. Now let's switch to cool down."

He led them in various stretching exercises, nothing too strenuous, until the alarm beeped on his phone. "Great job everyone!"

A group of three or four ladies broke off from those leaving the room, heading toward him. Griff said a silent prayer this didn't mean what he thought.

"Griff honey, did I ever tell you about my great niece, Amanda?" This from Phyllis, number two in years, only behind Miss Harriet.

This was exactly what he feared.

Griff smiled and shook his head. "I don't believe you have, Phyllis. But with the business and all, I don't really have a lot of time for dating right now."

"You're not getting any younger," grunted Gwendolyn.

"None of us are," Griff agreed.

"Don't get smart with me, young man," she responded. "Some of us are already married to the loves of their lives.

"Some of us have done that several times already," sniped Vera.

Gwendolyn glared at Vera, opening her mouth to respond. Griff waded in before things got testy.

"Ladies, I appreciate that y'all worry about me. Really, I do. But I'm fine. Once things settle down a bit here, I'll make sure I meet a nice woman." He made an X over his heart. "I promise."

Miss Harriet, quiet for once, stood at the back of the small group. Too late, Griff noticed the smile on her face and gleam in her eye.

"I think our young man has already met someone he fancies. Isn't that right, Griff?"

Young man? He was on the wrong side of thirty-five already. Griff cleared his throat. "No comment," he mumbled, hoping that would satisfy them.

"Who's caught our Griff's eye?" asked Gwendolyn. Her mouth curled down further. "Not that slutty Darla I hope."

"That woman's after anything in pants. Surely our Griff would have better judgment than that," added Vera.

They were right, but he wasn't about to badmouth another client to them, no matter how much he agreed. Instead, he headed toward the door, hoping they'd follow. "Now, ladies, as I said, I'm doing fine. Let's all get some water." Griff herded them out into the gym and toward the desk.

He loved his senior set, but matchmaking was an Olympic sport for them. Someone always had a single neighbor, niece, or granddaughter of a second cousin once removed. And he appreciated the sentiment, but he wasn't much for blind dates. He enjoyed them about as much as he did a good root canal.

Griff opened the fridge and grabbed waters, handing one to each woman. "Now, if you'll excuse me, there's a mountain of paperwork in my office with my name on it."

He hugged each before escaping to his office. And escaping was what it was. As much as he enjoyed their company, constantly dodging their endless set up attempts exhausted him. And he didn't kid about the work awaiting him, although the thought of it brought a scowl to his face.

If only he knew an accountant…

*****

As she expected, Sam had been over the moon with her text. In between her client meetings, Jamie read text after text, each more excited than the previous. And that's why she'd said she wanted to go forward with it. Sam would hold her to it. No backing out now. And she needed that, to be held accountable.

Jamie no longer cared for the rigidity of corporate life. What she wanted was her own firm where she could set the rules. For instance, if they wanted a bring your dog to work day, they could make it a thing. Not that she had a dog, and Fiona would hate it. People weren't her thing. But she might get a dog, someday. And she just might want to bring said dog to work. She at least wanted the opportunity to do so.

On impulse, she dashed off another in the seemingly endless stream of texts to Sam today, this one proposing a bring your pet to work day. Within a minute, a 'Heck, yeah" popped up on her phone. Jamie laughed and laughed, knowing they were moving in the right direction.

Hours later, after arriving home, wolfing down a frozen meal for one and feeding Fiona, she stretched, moving her head around on her shoulders. She'd been hunched over her laptop for hours and needed a break. Maybe some exercise. Maybe she'd go to the gym. Wait, what? Twice in one day? Pretty radical for someone who had never entered a gym prior to a few weeks ago.

But she felt restless and edgy after the day she'd had. Ideas for Operation Phoenix rolled through her head like a runaway freight train. Before she lost the momentum, Jamie jumped up, grabbed her phone and keys, and bolted out the door with a "See you later," to Fiona tossed over her shoulder.

On the short drive, Jamie rocked along to AC/DC on her

Sirius radio. Bless her friend Ben from college for educating her on classic rock. Her mind continued to race, but this time her thoughts revolved around Griff. Knowing he wouldn't be there this late (at least she didn't think so) made it easier. And harder.

A few minutes later, she pulled into the parking lot. She glanced around, noting only one other car off in the corner. Once again, she parked right near the front door. Better to be smart this late at night. Grabbing her phone and earbuds, Jamie left her car and raced inside. She spied one other lone female doing something insane with what had to be a truck tire, flipping it continually around the room where she thought classes might be held. The woman did not notice her, seemingly intent on besting her rubber foe.

Not for her, Jamie chuckled to herself, and jumped on her favorite treadmill. Tonight, she was determined to run. At least for a few moments. Something faster than a slow jog, which is all she had managed thus far. With no Griff as witness to her folly, she had no reason to put it off. She slid in her earbuds and stretched her legs for a minute. She watched others in the gym, hopefully in a non-creepy way, hoping to pick up tips. Like how to stretch to avoid hurting herself. Griff had been wonderful, but she didn't want to abuse their friendship, or whatever it was.

Satisfied she'd warmed up her muscles, Jamie hit play on her phone. Then she started the machine. She began at her usual slightly faster than a turtle pace. She needed to work on her speed but no reason to go crazy. Or kill herself.

After a few minutes, she increased the speed in increments, upping it every minute or so. Before she knew it, she was running. Running!

She kept at it, sweat pouring out of her. From every possible sweat gland. She swiped a hand across her face, trying to get the wet, clingy tendrils of hair from her face. And still she didn't stop. Not even when breathing became torture. Each breath burned, but she didn't stop. Then she looked up and spied Griff in the mirror. He stood behind her and off to the side.

"Well, look at you running," he called out to her.

Jamie pulled out one ear bud. "What? I couldn't hear you." Running and speaking? A new high for her.

"I just commended you for running. Way to go." He cocked his head to the side, studying her. "Are you okay?"

"I'm fine," she managed in between ragged breaths.

"It'll improve, the talking and breathing part, as you develop lung capacity."

"Well, unless it happens in the next five seconds, I may die." A stitch developed in her side, and she hit the stop button.

Seeking a nonchalance she didn't feel, she turned to Griff. "What brings you here at this hour? Not that you can't come at night. Or anytime you want of course." *Stop talking, Jamie!*

"You're cute when you're nervous."

That might have been the very last thing she expected to hear from his mouth. His oh so delicious mouth she was not staring at.

"Thank you, I think."

"I mean you're always cute, of course. But when you're nervous, you do this thing where you bite your lip." He bit down on his to demonstrate. "It gets me. Every time."

That she understood because watching him bite his lip made her want to soothe it, with her tongue. Instead, she looked down at her feet. "I felt restless tonight. So, here I am." She looked up at him. "I'll have you know this is a historic event. Usually restlessness equals too much Ben and Jerry's. My two favorite guys."

Griff clapped his hands a few times. "That's amazing, Jamie. Good for you. What made you come here instead of your long-standing date?" His green eyes danced with delight.

You she almost blurted and wondered how he might respond. "Oh, I don't know. New year, new rules. I'm trying to make better choices."

"And Charlie, of course," he muttered.

"Who? Oh, you mean Chad! Of course." For a moment, lost in the depth of his gaze, she had no idea what he was talking about.

"Of course. Well, I'll let you get back to it."

Griff turned and walked toward the back of the gym.

Jamie stood there, trying to figure out what had happened. They went from joking to his walking off in a matter of seconds. *Who could figure out men?* She got back up on the treadmill and restarted it.

*****

Griff piled more weight on the machine and pushed his body to the limits. Queen's "We Will Rock You" blared in his ears. His older brother had a thing for classic rock that he'd shared with Griff at a young age. The biopic of Freddie Mercury's life had renewed his love for their music. He sang along in his head, nobody needed to hear him singing, as he started yet another set of reps. He couldn't believe he mentioned Chad, the man who lurked between them. The guy may as well be a ghost, one that popped up at odd moments to ruin everything.

He finished his set and sat down on the bench, wiping the sweat pouring from his face. He shook his head. Chad or no Chad, Jamie was off limits. *No dating clients!* He made the rule for a reason. Of course, that had been long before Jamie popped into his life. Now the rule seemed stupid.

He had the worst luck. The first woman to catch his eye in longer than he cared to admit, and she had to be a client. Not to mention in love with some guy hundreds of miles away from her past. And that brought him right back to Chad. What was it with that guy anyway? Why did he have such a hold on Jamie?

Griff guzzled some water before putting his elbows on his knees and his head in his hands. Jamie was not a possibility. He had to remember that.

"Griff, are you okay?"

He watched impossibly small sneakers move into his range of vision. Speak of the devil.

"I'm fine, thanks. Just a bit tired."

He sat up. She stood a measly two feet from him. Biting that damn lip of hers. She really wasn't going to make this easy for him, was she?

"Oh. Okay. It's just you seemed a bit, well, maybe angry before. Was it something I said?"

Her tiny voiced ripped into his gut.

"No, of course not. I have a lot on my mind." *You, for starts.* But he wasn't telling her that.

A wide smile formed on her lips, spreading to her eyes. And now his gut dipped with a totally different sensation.

"I'm glad. I thought maybe I had said something to upset you. Well, I'm going to go home. Work is really ramping up. I need my sleep. See you."

"See you around," he agreed and gave her a small wave.

She returned the gesture and turned to leave. She walked slowly. Maybe his imagination ran wild, but she seemed almost reluctant to leave.

"Would you like to have dinner with me sometime?" he called before he could stop himself.

She turned to face him, only a few feet away. "Dinner?" she parroted.

"You know. The meal traditionally eaten in the evening."

"I know what dinner means. I wasn't expecting you to ask me, that's all."

"Would lunch be better?"

"Ah, no."

"No, lunch wouldn't be better? Or no, you're not interested in having a meal with me?" He mentally crossed his fingers, hoping for the first.

"I meant lunch is tricky. We get busy, and I usually eat something at my desk that I brought from home or order in."

"And dinner?" he asked, almost holding his breath in anticipation of her answer. "You do eat dinner, right? I saw you at Dusty's. You ate food," he joked.

To his delight, a swath of color crept into her cheeks.

"Yes, of course, I eat dinner."

Jamie jingled her keys in her hands, making him wonder if he made her nervous.

"Now that we know you eat dinner; would you like to eat it with me sometime?"

"I could do that. I have to go."

Before Griff could ask when, she bolted from the gym. He didn't go after her. Rather, he stood there with what he was sure was a goofy grin on his face. And then he raised a fist in the air and yelled, "Yeah!"

Chapter Twelve

"There is nothing clever about confusion."
-William Wyler

Jamie got into her car and drove on automatic pilot. She continued that way until she pulled into her driveway. "What just happened?" she muttered aloud in her car. One minute, Griff seemed angry with her, the next he'd asked her out. To dinner. With him!

She jumped out of her car and dashed to the front door. The late-night air held a bit of chill. Spring couldn't come fast enough. At least there wouldn't be any snow. That was one thing Jamie did not miss from living up north.

Once inside, Jamie tossed her keys in the bowl where they lived near the door and spied Fiona, stretched out along the back of her sofa. She lifted her head and stared at Jamie for a moment, blinking once, then laying her head back down upon the ancient quilt Jamie's grandmother had made for her as a child. Fiona had never been the wind-herself-around-your-ankles type. More like the why-haven't-you-fed-me type.

Jamie took a shower and got ready for bed. Not until she crawled under her downed comforter did she allow herself to think about what had happened. And then she texted Sam.

"Call me. Now!"

Within seconds, her phone rang.

"He asked me out on a date, and I said yes before pretty much running from the gym," all came out in one long breath.

"About time! It's been so long, I'm worried you might be a virgin again, honey."

The sound of Sam's laughter eased Jamie's frazzled nerves.

"Hold up. We are talking about Griff, right?"

"Of course, I am," Jamie squealed into the phone. "This is me we're talking about. I don't have a line of guys queued up to ask me out." She blew out a breath and then inhaled slowly; a trick she'd learned in college.

"First off, you absolutely could if you saw yourself the way I see you," Sam scolded.

"Not this old argument again," Jamie protested.

"Yes, again, and forever until you do. But for now, tell me everything."

And Jamie did, even the embarrassing part about basically fleeing from the gym after she agreed to dinner.

Sam's laughter didn't comfort her this time. She waited until the snorting ceased.

"Nice."

"I'm sorry, Jamie, I am, but you can't blame me. You *ran* from him as if he tried to kill you, not ask you out." Another round of laughing and snorting followed.

"In my defense, he'd acted weird a few minutes prior." She told Sam what happened.

"He sounds jealous," Sam stated, no trace of laughter in her voice.

"Jealous? Griff? Have you seen him? Better yet, have you lost your mind?"

"Yes, yes, yes, and no," Sam answered. "What were you two discussing when his mood changed so abruptly."

Jamie thought about it for a moment. "Ben and Jerry's ice cream? Maybe he's lactose intolerant," she joked.

"Did you not mention Chad right before he bolted?"

"Chad?" And then it hit her. "Actually, *he* brought up Chad."

"After you talked about changing your habits and living healthier, which you already told him was for Chad. And by the way, I think that's a terrible reason for this. Although I love you're changing the things you're unhappy with. Good for you! Good for Operation Phoenix!"

Jamie's mind whirled in a million different directions. "I did say that to him about Chad, but that was in the very beginning. How would he remember?"

"Think, think, think, as Pooh would say. Maybe he remembers because it affects him. Maybe he remembers because he sees this stupid Chad as a rival. Maybe he remembers because he likes you." The last bit she crooned through the phone.

Jamie shrugged, even though Sam couldn't see. "Back to have you seen him. Griff is gorgeous. Like take a second look passing him on the street gorgeous. And Chad was not stupid, just more focused on athletics." She had no idea why she felt the need to defend him years later.

"Chad never noticed you right under his nose. His loss."

"Aw, you're the best," Jamie commented.

"True, but back to Griff. Yes, the man holds a certain appeal. But so do you, Jamie. Between your gorgeous eyes and lush figure, not to mention your hair."

It became Jamie's turn to snort. "I do like my eyes. But lush? I am overweight. Say it with me."

"You are not overweight, Jamie."

"Okay, then I'm under-tall."

"I give up. What you are is a smart, beautiful, funny woman who has so much to offer some lucky man. And you're about to own your own business," Sam added.

"Well, that part is true at least. Oh, and I am funny. I've always thought of it as my one redeeming quality." The part about owning her own business, or owning it with Sam, set off a wave of flutters in her belly, part excitement, part terror.

"Jamie, Jamie, Jamie, how many times do I have to remind you? You are beautiful. Fine, if you feel you need to lose a little weight, I'd say ten pounds at the most. Will that make you feel better about yourself?"

Jamie could see Sam shaking her head in her mind's eye. She didn't have to be present to know. Her long red hair would be swishing back and forth, maybe hands on hips as well.

"If only I had ten pounds to lose. Try three times that. At least."

"Let's agree to disagree. Now back to this date. Where is he taking you? When? What are you going to wear?"

"I don't have an answer for any of those, especially the last. You know I'm hopeless when it comes to fashion."

"True, you really are. And you might have some idea about the first two if you hadn't gone running into the night."

Jamie half smothered a yawn. "Sorry. It's been a long, and interesting, day. I have to go to sleep now. See you tomorrow."

"Yes, in the dragon's lair. Night!"

Jamie disconnected the call and plugged in her phone on the bedside table. She grabbed her iPad and slipped between the digital pages of a romance novel. Her love life might be a mess, but she could at least count on a happy ever after in the book.

By the middle of the next afternoon, Jamie regretted staying up late reading last night. But the book was a real page turner. Would the hero learn to love again? Would the heroine stay or go? So what if she knew they both would. There weren't as many happy endings in real life; she'd take it.

Stifling a yawn, Jamie wandered out of her office in search of caffeine. She grabbed one of her favorite mugs from the cabinet, this one saying, "Not all who wander are lost." She'd picked it up in London three years ago. Jamie's biggest expenditure in life was travel.

With the craziness of her job, the insane hours during tax season alone, Jamie lived to travel. Sometimes Sam joined her. Others, she flew solo, much to the horror and chagrin of her parents. After all, if she were kidnapped and murdered in Greece, who would know? Jamie never let that stop her. Her bucket list pretty much consisted of places she hadn't visited, Australia, Scotland, the Maldives, Belgium, Belize. The list went on and on in her mind.

And sky diving. Jamie wasn't wild about heights, which had made the Eiffel Tower a bit difficult. What better way to conquer that fear than sky diving? She popped a pod into the coffee machine and waited. Coffee wasn't her first choice, but she drank a lot of it during tax season. And when she stayed up too late reading. Or watching Netflix, another of her vices. What an exciting life she led…

"Someone stayed up too late reading again, didn't they?" asked Sam as she sailed into the kitchen. She winked at Jamie before reaching for her own coffee pod. "I believe you said something about going to bed when we hung up, didn't you?"

"True, but you know how I am. And I don't see it changing." She looked around the area to make sure they were alone and lowered her voice. "Maybe another rule at Phoenix Accounting will be not starting until ten in the morning."

Sam stepped in and high-fived her. "That's my girl!" She eyed Jamie as if trying to figure out something. "What's gotten into you? I'm not complaining, mind you, but something is changing."

Jamie moved to the coffee machine, taking her mug and the empty pod out. "I feel free. Since making the decision to go forward with Operation Phoenix, I feel different, lighter."

"Maybe Griff has something to do with that," Sam commented.

Jamie shook her head. "This has nothing to do with him."

"Not even the tiniest bit?"

Jamie held her hand up, thumb and pointer finger almost touching. "Maybe this much."

Sam clapped her hands. "I'll take it." She looked Jamie's clothing up and down. "Now, to do something about your wardrobe choices."

*****

"I may have asked Jamie to dinner," Griff announced as he ate his lunch at his desk.

Jack looked up from his own meal. "You may have? Or you did?"

Griff grinned across the desks at his friend. "Oh, I did. And she said yes. Right before running for the door as though the hounds of Hell nipped at her heels." He shook his head, still wondering about her reaction.

"Well good for you. And who knows why women do any of the things they do?" He took a big bite of his apple, chewing and swallowing before proceeding. "And far be it from me to get in between you and some action, finally, but what about your rule?"

And just like that, the high Griff had felt dissipated.

"I have no idea. There's something about her. She's so sweet and yet sexy without even trying." He shrugged. "And she makes me laugh."

"Then it's settled. Go for it, I say."

"Of course, you would. Never were one for the rules."

"You got me."

"How are things with Sam, by the way?"

"Nice deflection, but I'll allow it." A frown bloomed on his face. "Things are fantastic, thanks for asking." A definite edge had tainted his voice. "Apparently, we're *friends*."

"Ouch." Griff wrestled with what to say next for a moment before opening his mouth. "Jamie mentioned to me that Sam wasn't really into relationships. Kind of warned me, or you, really."

"How cute is that? Jamie's worried about me. Did she happen to mention why?"

In for a penny, in for a pound as his dead granny would say. "Apparently, she doesn't 'do relationships.' Doesn't believe in them. Jamie mentioned that she dates a lot. 'She goes on a lot of first dates' is what Jamie said."

Jack leaned back in his chair. "Have you seen her? I'm sure she does date a lot. And a lot of first dates means they aren't worthy of her."

"Does that mean that you are?" Griff asked.

"I'd like to think so. Of course, she has to give me a chance to prove it."

Griff's mouth dropped open. "What? She still hasn't fallen for the Whitaker charm?"

Jack shook his head. "She mentioned that her parents divorced many years ago. I got the feeling it wasn't an amicable one."

Griff nodded. "Hard to get past that."

"Might explain why she's commitment phobic," Jack guessed

"Maybe she'll come around."

"Too soon to tell, my friend. But I like her. A lot."

The smile, tinged with sadness, on Jack's face told the story. Something tightened a little in his chest. He knew the feeling.

"Well, gotta go. Have a new client coming in for their first training session. Wish me luck." Jack grabbed his phone and water bottle, heading out the door.

Griff slid his finger across the mouse pad of his laptop, waking it up. Bringing up the day's schedule, he saw that he had a little time before his next class. That gave him a moment to plan out the date Jamie had agreed to before fleeing the gym. He hoped her behavior last night said more about her nervousness than how she felt about him.

Chapter Thirteen

"Along with any great joy comes a good deal of anxiety and nervousness."
-Chris Sullivan

You've got this! Jamie sat in her car in the predawn darkness and chill, staring at the front of Getting It Done. *Go in already.* She'd skipped yesterday's morning workout, telling herself that two times at the gym the day before made up for it. And if it also meant avoiding Griff for a little longer, then even better. Her cheeks burned as she thought about running out on him the other night. In her defense, the dinner invitation seemed very off the cuff and caught her off guard. Jamie didn't get a lot of spontaneous offers of dinner. That was Sam's forte.

Knowing she would sit there until it was time to get ready for work, Jamie left the security of her car and headed into the gym. She bypassed her usual treadmill and chose a recumbent bike. How hard could this be? Griff had taught her the importance of adjusting the equipment for her height (or lack thereof), so she did before getting on. She put her earbuds in and chose some fast music to get her going. Picking an interval program for the bike, she sat back and started peddling.

This seemed way easier than the treadmill, she didn't even have to stand. Mentally high-fiving herself for her brilliant choice, she closed her eyes and tried to lose herself in the music. Which lasted for about a minute before thoughts of Griff creeped in. Griff lifting weights. Griff laughing at something she said. Griff looking way too hot in shorts and a sleeveless shirt. That last thought caught her breath, making it ragged.

Then she realized the peddling had grown harder. Must be that interval stuff Griff had taught her. She focused on her breathing and peddled away, delighted as the calories burned ticked higher.

When the interval changed again and it got easier to peddle, Jamie let out a long breath. *Whew!* It could only have lasted a minute or two, but she really struggled near the end of it. At least now she could catch her breath. She closed her eyes and tried to relax as her breathing and heart rate dropped out of the alarming range.

She wondered where Griff could be. Maybe he slept in late. No, don't think of him in bed, she chastised herself. Maybe he had to get to work early. Goodness knew her job demanded strange hours.

Her eyes popped open when the difficulty increased again. The machine displayed a mountain road. What was she doing, climbing the Alps? Jamie sat up straighter, gasping a bit for air. Her calves screamed as she peddled. Her lungs began to burn. *She really was out of shape!*

When Jamie thought she'd have to hit the emergency stop button, the interval dropped again to a slower pace. Jamie panted as she pushed damp hair from her face. She'd forgotten to put it in a ponytail in her rush to leave this morning. Now the heavy, past her shoulders hair clung damply to her. When her lungs burst, that wouldn't matter.

She tried to focus on her breathing. In through her nose, out through her mouth like Griff had taught her. Good thing he wasn't here; she'd kill him. Somehow, this had to be his fault, always encouraging her to try new machines in the gym. Various methods of body disposal danced through her head as she focused on the screen in front of her.

Here come the mountains again. Knowing the tougher interval at least didn't last long, she leaned forward, putting everything she had into it. *Remember to breathe!* When she got tired or overwhelmed in the gym, she often forgot to breathe properly. Jamie pumped her legs while breathing in and out. In and out. Each breathe felt like her last, but she continued to pedal. Only knowing this interval would end kept her going. Words she'd never been allowed to say as a child streamed from her mouth.

Her battle against the mountain continued until her twenty minutes ended. Screw cool down. As soon as the bike entered that phase, she hit the stop button. Jamie let her feet slide from the pedals. She leaned forward, resting her elbows on her knees, and panted for air. She'd feel this in the morning, but for now, excitement coursed through her tired body. She'd done it!

When breathing no longer felt like a knife ripping through her chest, Jamie slipped from the bike, standing cautiously. She wasn't sure her legs would hold her. She stood, grinning when she didn't fall over. She didn't die after all.

She turned and spied Griff a few rows away, grinning at her. He'd probably heard all the swearing the bike and the damned Alps had wrung from her body. Not to mention her loose, sweaty hair clinging to her face. Didn't matter. She was too tired to care. Instead, she stood straight and waved at him. Then she watched as his lean form approached her. *God, that man was put together well.*

"Nice job," he called.

"Have you been there long?" *Please say no.*

"Maybe a few minutes. I waited until you were finished. Didn't want to scare you again," he said with a grin. "Can't have you falling off another machine."

"True. Not sure my dignity could survive it. Although if you heard what I just said to the bike, I may not have any left to kill."

"No worries. You're not the first to yell at a machine."

Good, maybe he didn't hear me curse.

"Or curse for that matter. Although, you do get points for originality. Not sure I've ever heard that combination or words before today."

So much for that thought. "Oh, well you should hear me when I cut myself shaving in the shower."

His eyes warmed, and Jamie realized what she'd said. She knew the heat in her face had more to do with her words than the bike.

"Uh, I just meant." She stopped and blew out a breath. "No point trying to salvage that."

Griff chuckled. "I knew what you meant."

When he didn't say anything else, she leaned against the bike. At least he was a gentleman and let her comment slide. Maybe she'd get out of here easily.

"About our dinner plans," he began.

Or not.

"Yes?" Brilliant but the best she could do.

"Have you thought about when? I think your schedule may be a bit tighter than mine in the evenings."

"Oh, I hadn't really thought about it." *Blatant lie...*

"Oh."

His shoulders sagged the tiniest bit, making Jamie feel bad for what she'd said.

"Let me rephrase that and start with an apology." She watched his eyebrows climb toward his hairline. "I sort of, uh, bolted the other night. And I am sorry. You caught me off guard. I'm not used to cute guys asking me to have dinner with them."

His face broke into a grin. "You think I'm cute?"

She held his gaze, even though she wanted to look everywhere else instead.

"Have you seen yourself? Cute doesn't cover it. But don't let that give you a big head. There are other qualities more important."

And now she sounded like a frustrated school principal.

Griff stepped forward and tucked the damp hair behind her ears on either side of her face. "I happen to think you're cute also."

Jamie burst out laughing. She couldn't help it. She glanced down at her sweaty self. She barely qualified as cute on her best day. This was far from her best day.

"That's very sweet of you, but I know what I look like."

Instead of replying, Griff turned her by the shoulders and walked her to the mirror. "Look at yourself, Jamie. But see what I see. Your face is flushed from hard work, and the color makes your eyes pop."

She glanced up, her eyes meeting his in the mirror. He was right. Her high color brought out the gold flecks in her eyes. She met his gaze in the mirror and smiled.

"Well, my hair is a wreck. But my eyes are sparkling. I've always thought my eyes and my hair are my best features."

She held her breath as he raked his gaze down the length of her. Standing up close to him brought out the difference in their heights. He had over a foot on her short stature and standing close to him made her feel delicate; a new feeling for her.

"I kind of like the whole package," he murmured, never breaking eye contact.

"About dinner…" She broke off, not knowing what else to say. *Sorry I was an idiot and bolted?*

He continued to hold eye contact with her in the mirror. "About dinner?"

She blew out a breath. He wasn't going to make this easy for her.

"Again, I'm sorry about running out the other night." She turned to face him. "Your invitation surprised me. That's all."

His dark brows drew together. "Why? I'm sure you get asked out all the time."

"You'd think, right?" She laughed then, wiping her hands on her sweats. "But no, not so much. I work a lot. And then when I go out with Sam, I sort of become invisible."

"I find that hard to believe. The invisible part I mean."

"Have you seen Sam? She's ridiculously gorgeous. That fiery red hair and blazing green eyes. Then there's her legs that go on forever. Are you blind?"

"No, and I've seen Sam. And yes, she's very pretty. But, she's not you. You make me laugh. I admire what you're doing, working hard for the goals you've set for yourself." He reached out with one finger and stroked it along the line of her jaw. "And maybe I prefer curvy brunettes with eyes I could get lost in."

And she forgot to breathe.

"Back to dinner. Tell me what works for you since you have the crazier schedule," Griff offered.

"Right now, weekends are better." She sighed. "This is the

part where I chant, I love my job, I love my job."

"About that. If you hate it so much, why don't you do something about it?"

"Funny you should ask." She told him about yesterday, texting Sam about starting their own firm. She chewed her lip when she finished, waiting him to say something. "Well? What do you think?" she asked when she couldn't take the suspense anymore.

Griff lifted her off her feet and swung her around in his arms. "What do I think? I think that's amazing!"

He placed her back on her feet, and she immediately missed the feeling of his strong arms around her.

"Really?" she asked.

"What's not to love? You're getting away from what sounds like a toxic situation. You'll be your own boss. Well, you and Sam."

"It's a big step, Griff. What if we fail?"

"What if you don't?" he countered.

"I'll be eating Ramen for months if not years."

He threw his head back and laughed. "I doubt you'll be forced to do that. Do you have a business plan? Do you have savings?"

She nodded. "Yes to both of those. I make decent money at the firm, and other than travelling, I don't spend a lot. I have always been on the thrifty side, but once we discussed doing this, I started shoveling away any money I could."

"Then you're already way ahead of most small business owners. You have a plan and a great partner." He reached out and squeezed one arm. "I'm not saying this will be easy. Starting out is rough, but this is what you want, so any sacrifice will be worth it."

She wondered how he knew so much about starting a

business and then remembered she still had no idea what he did for a living. She opened her mouth to ask when he started talking again.

"Not that I'm trying to rush you out of here, but don't you have to get to work?"

"Huh, work?" Jamie glanced at her phone and gasped at the time. She had no idea they'd been talking so long. "Oh my gosh, I have to go." She swiped her phone open. "Can I get your number? Then we can talk about when this dinner of ours is going to happen."

Griff smiled at her. "I love a woman who takes control," he joked. He rattled off his number which she entered into her phone.

"I really have to go, but I'll call or text you. Bye." She waved then jogged toward the door.

*****

Griff laughed at her retreating form. She really had brought a lot of that to his life. Building their business with Jack had been his focus for almost two years. One reason Sheila gave for leaving him, beyond the obvious of his friend's trust find, was he was never around to have any 'fun.' She didn't seem to understand the time and effort building Getting It Done demanded.

When he thought about it, Sheila leaving him barely created a ripple in his life. He never loved her. They probably stayed together out of habit. Life, and love, should be more than habit. If he was being honest, other than hurt pride, Sheila's leaving brought relief, not heartache. They had fought a lot the last few months they were together. She wanted to go out every night. She didn't understand why he always had to work.

Starting the gym was rough, as he had told Jamie. But maybe, if he'd cared more for Sheila, he would have made more time for her. Chewing on that thought, he jumped up on one of the treadmills and started his daily five-mile run. Most days he preferred to run along the beach but not until the weather warmed up a bit.

Although he got a fair bit of exercise during the day, helping clients, he always liked to start his day with a run. It centered him, allowing him to clear his head for the new day. But today, his head filled with thoughts of Jamie. He hoped she texted or called him today so that he had her number. That thought made him shake his head. Now he sounded like a teenage girl. Jack would pull his man card for sure.

But he couldn't help how he felt when he thought about taking her to dinner. Unlike Jack, Griff preferred a casual restaurant. One where they could relax, talk, get to know each other better, and not worry about which fork to use. Did she like Italian? Mexican? Maybe he could ask Jack to ask Sam. No. He rejected that idea as soon as it formed in his head. He'd figure it out.

Pushing the speed and incline further now that he felt warmed up, Griff concentrated on the pounding of his feet on the treadmill. The repeated, rhythmic noise centered him. When he'd served in war zones with the Marines, running had saved him. Even if he only ran within the perimeter of their compound. He ran every day to block out the sounds and memories. He didn't always agree with what they were doing over there, but he was proud of his service. And it had allowed him to save a lot of money over the years.

When he and Jack finally opened Getting It Done, his father had taken him aside and asked if he needed any money. And although he appreciated the gesture, he'd been able to tell him no. Between saving and some smart investments, he'd grown the money to give him a comfort zone while the business took off.

Thoughts of the gym brought him right back to Jamie. She still didn't know he owned it with Jack. And she was still one of his clients, even if she didn't know that. Which meant he still wrestled with dating her.

But Griff had learned a long time ago that life was short and lacked any guarantees. His years in the service taught him that lesson. He genuinely liked Jamie, enjoyed being in her company. And she was the first woman here he'd been even remotely attracted to. And dinner wasn't a proposal. So what if he was rationalizing?

He looked at himself in the mirror and spotted the huge grin right away. He and Jamie were going to have dinner together. He'd let the chips fall where they may.

Chapter Fourteen

"I'm a Libra. That means I can make a decision but only after much thought."

-P.J. Harvey

For probably the millionth time that day, Jamie stared at her cell phone. And as many times, she'd picked up and started to text Griff. And then she placed it right back down. Silly, really. How hard could it be to send a single text? Almost impossible, as it turned out. Should she just say 'hey'? Nah, too informal. Or should she text something about looking forward to their dinner? That felt a bit pushy. Maybe something along the lines of, 'thinking of you'? Ugh!

"Oh, for the love of Pete! Whoever Pete might be. My dead Grandma Vera used to say it all the time. And I believe this is a correct instance to utilize it. Text the man already."

Sam swept into Jamie's office and plopped herself down in the chair in front of the desk. Jamie smiled thinking Sam might be the only person to have ever sat in the chair.

"I will when I think of the right thing to say, or text. You know what I mean."

Never one to let matters drop, Sam stretched forward and

plucked Jamie's phone from her desk. "No time like the present. Another of Grandma Vera's famous quotes." She tapped a long, red fingernail on the desk. "Now, what to say?"

"Give it back," Jamie demanded in a hushed tone. She glanced up toward her open office door to make sure the dragon wasn't within earshot.

Sam handed the phone back with a laugh. "You know I wouldn't have actually texted him anything." She glanced up at the wall clock. "But honestly, Jamie, its already late afternoon. What if he's languishing by the phone, awaiting your call?" She threw a hand to her forehead for good measure.

Jamie couldn't help but bust out laughing, which she knew was the desired effect.

"You're impossible. First, I haven't exactly been sitting around all day eating bon bons. Second, and most important, no one has ever 'languished' by a phone for me."

"You don't know that for sure. He likes you, honey. Why else would he ask you out to dinner? And still want to go after you bolted from the building?"

"Good points, Sam." She glanced at her phone yet again. "But you're much better at this stuff than me. What do I say?"

Sam rolled her eyes. "Say anything. You're only texting him to give him your number. Say hello. Or hey, how are you. Or how about 'what are you wearing?' Guys love that!"

It was Jamie's turn to roll her eyes. "You're impossible. You know how I am. I reread every email I send. I was way worse in college. I'd sit there, staring at my paper, agonizing about how to make it better. Pushing send always terrified me."

"As Nike says, 'just do it'."

She was right. Jamie knew Sam was right. She sucked in a shaky breath and typed out *'Hey, this is Jamie. You're it.'*

And then for the first time ever, she hit send without a

second thought. And then thought she might vomit. "Ugh, what have I done?"

Once again, Sam grabbed the phone, but this time from Jamie's cold fingers. "Let me see." She glanced at the phone and smiled. "Brilliant! Now was that so hard?"

Jamie nodded and wrung her hands. "What if it's too flippant? What if he…"

"Never mind all that second guessing, he's texting back!" Sam turned the phone, and they both watched the tiny bubbles.

"What? Already? Let me see!" Jamie took her phone back, cradling it in her hands with a grin on her face. "He really is."

"Took you long enough, but now I have your number," Jamie read aloud and giggled.

"Guess he didn't find it too 'flippant'," Sam joked.

"Oh, he's writing again." Jamie watched in wonder at the bubbles. She felt like a teenager all over again.

"All I need now is your address. And whether or not there's any type of food you really hate or would die if you ate it."

Jamie smiled and held the phone aloft for Sam to read his text. She couldn't top the grin from spreading even if she wanted to.

"He doesn't want me to die at dinner. He cares about me."

If she hadn't been at work, she'd jump up and do a happy dance about now.

"You're a mess," grunted Sam, but her smile softened the words.

Jamie typed back, *"That is very considerate of you. No allergies so far, and I can't stand mushrooms. They're slimy and gross. Anything else is fair game."* She added her address.

She glanced up to see the dragon passing by her door, shaking his head. Jamie dashed off a quick text tell Griff she needed to get back to work.

"Well, I guess we should get back to it." She pulled open a desk drawer and placed her phone inside, face down, after turning off the volume. Maybe if the phone were out of sight it would be out of mind as well. *Yeah, right.*

Sam rose, smoothing unseen wrinkles from her black pencil skirt. "I suppose." She pointed a finger at Jamie. "Remember, someday we won't have to hide our phones at work. It will all be worth it." She waved and left Jamie's office.

When her stomach rumbled in protest, Jamie opened another drawer and surveyed her options. Since joining the gym, and trying to lose weight, she replaced all her old, bad choices with newer, healthy ones. She pulled a mini power bar and unwrapped it. Might not be a Snickers, but at least it had chocolate.

*****

Griff stepped out of the gym's shower and wrapped a towel around his waist. He rolled his shoulders, easing away fatigue the hot water had missed. What a day! He loved this thing that he and Jack were building, but some days were better than others. First, he had to referee a fender bender in the parking lot. Apparently, Mrs. Applebaum had been 'jamming to some Jay-Z' and didn't notice Mr. Peterson behind her as she backed her mammoth Caddy out of its space. At least that's what she told the officer who arrived to take the report. In between flirting with the poor man who was young enough to be her grandson. Mr. Peterson gave a different, and slightly spicier, version of events.

At least he did until he clutched his chest. Another call to 9-1-1 brought an ambulance to take Mr. Peterson, and his angina, to the emergency department. The man, who was pushing eighty, threatened to sue Mrs. Applebaum for 'hitting his car and her terrible taste in music.' All Griff could do was calm the older woman and shake his head.

Then one of the toilets in the ladies' room decided to quit on him. Jack, conveniently, had run to the local box store to stock up on paper products, leaving him with a plunger and Darla in way too tight of a space. That woman didn't know how to take no for an answer. The fine line between staying professional and telling her to find a new gym blurred.

On top of all that, he and Jack had a busy day of classes and meeting with new clients. All good, as it meant Getting It Done continued to grow. If only he hadn't checked his phone every ten minutes. Now he knew how women felt. And he didn't like it. By the time Jamie had finally texted him in the late afternoon, he'd kicked himself for not asking for her number instead. How long had it been since he had waited to hear from a woman?

The locker room door swung open, and Jack strode in, dressed in khakis and a button-down shirt.

"Let me guess, off to see Sam again?" asked Griff.

Jack leaned into the mirror, fingering his short, dark hair into place. "You know it. She's 'allowing' me to take her to dinner. As *friends*." His expression told Griff how his friend felt about that. "Speaking of dinner, set a time and date for dinner with Jamie yet?"

"Not yet. Now that I know it's anything but mushrooms, I have to find the perfect place."

"Seems like a lot of pressure for dinner with someone you're not dating because she happens to be a client." He laughed at the glare Griff sent his way, not impressed. "Just saying."

"I am taking Jamie to dinner because we're friends. And I

would like to get to know her better." *Oh, the lies we tell ourselves.* Jack would never fall for that line.

Jack laughed long and hard. "Sure, you are. Getting to 'know her better.' Got it."

Griff threw up his hands. "What am I supposed to do? She's the first woman who's caught my attention in a long time. So, of course, she's a client."

"A very long time," Jack corrected. "You know my feelings on the matter. Go out to dinner, get to know her better, see if this is heading anywhere. But at some point, you have to tell her you and I own Getting It Done."

Griff ran a hand through his hair. "Don't you think I know? The best time would have been the moment we met."

"Agreed."

"You didn't let me finish. When we first met, Jamie mentioned not caring to take advantage of the free lesson for new clients; something about musclebound guys laughing at her. And now, it's been too long to bring it up."

"What's your plan? You're never going to tell her?"

"I know," Griff groaned. "Anyway, don't you have to be somewhere?"

"I do. Tell her. And now I am off to pick up Sam. See ya."

Griff turned to the mirror, swiping a hand across it to see his reflection. Jack was right. This seemed stupid really, her not knowing he was a part owner of the gym. But, in his defense, his occupation had never worked its way into conversation. *But it would over dinner.* He shook his head and finished getting dressed. He had to figure out the perfect place for their date.

Griff headed out, waving to Kara, their evening part-timer. He left before anyone asked him to fix one more thing.

By the time he got home, Griff wasn't any closer to figuring out where to take Jamie for dinner. He pulled his cell from his pocket and opened it to the text from her. Maybe he needed a bit more information.

"No mushrooms isn't a lot to go by. Care to share any more tips?"

Griff sent the message, steering clear of any emojis. He'd overheard a conversation in the gym the other day about what other meaning various ones held. He had walked away feeling old.

Setting his phone on the breakfast bar, Griff rummaged in the fridge for dinner. He pulled out a package from Fresh Ideas to You, a local company who made precooked, healthy meals. Pulled chicken burrito was tonight's choice. After popping it in the microwave, he avoided his phone. She would answer when she could. He wasn't going down that road again, glancing at it again and again.

Instead, he thought about the meal warming up in the microwave. He knew the owners, a young married couple with a couple of small kids. They were members of the gym. He'd had a conversation with the husband one day about their company and was impressed that they had left corporate jobs to open Fresh Ideas to You. He and Jack needed to think about partnering with them to offer meals for sale in the gym. Many members struggled with their weight and asked him for nutrition tips.

The microwave and his text alert dinged at the same time. He abandoned his dinner to check if the text came from Jamie. His pulse bounded in his chest when he saw her name on the screen.

"Now what fun would that be?"

A winking emoji followed the text. Griff grinned.

"Challenge accepted," he typed in response. He could do this. He could find a place that wasn't too uppity but not too

casual either. He could find something that would make her eyes light up. Challenge accepted indeed.

*****

Curled up on her couch with her work laptop, Jamie ignored the file opened in front of her and stared at her phone instead. *Had she really sent a winking emoji?* She glanced at the text thread. Yep, she really had. She smacked her hand on her forehead. What had she been thinking? What if that particular emoji held some hidden meaning? She'd overheard a couple of millennials in the supermarket the other day giggling over the other meanings for them. *Great!*

She set her phone down only to have it ding again. His short but to the point message made her laugh. What could Griff come up with for dinner? Should she answer? She gnawed on her lower lip. Fiona blinked at her from the top of the sofa.

"What do you think, Fiona? Will he come up with something different for dinner? Will I be impressed? Do I even want to be? After all, the busy season has already started. And as if that weren't enough, Sam and I are plotting out new business."

And then there's Chad. Funny how since meeting Griff she only thought of Chad when she spied the reunion reminder on her fridge.

"Tell me, Fiona, what should I do? Is this dinner a real date? I don't really know anything about Griff, other than he's smoking hot and makes me laugh."

Fiona, not great with advice, blinked again and proceeded to wash her lady parts.

"Gee, thanks," Jamie muttered. "You've been a real help."

Fiona, not aware of sarcasm, continued bathing.

Jamie closed the program she'd been working in and opened a file entitled Operation Phoenix. When she and Sam had first conceived it, she'd created this word document as a place to store ideas. Right now, it consisted of random thoughts such as location, need for a catchy logo, was having a margarita bar at work a bad idea? If they worked out of their homes initially as planned, the margarita bar might not be such a bad thing.

She glanced at phoenix images she'd stolen from the web. Even though their plan had been conceived in a Tequila fueled daze, the idea of moving forward with it (and leaving the dragon in their wake) brought hope. Jamie closed her eyes and imagined crisp, white stationary with their new logo and their names underneath it. How cool would that be with the bold phoenix rising from the page?

Maybe, just maybe, this dream of theirs would happen.

Chapter Fifteen

"Carpe diem…"
-Horace

Griff beat Jamie to the gym the next morning. He'd planned it that way. Ideas for their dinner together swirled in his head, but he wanted to learn more about her before deciding. He picked up hand weights and started repetitions. Never before had he put this much effort into a first date. A date he shouldn't even be having, he reminded himself. He shook his head to clear it and lost himself in the reps.

Thirty minutes later, Griff spotted Jamie coming through the door. He noticed an air of confidence she'd lacked the first time they'd met. He loved that about this place. People came for all different reasons, exercise, health, strength training. But the reason didn't matter as much as the benefits they received from hard work; from pushing themselves.

Griff knew the moment she spotted him. Even from across the room, he could see her face light up, her pace quicken. He returned her small wave and headed across to meet her in the middle.

"You're here early," she remarked.

"Trying to get a jump on my day." His glance raked over her from head to toe. "New workout clothes?" he asked.

Jamie glanced down at what she wore. "Sam threatened to buy them for me if I didn't. Said I shouldn't be seen in public in what I wore. As if anyone at the gym cares."

I care. But he kept that thought to himself.

"It's more about comfort. But you look great." He hid a grin at the light color washing across her face.

"Thanks. She also insisted I buy things that 'don't fit like a potato sack.' Apparently, my old sweats offended her." She shrugged her shoulders before climbing up on the treadmill. "God forbid I wear old, baggy sweats in public. Someone might know Sam and I are friends." Her chuckle hit him right in the gut.

Griff chose the machine next to her and started at a slow jog. "She has a point. Clothing can give you confidence, set a tone."

She glanced over at him. "Huh. I never thought of it that way. Kind of like wearing a suit to work every day even though we've gone to mostly business casual."

"Exactly."

"Sam says that's the first thing to go when we open Operation Phoenix. She hates wearing business clothing. Says they don't 'fit her personality.' Between you and I, she doesn't care to follow rules."

Griff turned up the speed on his treadmill, breaking into a faster pace. "I can see that. Sam seems like a free spirit."

"You figured it out already, huh? Doesn't take long. It's one of the many things I love about Sam. She does what she wants. She goes through life thumbing her nose at the rules." Jamie sighed before increasing the speed on her treadmill. "I wish I could be more like her."

"In what ways?" This was more than Jamie had ever revealed about herself, and Griff hung on every word.

Jamie stared straight ahead for so long, he wondered of she'd heard him. Or if she intended to answer.

"We had a similar upbringing, Sam and I, at least in some ways. It took me longer to break away from the expectations, completely unrealistic ones."

"You escaped."

"Exactly. All the way to South Carolina. I love my family, but I don't understand them. Nor do they understand me. And while that makes me sad, it is what it is. I've always believed that family is not only defined by biology. Sam is my family, and I'm hers."

"I get it. Jack is closer to me than my oldest brother. Zach is great but enough years older than me that we never really clicked as kids."

Jamie had chosen the interval program this morning, and the treadmill kicked into higher speed and incline. He watched her from the corner of his eye and marveled at the change in her. She didn't have a death grip on the bars.

"Melissa and I are under two years apart, but that didn't help us be friends." She wiped her face with a towel. "About this dinner."

Griff caught her gaze in the mirrored wall. "Yes? What about it?"

She gnawed on her bottom lip, and he couldn't blame the workout for his pulse shooting up.

"Did we decide on a day and time yet?"

"Well, no. You said weekends are better. How about this Saturday? Would that work? Maybe six o'clock?"

"Yes, yes, and yes," Jamie answered. "That would be great. And one more question. What should I wear?"

After listening to her talk about her family, Griff had a better idea on what to do for dinner.

"Wear whatever you want to wear, whatever you're comfortable in. I don't care about stuff like that." He didn't add that she could wear nothing at all, and he'd be happy.

"If the weather cooperated, I'd say capris and flip flops. Much to Sam's chagrin, I'm not much of a clothes horse."

An idea sprang to life in his mind, something she could wear flip flops for. Something Sheila would have hated. Perfect!

"I know just the thing. And feel free to wear your capris and flip flops. I will be casually decked out as well." He grinned at her. "Now, which machine are you tempting today?"

She tilted her head to one side. "Tempting?"

"You know, to kill you. Not that I've seen one even try yet."

"Ah, now I get it." She shook a finger at him then wiped down the treadmill. "Joke all you want, but I know the truth. And once they've tasted blood, there's no going back. You won't be laughing then, Griff."

He threw back his head and did just that. "I'll take my chances. Let me introduce you to my friend the incline bench. You'll be the only moving part. How does that sound?"

"Dangerous," she answered without hesitation.

*****

Early Saturday evening, Jamie stood in her closet, wondering what to wear. Should she take him at face value and wear capris and flip flops? He did say to and that he would be equally casual. Hmmm… She clutched the oversized towel to her and wished for the first time ever she was more like Sam. Jamie never thought about clothes. She reached into her closet and put on whatever her fingers found. And even though she didn't like her boss, she loved having a 'uniform' of sorts for work. No thought involved in picking a suit each day. In fact, she'd assign each suit to a day of the week if she thought Sam would let her get away with it. The thought of Sam's face if she tried made her laugh.

Unsure still of what to wear, Jamie headed back into the bathroom. She put on a set of matching underwear Sam had bought her for Christmas. For 'if you ever get lucky again' her friend had said with a laugh. Not that she was planning on 'getting lucky' tonight. She barely knew Griff. But still, knowing she wore them under whatever else she came up with gave her confidence. Made her feel good.

Jamie dried her hair, something she rarely did, to give it a little more body. She applied a touch of mascara and lip gloss, otherwise leaving her face bare. Makeup had also never been her thing. Another thing Sam didn't understand. Then she returned to her closet, determined to not make herself crazy. Griff said casual, so casual it would be. She grabbed her favorite pair of olive colored capris and a bright T-shirt with three-quarter-length sleeves. The aqua blue color reminded her of the Caribbean, which she loved.

She stepped into the capris prepared to suck in her belly a bit as she'd done the last time she'd worn them. But to her surprise, they buttoned with ease. Maybe killing herself (and skipping her favorite candy bar) was paying off. She slid her feet into her favorite pair of flip flops and decided she was ready.

Now to kill time. She hadn't been on a first date in a long time. She hadn't been on a first date with someone who gave her butterflies in the pit of her stomach in even longer. Maybe never.

"Meow," came from the kitchen, followed by the sound of metal clanging. Fiona's way of telling her she'd been a bad cat mom.

Grateful for the disruption and something to do, Jamie went to the kitchen. "Hello there," she called to her cat as she bent down to pick up both bowls, filling one with fresh water and the other with some kitty kibble. "I might remind you that you're eating earlier than you would be if I was working today."

Fiona met her stare and blinked, not deigning to answer.

Jamie laughed and placed both bowls on the floor. "A dog would appreciate the food given to them." She stroked one hand down Fiona's soft back before leaving her to her meal.

Not wanting to do any work but needing to kill more time, Jamie sank into her sofa and turned on Hulu. She clicked on a favorite episode of *Criminal Minds* and settled back to watch. She loved this show and anything to do with crime fighting, true crime being her favorite. TV became a luxury in the busy season. She tried to watch the shows she loved when she could.

She had no idea how much time had passed when the doorbell rang. She sprang off the sofa and bolted for the door. She ran her hands through her hair, fluffing it. Nothing she could do about the flutters in her stomach. She glanced down at herself one last time and hoped she had chosen correctly before opening her front door.

All wardrobe doubts fled, along with rational thought, when she spotted Griff on her front porch.

"Good! You took me at my word." He handed her a bunch of colorful flowers. "I wasn't sure what kind to get, but somehow roses didn't seem like you. Too predictable. I hope you like them."

She took the flowers with shaking hands. "They're

gorgeous, thank you. Come on in."

Jamie stepped aside for him to pass, and she caught the slightest hint of something spicy as he did. She'd only seen him outside of the gym once and was glad he didn't subscribe to the 'more the better' school of thought when it came to cologne. The memory of a first date last year who had sent her into a sneezing fit with his cologne made her giggle.

"Let me put these in some water."

She closed the door and headed for the kitchen. The open floor plan of her small home essentially held one large area, divided into living room and kitchen. She wandered to the sink, grabbing a vase from a cupboard above it.

"You must be Fiona," drifted in from the living area.

Jamie turned to see her not too fond of men cat weave her way around Griff's ankles. She watched in shock as Fiona allowed him to pet her under the chin. Then she rewarded him with a deep purr. She'd never been jealous of her cat before.

"Now I know Fiona has been abducted by aliens and replaced with a body double. She never lets people pet her like that. And she doesn't even purr for me. How did you do that? Are you a cat whisperer?"

Griff straightened and chuckled. "No, not that I'm aware of anyway. I'm not even a huge fan of cats. But my sister has them, so I've been around one enough I guess."

Jamie shook her head. "But Fiona barely tolerates me, and I keep a roof over her head." She leaned in and sniffed him, earning her one raised brow.

"I showered. I promise," he joked.

Jamie laughed. "Sorry. I just wondered if you had rubbed cat nip on yourself before picking me up. She really isn't like this with anyone. Ask Sam. The two have at best an armed détente."

Griff smiled. "I guess Fiona has good taste. Are you ready to go?"

"Let me grab my purse." Jamie made sure the slider leading to her small backyard was locked then grabbed her purse. "Ready."

She bent to pet Fiona. "Now remember, make good choices. No boys over."

And then she remembered Griff stood well within ear shot. "I, uh, always chat with her before I leave."

"There are just so many sides to you, Jamie Lawler. Now who's the cat whisperer?"

Relieved he hadn't thought her mad, she shrugged. "In my defense, I didn't actually whisper."

Griff threw back his head and laughed. "I love that I'm never sure of what's going to come out of your mouth every time you open it. Let's go. Our adventure awaits."

They walked outside, and Jamie paused to lock the door behind them. When she turned, Griff stood next to her arm extended. She hooked her elbow around his.

"Adventure, huh? I thought you said dinner."

"Oh. There will be dinner. Later. But first, I have to make sure you work up an appetite."

Chapter Sixteen

"As Daddy said, life is 95% anticipation."
- Gloria Swanson

Jamie's heart pounded in her chest at the word 'appetite.' *What did he mean by that?* She followed him to his car, or truck actually, and waited while he opened the door for her. She really loved the southern manners she'd grown accustomed to.

"Thank you," she murmured through tight lips when he helped her up into the cab. She waited until he came around got in the driver's side. "This adventure of which you speak. Care to give any clues?"

"No," Griff responded and started the car.

"Oh."

He turned to her and grinned. "And ruin the surprise? What would be the fun in that?"

"Have I never mentioned I'm not a huge fan of them? Surprises, I mean." She fiddled with her purse strap, unsure what to do with her hands.

He stopped for traffic at the entrance to her development. "If you really want to know, I'll tell you."

She shook her head without even thinking about it. "No, that's okay. A surprise might be fun. As long as this doesn't involve snakes." She turned to face him, placing a hand on one arm. "There won't be snakes will there?"

"Snakes never seemed appropriate for a first date. Maybe a second or third?"

"Griff!" she shrieked in a tone that set off dogs for miles. "I am not kidding about the snake thing. I don't just hate them. I'm deathly afraid of them."

She looked at him and saw his shoulders shaking and punched him in the arm.

"You rat! You were kidding the whole time."

"I'm sorry. Okay, maybe not that sorry. But your face! You actually thought I was taking you to a place with snakes?"

"I can't help it. I babble when I'm nervous."

She stopped talking then and hoped he hadn't heard that last bit.

"I make you nervous? In a good way, I hope."

No such luck!

She cleared her throat. "I haven't been on a date in quite a while. I'm out of practice."

"But still, I make you nervous?"

She shifted in her seat, trying to find a more comfortable position. Or one that would make her disappear altogether.

"Yes, okay? You make me nervous. You with your handsome face and that body." She waved a hand up and down as if pointing these things out to him. "Oh crap. I'm going to shut up now."

"Please, continue. This just got interesting."

He turned and grinned at her, a wide, toothy one that made his dimples pop. Jamie tried to not stare, but who could blame her? The man was hot!

"Give me a break. You own a mirror. You know what you look like."

She said a silent prayer to the universe that he would let it drop.

"Would you think I'm vain if I asked exactly what about me you find appealing? Something about my face? Or is it my body?"

Yep, he went there. Even though the universe had disappointed her, she thanked it for the dim light of the truck interior. She felt her face burning. *How to answer him?*

"You know I'm kidding, right?" He snuck a glance at her. "Please tell me you know that."

"Of course I did. I did go out to dinner with a guy who would have taken that to heart."

"Let me guess. You didn't have a second date."

"No, I did not. Someone who uses more hair product than I do isn't worthy of a second date."

"Good to know. I'll keep that in mind."

Jamie glanced at his hair. He wore it short, which spoke of his military service. She doubted he used anything in it. It looked soft, though. The kind of soft that made her fingers itch to run through it.

"What other pitfalls should I know about? There has to be something other than snakes and an inordinate amount of hair gel."

"Well, most women, if they're honest, keep a running list in their heads."

"Do they now? Care to share?"

"Where to start? Please don't ever order for me unless I ask you to do so. And I won't. It's belittling and not in the least bit macho. If you say you're going to call, then call. And not a week later when you suddenly remember you said you would call. If you're not interested, I'd rather you tell me that instead of 'I'll call you'."

She tapped one finger to her forehead. "Let me think.

What else?"

"There's more?"

"I'm not a fan of Valentine's Day. It's a holiday made up by the greeting card industry. No overpriced roses or chocolates I certainly don't need please."

"Duly noted."

"And last but certainly far from least. I cannot stand dishonesty in any form. Lying, cheating, it's all the same to me."

When he didn't respond right away, Jamie gnawed her lower lip. Had he been cheated on? Is that why he didn't say anything. Then a worse thought occurred. Her stomach rolled. *What if he's cheated on someone?* She didn't want to believe it about him, even if she didn't know him that well. Griff came across as an aboveboard kind of guy.

He pulled into a parking lot and put the car in park. Griff turned toward Jamie but didn't say anything for a few moments. Her heart beat a wild tattoo in her chest as she thought of all the horrible things he might be trying to say.

"I have a lot of faults. We all do. No one is perfect. But I would never cheat on someone. Ever. I never have and never would. And before you ask, yes, I have been cheated on, so I know how it feels."

Jamie blew out a long breath she didn't even know she'd been holding. "I'm sorry." The words felt inadequate, but they were all she had.

"Why? You didn't cheat on me." He gave a small smile that didn't reach his eyes. "Her name is Sheila, and we were together for over a year before she left town. With my friend, Dan. Well, former friend." He took one of her hands in his and looked into her eyes. "But I need you to know that long before that happened to me, I still never considered cheating on anyone. I've always felt if you're not happy, then end the relationship. Do the right thing."

Jamie didn't know whether to feel relief or sadness. Maybe both.

"Thank you for telling me that. And even though I was not the person who hurt you, I am sorry it happened." She hesitated for a moment, not sure how to continue. "Did you love her very much? You obviously don't have to answer. It's really none of my business."

"You're fine. We're getting to know each other. Looking back, I'm not even sure I was in love with her."

He ran a hand through his hair, leaving finger marks in it. Jamie had to stop herself from reaching up to smooth it.

"Still she didn't treat you well. Nor did your friend."

"Jamie, I have to tell you something else. In the interest of full disclosure. And because I never want to lie to you, even by omission."

The rapid heart rate returned with a bang. "Are you dying?"

"What?"

His furrowed brow cracked her up.

"Sorry," she muttered. "As you probably already know, I babble when nervous. Go ahead. You were saying?"

"Well, after that, what I have to tell you doesn't seem so bad."

Jamie closed her eyes for a moment before opening them and staring into his. "Okay, I'm ready for whatever you have to tell me."

"I own the gym with Jack. Getting It Done? It's our joint venture. There, I said it. Feel free to judge that."

Jamie's mouth dropped. Literally. She sat there, mouth hanging open while her mind whirled in a thousand different directions. *Get it together!*

"That's your big secret? That's what you didn't want to tell me?"

"Well, when you put it like that... Yes, that's the thing. I have to admit I feel a lot better having told you now."

Jamie rubbed her temples. "But why? What's wrong with owning a gym? Good for you! Well, good for you and Jack!"

"Do you remember the morning we met?"

"You mean the morning you caught me talking to machines? Yes, of course, I remember. Why? What does that have to do with this conversation?"

"I asked you if you had taken them up on the free introductory lesson when you joined. Remember?"

"Yes, of course. I might have been busy wishing the earth would open up and swallow me whole, but I remember. And?"

"You said you had not taken advantage of the offer. Do you remember why you hadn't? Or what you told me?"

"Not really. I..." And then she did remember. *Oh no!* "I, uh, probably said something about not wanting to embarrass myself in front of someone," she ended weakly.

"Or you might have said you didn't want some 'muscle-bound guy judging you.' At least that's how I remember it."

"Oh." She resisted the urge to fan her heated face. "I may have said something along those lines."

"And in that moment, I didn't want you to view me as 'some muscle-bound guy.' Not that I would ever laugh at you."

"Oh." She did seem to say that a lot around Griff.

"I know I lied by omission. And I know that there were countless opportunities since then to tell you. But to be honest, the longer it went on, the harder it became. It felt like a lie to me. And that's not who I am. So, I am sorry for lying to you."

"Thank you for telling me, although you didn't technically lie to me." She laughed and cocked her head. "In fact, this is kind of funny now that I think about it. A couple of times, I meant to ask you what you did for a living. But, usually as my brain works, I didn't think of it until I was already home or at work."

"Well, that is the thing that usually comes up. Things like what you do for a living or where did you go to school."

"Are you a dog or cat person. That's an important one," Jamie added.

"Of course. Right up there with do you want kids," he joked.

Before she could stop herself, Jamie leaned out and poked him in the chest. "Don't make fun of me. It's crucial. What happens if you fall in love only to find out he's a cat person?"

One eyebrow met his hairline. "You have a cat. Why would he being a cat person be an issue?"

"Well, I'm really a dog person who currently has a cat. I can't really say that I 'own' Fiona. You've met her. She's her own cat. In fact, most days, it feels like she lets me live in my own house."

Griff grinned at her.

"I see. And by the way, I consider myself a dog person also. I've never liked cats; too sneaky. But I'd make an exception for Fiona, seeing how she likes me so much."

"Very funny. Yes, she likes you better than she likes me, even after only a few minutes. And I didn't set out to adopt Fiona. I went to the local shelter to look for a dog. Mind you, I was just looking. I want a dog, but my hours are crazy. And there was Fiona. Her elderly owner had died months before. She had lived in the shelter ever since. No one wanted an older, hard of hearing, half-blind, cantankerous at best cat."

"You did."

"I did. I got Fiona. She's not young or in perfect health.

Most days she tolerates me and only because I feed her. I told myself cats are less maintenance. She wouldn't mind my being gone for most of the day."

"You fell in love with her," he accused in a soft tone.

"I did. Despite her disdain for me. What does that tell you about me?" she joked. Well, sort of joked.

"It tells me you're a softy with a big heart. In this world, that's not such a bad thing to be."

"Well, that's sweet of you to say."

"Calling it like I see it," he quipped. And then his smile disappeared, taking those delightful dimples with it.

"Is something wrong?" Jamie asked. *Please don't let it be something awful.* The more time she spent with him, the more she liked him.

"It's about my being a part owner of Getting It Done."

He dropped his gaze, no longer holding hers. Her heart plummeted with it.

"Tell me. Whatever it is. Pretend it's a bandage; just rip it off."

"The thing about owning the gym is the rule that comes along with it."

"Rule?"

"Yes. The one about not dating clients."

Chapter Seventeen

"Sometimes life hits you in the head with a brick. Don't lose faith."
-Steve Jobs

If her life were a cartoon, or a comedy, the heroine at this point would be sticking a finger in her ear to make sure she'd heard right. But this wasn't a cartoon or comedy. This was Jamie's life. And she had just heard Griff tell her he doesn't date his clients.

"I see," she responded. Not that she did, but she had to say something.

"Do you? Because I'm not sure I do."

"If you don't date clients, and I'm your client, what are we doing right now?"

"I don't know that either." He sighed. "When I made that rule, I didn't have you in mind. I wanted to protect us, Jack and me, from any legal entanglements that might arise."

"That makes sense," she agreed. "When Sam and I get Operation Phoenix off the ground, that can be our first rule. Well, after we establish Bring Your Dog to Work Day."

"You don't have a dog," he reminded her.

"I know, and Fiona would hate it. Too many humans. But I will have a dog someday. I want to be prepared. But that's not what we are discussing."

"No, though I like it better. Like I said, I had, have, my reasons. Sound ones, too. And then I met you, and you make me laugh. When I'm with you, I want to stay with you, not have you run off to work."

"Despite my being one of your clients. And one of the clumsiest people you've met."

"Yes to the first part. As for the second, you're not that bad."

"We'll agree to disagree. About the clumsy thing. But what about this date?"

"You mean the one that hasn't even started, and I like it better than any I've ever actually had?"

She almost forgot to breathe. Luckily, her lungs did not.

"Yes, that date."

"I don't know." He held up both hands as if in surrender. "I'm sorry. This is uncharted territory for me."

Jamie's shoulders slumped. Griff was the best man to come along in, well, a long time. And here, on their first 'date,' he tells her he can't date her. Because she is a client of his gym. And that's what she got for trying to be healthy. Fate must be enjoying a good chuckle over this.

"Do you want me to take you home?" he asked.

She shook her head. That was the last thing she wanted. "What if this wasn't a date? What if it was an un-date?"

He cocked his head. "An un-date? You mean like two people having dinner together; two friends?"

"Yes, exactly. We could be two people just hanging out, getting to know each other better."

"I could do that. If you're sure."

"I'm sure. Let's do this."

Griff turned the car back on, that killer smile once again in place.

"Well, friend, you're going to love this."

"Can't wait."

And she couldn't. She had no idea what they were really doing, but she wanted to see what it might become.

*****

Griff led the way inside, holding one hand loosely over Jamie's eyes. "Okay, there's a door here. I have it open. Keep your eyes closed for me."

"I promised, didn't I?"

He watched her step hesitantly over the doorway. Griff loved that she was game for this.

"Now, before you open your eyes, remember I wanted to take you somewhere fun."

"Fun. Got it."

His stomach did a little roll as he waited for her to see where they were. He really meant for this to be fun.

"Okay on the count of three. One. Two. Three." On three he removed his hand from in front of her eyes.

Jamie squinted for a moment, her eyes adjusting to the light. Or relative darkness in this case.

"Mini golf?" she squealed, clapping her hands together. "You brought me to play mini golf."

She threw her arms around him, and something unfurled in Griff's chest. A tightness he hadn't noticed there. He hugged her back for a moment before taking a step back to see her expression.

"I take it you approve."

"Approve? Are you kidding me?" She turned around, taking it all in. "This is amazing!"

He did the same, trying to see Goofy Golf Under the Sea through her fresh eyes. Black light bulbs popped the Day-Glo paint. Scene after scene featured sea creatures of all shapes and sizes.

"It looks the same. I can't believe it."

"Do you take all your dates here?" she teased.

"Well, I did come here with Becky Wrigley. But I didn't have a good time. She tried to hold my hand."

A giggle escaped from Jamie's lips, drawing his attention to them. As if he needed anything to help him with that.

"She sounds pretty brazen, your Becky Wrigley."

"For third grade she was. And we were on a school field trip. Mrs. Stewart was not pleased."

"Your teacher? I'll bet." She giggled again.

"Neither was Becky. I wouldn't let her hold my hand." He shuddered. "Girls had cooties back then."

"As did boys. I remember it well."

"Are you ready to golf?"

"Are you?"

"Let's do this."

Griff led the way to the counter, paying for a round of eighteen holes. After picking their clubs and balls, orange for her, yellow for him, they approached the first hole.

Jamie stared at the huge, brightly-colored octopus in front of them. Its tentacles swayed back and forth, forcing the golfer to time their putt carefully. She took her small purse and looped the long strap across her body.

"Need my hands free," she said by way of explanation. "Oh, and by the way, be prepared to lose. I happen to be a former mini golf champion."

Griff laughed. "Champion, huh? Did that include a trophy?"

"I'll have you know that while Melissa excelled at tennis, and everything else, my college years were spent playing mini golf with my friends. It seems I have just enough coordination to pull this off."

"We'll see about that."

The truth was, he hadn't been here since Jack's tenth birthday party. He also didn't golf, as in real golf, despite there being a ton of golf courses in South Carolina. But he couldn't have cared less. Seeing the joy on her face was enough.

Jamie placed her ball on the green mat. She gripped the club and eyed the octopus. Her serious expression bespoke one going into battle, not about to whack an orange ball through the tentacles of an octopus.

She raised her head and grinned at him. "Prepare to lose!"

With that, she hit the ball. Griff watched as it sailed right through a small space between the swinging tentacles.

Jamie ran to the other side, jumping up and down. "Hole-in-one!" she cried.

Griff placed his ball on the mat.

"Just a lucky shot." He aimed and hit it. Right into the bright, purple tentacle. With a resounding 'thwack,' his ball ricocheted back to him, sailing past his foot and into the crushed stones behind him.

"If I'm not mistaken, that's a one-stroke penalty," Jamie crowed, popping up from the other side of the hideous octopus.

"By the gleam in your eye, I'm sure you have no doubt of it."

He took another swing, this time making it through to the other side. With one more stroke, he sent the ball into the cup.

"Would have been cool, if not for your, uh, false start." She pulled the score card from the back pocket of her capris. "Let's see, that's one for me and three for you." She batted her eyelashes at him. "Don't worry, Griff, you still have seventeen holes to catch me."

"Good thing we didn't bet anything," he joked.

"There's still time," Jamie challenged.

He shook his head. "No can do. The international mini golf rules clearly state all wagers must be placed prior to the first hole. Sorry, Jamie, nothing I can do about it."

"Well, I guess if we're following the international rules…"

She led the way to hole two. This time, a bright blue shark challenged them to putt straight into his mouth. Up a very narrow indoor grass-covered board. He was toast.

By the time, they completed the eighteenth hole, Jamie had stopped keeping score in deference to his 'fragile male ego' as she called it. Griff couldn't care less. Watching her laugh and strut her stuff around the place was worth the price of admission. And more.

They turned in their clubs and left the building. Outside, the wind had picked up a bit, bringing a nip to the night air. Jamie shivered as they walked to his truck.

Griff used the remote to unlock it, helping her into the passenger seat. He reached behind him and grabbed an old sweatshirt of his.

"Here, put this on. You look chilly."

"What gave it away, my blue lips or chattering teeth?"

When he got in the truck, she'd already pulled it over her head and fastened her seatbelt. She sat there, rolling up the sleeves a few times. The sweatshirt swamped her, but it had never looked this good on him.

"Thank you so much. I didn't think about a jacket for some

reason."

He hoped she'd forgotten because she was excited to see him.

"That's okay. I keep it in here for just that reason. The weather has been fickle this winter. One minute, you're wearing shorts. The next, you need layers." He started the truck, turning on the seat warmers. They'd come already installed with his truck, and now he was thankful for them.

"Oh, that's lovely," she gasped. "Now, you did promise to feed me."

"I did indeed. The place we're going is just down the road."

They drove for a few miles, listening to the local country station. Even though this wasn't a true 'date,' Griff couldn't help comparing Jamie to Sheila. His former girlfriend never felt comfortable with even a moment of silence, always filling each one with babble about things he neither understood nor cared to. Jamie didn't seem to have that problem. Not that this was a date, he reminded himself.

A few minutes later, he pulled into Mama's Cucina restaurant. After parking, he turned to Jamie.

"I hope you like Italian."

He jumped out before she could answer, coming around to help her down.

"I love Italian. It might be my favorite. Although there's Mexican also." She sighed. "All the things I shouldn't be eating."

"You can eat whatever you want, Jamie. Everything in moderation. That's what I tell my clients."

The reminder she was exactly that, his client, put a pin to the fun they'd been having. He held open the door for her, happy she didn't seem to notice, or make a big deal, out of what he'd said. They crossed the lot and he once again held the door for her.

"Griff!"

The exclamation was followed by a hug and kisses on both cheeks from Mama Rosa herself. He hugged her back.

"Mama, it's great to see you."

"Hmmm, is it? Then why is it so long since you last visited? I started reading the obituaries, looking for your name."

The older woman spied Jamie next to him and clapped her hands. "And who is this beautiful girl?"

Before he could make the introductions, Mama engulfed Jamie in her ample arms. When she finally let her go, Griff cleared his throat.

"Mama Rosa, this is my friend, Jamie Lawler. Jamie, this is Mama Rosa, the best cook this side of Sicily."

"Any friend of Griff's is a friend of mine." She turned toward the kitchen. "Luca, come out here."

She turned back to Jamie. "Griff and my Luca went to high school together. Let me tell you, a bunch of scallywags they were." She broke off, muttering something in Italian. Griff was glad he'd never learned the language.

"Luca!" she cried again. "Ugh, that one is always too busy with the food. Come my friends, I will seat you at our best table. I'll send Luca out to you with some warm bread and dipping sauce."

"That sounds delicious, Mama Rosa. Whipping Griff in mini golf sure worked up an appetite."

The older woman clapped her hands again. "Wonderful! I love a woman with a healthy appetite. Girls today, they pick at their food. Don't do Mama Rosa justice."

"Well, I've never had that problem, as you can see."

"What? You are a skinny girl. But don't worry, Mama Rosa will fill you with pasta and love."

She placed two menus on the table and waddled away.

"Wow, she's lovely," remarked Jamie. She glanced around the dim interior. "It all smells delicious. What do you recommend?" She opened her menu.

"Everything. Especially since you 'worked up an appetite.' I love the lasagna."

"Oooh, sounds delicious." She ducked her head back into the menu. "But then there's fettucine alfredo. And who doesn't love a good alfredo sauce? How will I ever choose?"

"If it helps, Mama makes the best alfredo sauce in the world. The whole world."

"Ugh! How was that supposed to help? Now I want it all."

"I know. How about we get both and split them?"

"Really? You'd do that?"

"Of course. Why wouldn't I?"

"On one of my first dates, the guy, trying to be 'helpful,' suggested I eat less. Or at least take some home for another meal."

Griff felt a burning in his chest.

"I'm guessing there wasn't a second date."

"What do you think? I told him exactly what he could with his ideas and walked out of the restaurant."

That's my girl! Not that she was his girl. Or ever would be.

"Look what the cat dragged in."

They both turned at the booming voice over Griff's shoulder.

"And who is this charming beauty with my ugly friend?"

Jamie laughed, but Griff didn't notice the telltale signs of instant lust that followed Luca everywhere. Interesting.

Griff stood, enfolding his old friend in a bear hug. "Luca,

it's been way too long." He turned to Jamie. "This is my friend, Jamie. Jamie, this is Luca, Mama's youngest, and ugliest, son."

Friend! The word burned into his brain. That was not how he wanted to think of her. Damn his own rules…

"How lovely to meet you, Jamie. Mama told me of a beautiful young woman with this guy." He pointed a thumb in Griff's direction. "This I had to see for myself."

Jamie's eyes sparkled with laughter. Griff found himself watching their interaction very closely.

"Delighted to meet you, Luca. And Griff isn't so bad."

She had spunk; he'd give her that.

"Move over," Luca instructed Jamie, sliding into her side of the booth until he was practically pressed against her. "Now tell me all about you."

Griff stifled a groan at the blush on her cheekbones. Luca had always had a way with the women.

"There's not much to tell, Luca. Griff and I met at his gym." She arched a brow in Griff's direction as if reminding him she had just discovered the fact. "I'm an accountant. Don't worry, I won't bore you with the details. Your friend here tells me your mom makes the best alfredo sauce in the world. I'm excited to try it."

Luca leaned in and whispered, "Second best, but don't tell her I said so." His trademark grin lit up his face.

Griff has seen a lot of girls, and now women, fall for it. His gut tightened some more.

"I heard that."

Mama placed a basket of fresh garlic knots on the table. Griff's stomach grumbled.

"See, my knots are to die for. His stomach already knows." She turned on her son. "Luca, you were not raised by wolves. Get up from that table." She muttered something in Italian half under her breath. "Can't you see they are on a date?"

Griff hoped she'd pull him out of the booth by his ear. It wouldn't be the first time.

"But, Mama, he introduced this beautiful woman as his 'friend.' What was I supposed to do? If he is so blind..." He shrugged. "Jamie, I'm pleased to meet you. Let me go prepare your dinner."

"Ignore my son. I'm afraid I dropped him on his head one too many times when he was little." She gestured to the hot bread. "Eat, eat." Then she left them alone.

"Wow," breathed Jamie, sitting back in her seat. She pulled a garlic knot from the bunch, setting it on her plate.

"I'm sorry about that. The Rinaldi family gets a bit, uh, theatrical, at times."

She poured some dipping sauce on her plate. "Are you kidding me? I loved it. Growing up our meals were either silent or interrogations."

She popped a bite in her mouth and groaned around it. He felt in all parts south.

"I ate more meals at their house as a kid than I can count. Luca's family is always like that-loud and entertaining. But wonderful."

Jamie sighed. "That must have been amazing." She took another bite. "If these are any indication, dinner will be mind-blowing."

Griff nodded. "You have no idea."

Mama appeared at their table again. "Have you decided?"

"Jamie, what do you think? The two we discussed?"

"Oh, yes, please."

"We will have the lasagna and fettucine alfredo. I told Jamie we could share both, since choosing only one masterpiece from the menu would break her heart." He grinned up at

Mama.

"Oh, you rascal," she crowed. "Watch this one, Jamie. Heart of gold but always a handful. I will see to your dinners."

Griff watched her go then turned back to find Jamie staring at him with a smirk on her face.

"I feel like there might be a story there. Or maybe several. Go ahead, tell me all about your misspent youth."

Chapter Eighteen

"I like to fly close to the edge. I like to play with fire."
-Dean Ambrose

Jamie delighted in watching Griff squirm in his seat. There must be some truth to Mama's claim. She let him dangle for a little while more while she finished her garlic knot.

"It's okay. You don't have to tell me. I'm sure Mama, or Luca, would be happy to do so."

His face paled a bit at her words. "I'm an open book," he said. "Ask me anything."

"Tell me about Luca."

She knew she was playing with fire. And didn't care. He might be determined to keep her in the 'friend zone' but she'd seen his face when Lucas slid in next to her in the booth.

"Luca is the salt of the earth. His whole family is."

He took one of the garlic knots, moving it around his plate without eating it. When he started to pull it apart, Jamie bit back a grin. 'In for a penny, in for a pound," as her Grandmother Lawler used to say.

"That doesn't tell me much. Is he single?"

"Luca is perpetually single."

The shreds of the garlic knot became smaller.

"Well who could blame him? The guy is GQ handsome. I'm surprised he's not off modelling somewhere."

"Not only is the lady beautiful but smart as well." Luca placed wine glasses on their table and held aloft a bottle. "On the house, courtesy of Mama. I tried to tell her it's just Griff, but she insisted." He poured a glass for each. "Your dinners will be out shortly."

Jamie returned his smile, because why not? He really was drop dead gorgeous. And because she knew it would piss off Griff. She turned back to face him.

"You were saying?" she asked him, voice all light and innocent.

He took a healthy sip of wine and placed his glass back down. "I was saying that he's perpetually single because Luca knows exactly how handsome he is. He uses it to his advantage. And you said you don't like wine." He pointed at her glass.

"I'm not a wine aficionado, but I didn't want to be rude." She took a small sip, trying to not make a face. She really wasn't a wine person.

"I can see how much you enjoyed it," Griff smirked.

Before she could come up with a remark, another handsome Italian looking man brought their dinners.

"Fettucine for the lady. And lasagna for you, Griff." His grin took away from his formality.

"Nico, good to see you, man." He shook hands with him. "Nico, this is Jamie. Jamie, this is Nico, Luca's cousin. This is a family business. Come often enough, and you'll meet everyone."

"You forgot to mention more handsome cousin." Nico bowed over Jamie's hand, brushing it with his lips.

"Nice to meet you, Nico. I'm impressed with the family

business."

"Thank you. I will tell my aunt. And now, I must go. Bon Appetit!"

The scents rising from their dishes made her mouth water. "Thank you, Griff, for bringing me here. Dinner smells divine."

"You're very welcome. They're a wonderful family when they aren't busy busting my balls. Dig in."

The next few minutes passed in relative silence, the only noise coming from their forks and knives scraping the plates. And the occasional moan of delight, and not only from her. When they'd each had some of their own dish, they divided up and traded.

Jamie took her first bite of his lasagna and set down her fork. When she had finished chewing and swallowing, she wiped her mouth on a napkin.

"I've never had Italian this good. And Philadelphia is known for its good food."

"I thought Philly was known for cheesesteaks and Rocky," he joked.

"Those, too, but there are sections of the city for almost any kind of food you could imagine. And not to knock South Carolina, but good pizza is hard to find down here. I don't suppose Mama makes that, too."

Not that she needed to be eating pizza. Or the two thousand calories she was currently consuming. But tomorrow was another day. She'd run longer on the dreaded treadmill. And by that she meant a fast walk for most of it.

"Of course, she does. Her Sicilian makes me think I've died and gone to Heaven."

Jamie groaned and stabbed another chunk of lasagna. "I can't imagine anything tasting better than this."

"You say that now. Wait until you taste it."

She watched him enjoy his food, wondering if he would ever bring her here again. Probably not since he had that silly rule about dating clients. Well, no reason she couldn't come alone or bring Sam.

"What are you thinking? I can almost hear the wheels turning over here."

"Oh nothing. Wondering when I would come back here. I'll have to bring Sam. That girl loves to eat."

An odd expression flashed across his face. It only lasted for a second, but Jamie would swear it looked like regret.

"Mama loves to cook for people. She'd appreciate the return business."

Jamie thought about mentioning Luca but dismissed it. No reason to be mean.

The rest of the meal passed without much in the way of conversation. The tension between them pulsated, and Jamie was grateful when the check arrived.

Mama smiled at them both. "No room for dessert? I make a tiramisu that brings tears to your eyes."

Jamie laughed. "I'll take your word on that and a raincheck. These pants started the night feeling a bit looser than I remember. But the pasta took care of that," she joked.

"Tsk, like you have anything to worry about Jamie. You are beautiful as you are. Don't ever let anyone tell you otherwise."

"She's been working hard at the gym," Griff commented. He pulled some cash from his wallet and slid it into the bill folder.

Standing, he bent down to hug Mama. "Thank you for dinner. I'll see you again, and I promise to not wait as long next time."

Jamie slid out of the booth and hugged her also. "Yes,

thank you. That rivals any food I've ever eaten in Philadelphia, or New York for that matter. And I understand you make a mean Sicilian pie. I'd love to try that."

Her compliments earned her two pinched cheeks. "This one is a gem, Griff. You make sure you bring her back to me soon. So much better than that other one."

Jamie's eyes rounded when the older woman made a spitting sound. If they had been anywhere but a restaurant, she was convinced the woman would have done just that. Obviously not a fan of Griff's ex.

"I will, Mama, I promise. See you soon."

He kissed her cheek before placing a hand in the small of Jamie's back. Even through the thickness of her borrowed sweatshirt, she felt branded. When they left the restaurant and reached his truck, Jamie waited for him to open the door.

"Well, if this is what you do on an un-date, I can't imagine a real one."

*****

Griff stumbled at her words, reality raining over him like a sudden rain shower. He helped her inside then shut her door without comment. Un-date or not, what he wanted to do was kiss her until memory of all men everywhere vanished, including Luca and what's his name. Instead, he got into his truck and started it.

He didn't say anything at all for a few blocks, but he knew he was being an ass. This wasn't Jamie's fault, and she deserved better.

"You never told me about Carl," he said to her at the first red light.

Guilt ate at him when she sucked in a quick breath.

"Not what I expected you to say, but since this is an undate, why not? What do you want to know about *Chad*?"

"Anything you want to tell me." *Like why he holds such fascination for you after all these years.*

Jamie sat for a moment without talking, and he wondered if she would answer his question. "Chad was the golden boy of our class, of the whole school really. He made varsity football as a freshman and never looked back."

Great! No competition there, not that he was in this race.

"Seems like an odd choice for you," Griff commented, hoping it didn't sound as off to her as it did to his own ears.

"Why?" she asked.

"I just mean you always kid about how clumsy you are. A star athlete doesn't seem like your type, that's all."

He glanced over in time to see a small smile play about her lips.

"And what sport did you play, Griff?"

"Baseball, but we're not talking about me."

"Well, if he had just been a 'dumb jock,' Chad would not have held my interest. I mean besides the fact that he was gorgeous."

"Oh, so he had layers, did he?" *Really? What was wrong with him?*

Out of the corner of his eye, Griff saw her turn toward him. He wished he weren't driving.

"I got to know Chad when I tutored him in math. We were in the same grade, and as you can probably imagine, math has always been my thing." She gave a soft laugh he felt to his toes. "Not so much *his* thing, though."

"Still doesn't sound like your type." *Shut up, Griff!*

He didn't dare glance at her, told himself to keep his eyes on the road. Yeah, that's the reason he'd use…

"I got to know him over the course of time. I mean weekly hours together in the library practically the whole four years gave me ample time. He made me laugh. I mean, no, he wasn't the brightest bulb, but he was...well you know. I'm sure the girls swooned over you in high school."

"No, not really."

Griff stopped at a red light and turned to look at Jamie. She was grinning at him.

"Oh, please. They did. And you never would have given anyone like me a second glance."

"That's not true," he protested. The light changed, and he drove on, bringing his eyes back to the road.

"Pfft. Like I'm going to believe that," Jamie scoffed.

"And exactly what kind of girl were you? You said, 'anyone like me'."

He heard her shift around in her seat. When he stole a glance, Jamie was looking out the passenger window. When she answered, he had to strain to catch her soft voice.

"I was the kind of girl not noticed by athletes, Griff. Quiet, shy, always had my nose shoved in a book. I wasn't a cheerleader or popular. But I had good friends, made good grades, and that's all that mattered to me."

Except not gaining the attention of a certain football player. But he kept that to himself. Because he didn't really know what to say anyway. He wondered if she was right. Would he have ignored her in high school? Had he been that shallow?

All too soon, he pulled into her driveway. Before she could say anything, he shut off his truck and ran around to her side, opening the door.

Jamie smiled at him, a look that sent heated blood coursing through his veins.

"I had a wonderful time tonight, Griff. Thank you."

She pulled her keys from her tiny purse and glanced at her door.

"Me, too. I mean I had a great time, too." He flashed a grin at her. "And you're welcome."

"Okay then."

She glanced at the ground as if she didn't know what else to say.

"Let me see you to your door."

"That's not necessary," she demurred.

"Where I come from, it is. My mother would skin me alive if I didn't."

And that was the truth. He'd been raised to respect women. But he had another reason for wanting to do so. It bought him a few more moments with her.

"Well, I wouldn't want to be responsible for that happening," she joked, leading the way to her front porch."

"This suits you," Griff commented as he glanced around at the things he hadn't noticed when he picked her up earlier.

A swing graced one end of the porch, while a pair of bright blue rocking chairs flanked a small table in the middle.

"I can picture you out here reading when it gets warmer."

"That's what I thought when I bought the place. And I do, but there's a small window for that before it's too bloody hot." She laughed and fumbled with her keys at the door. "On those days, I choose the window seat in my staircase or anywhere else that has air conditioning."

"Smart lady. I guess the heat and humidity down here take some getting used to."

She turned from the door and looked at him before laughing.

"I've been here since I graduated from college, Griff. If I'm not used to it by now, I never will be. And believe me, we know a thing or two about humidity in Pennsylvania. They don't exactly enjoy a dry heat."

Griff watched her play with then keys in her hands, passing them back and forth from one to the other. Good. He wanted her a little nervous.

"Well, I better go inside. Believe it or not, I have some work to do tonight. Thanks for the best un-date I've ever had."

He knew he shouldn't, but he didn't care. Griff leaned into her until he trapped her body between his and the door.

"Agreed," was all he said before pressing his mouth to hers. He didn't touch her. Didn't push his hands into her thick hair as they itched to do. He didn't mold her shape to his. He did none of those things because Griff knew he would be lost if he did.

He also knew the very moment Jamie returned the kiss. She emitted a soft sigh and parted her lips, giving him entry. Griff took it. He swept his tongue inside her mouth, tasting garlic and a hint of wine. But the sweetness he sampled was all her. His hands clenched into fists at his side, anything to keep him from touching her anywhere other than his lips.

And then Jamie pulled back, and he felt the loss of her heat all the way through his bones.

"Goodnight, Griff," she murmured before slipping into her home.

For a long moment, Griff stood there, hand upon her bright blue door. It felt warm to the touch somehow, almost as if he touched her instead.

Chapter Nineteen

"You can't blame gravity for falling in love."
-Albert Einstein

Jamie's purse and keys slid from her hands, clattering to the hardwood floor. She turned toward the door, leaning her forehead against the wood. Her heart hammered as though she'd just run a marathon instead of kissed Griff. She didn't hear his truck pull out of the driveway and wondered if he still stood on the porch. Afraid to know, she turned and walked into her kitchen. She said a vague hello to a sleepy Fiona and poured herself a glass of water. Anything to keep her hands busy. Anything to stop herself from running to check. Because if he still stood there, just on the other side of her front door, Jamie had no idea what she might do.

She drained the entire glass then placed her fingers to her still heated lips. One kiss! Mind you, one wonderful, pulse raising, felt it in every cell of her body kiss. But still, it was only a kiss. That kiss was the perfect ending to the best first date ever. Even if it was an un-date.

The thought sagged her shoulders and dropped her hand to her side.

"What am I going to do?" Jamie asked out loud.

"Mreow," complained Fiona from next to her empty food bowl.

"You're lucky to be a cat. Your biggest worry is whether or not you'll eat again."

She picked up the bag of kitty treats from the counter and poured a few into the bowl. "That's all you get, Fiona. We have to watch your girlish figure."

Fiona chose to not answer, pushing her face in the bowl.

"I, on the other hand, don't care about mine."

Jamie grabbed a carton of ice cream from the freezer. And a spoon.

"One of the many perks of being single," she informed the disinterested feline. "No need for a bowl."

She took her treat into the living room, curling up at one end of the sofa. Picking up the remote, she flicked on Netflix and chose the latest documentary on Ted Bundy.

"No one needs a romantic comedy right now," she said to the empty room and sighed.

Her romantic life was a joke, just not funny. She finally meets a great guy; funny, intelligent, kind. And he happens to have a moral code. That happens to make it impossible for them to date.

An unexpected pang erupted in her chest. This isn't a big deal she told herself. They'd only met a few weeks ago. She couldn't care about him already. Could she? Jamie shoved a huge spoonful of New York Super Fudge Chunk into her mouth, savoring the flavor. Ice cream would never break her heart.

And then it hit her. Without Griff to muddy the waters, she could focus on Chad and seeing him again after all those years. She didn't know if he still appealed to her. Still, she would march in there, with her new and improved body, and show him what he'd missed.

With a last, longing look at the pint of ice cream, Jamie got up and carried it to the kitchen. She put it back in the freezer and placed the spoon in the dishwasher. Then she eyed the fridge. It wasn't enough.

Crossing back to the fridge, she ripped open the freezer door and grabbed the ice cream. Knowing it lay waiting in there for the next emotional upheaval meant too big of a risk. She grabbed a new spoon and dug out the contents, throwing the most delicious ice cream ever into the disposal gave her hope. Her heart felt lighter. She was in control of her life, not Griff. And not her other two favorite guys, Ben and Jerry.

She filled her glass with more water and walked into the dining room to catch up on some work.

Bright sunlight hit Jamie's eyes the next morning. She reached blindly for her phone on the nightstand to check the time. Almost noon! But then, she'd stayed up until three, working on her biggest client. Things would get crazy for the next few weeks.

She used the bathroom and put on more of her new exercise clothing. Sam had taken her shopping, insisting on Jamie looking the part of a 'gym rat' as she called her. Glancing in the mirror, Jamie had to admit her friend had been on to something. The spandex pants fit better than her baggy old sweats without feeling skin-tight. No need to flash all of her sins to the world. The dimpled flesh of her thighs remained well covered.

Grabbing a protein drink and a banana, Jamie headed out. On the short drive to the gym, her thoughts consisted only of will he be there or not, was she ready to see him so soon after *that kiss.* Did that kiss even matter to him as it did to her? She touched her lips with a finger, swearing she could still feel the tingle he'd wrought.

After pulling into the gym lot, Jamie pulled down the visor and opened the mirror. "You are not that woman, Jamie Lawler. You do not fall apart just because a man kissed you. So what if he's gorgeous and wonderful? You are not that woman." There, she told herself. All better now. She got out of her car and walked right into Griff.

So much for not being affected by him.

"Sorry," she mumbled.

"Good morning," he said at the same time.

"I meant to get here earlier, but I slept in." Great! Now they were reduced to small talk.

"I try to not come in on the weekends, but I felt like blowing off some steam," added Griff by way of explanation. "And it's not quite warm enough to run on the beach."

"Well, it is your place. You can come whenever you want." She glanced at the building, her feet, the sky. Anywhere but directly at him. Even thought they'd only enjoyed one date, or un-date as it were, the idea they wouldn't have another saddened her.

"Yes, of course. I try to not come now, you know, to take a break from the place. Plus, Sundays are usually the day for things like groceries and laundry." He barked out a laugh. "Exciting life I lead."

She glanced at his handsome face. The dimples drew her in. "Not much different from mine. Anyway, I should get started. Didn't get much work done last night, so I have that much more to do today."

"Sure. Well, I was headed inside, I'll just walk with you. If that's okay."

"Of course."

By the time they made it the few yards into the building, Jamie wanted to scream. She wished they'd never had their stupid date. That wasn't entirely true. Last night had been terrific. Goofy Golf! Palm Harbor had been her home for more than a decade now, and she'd never gone mini golfing. But still, this weirdness, or whatever it was, between them sucked.

"Thanks," she threw over her shoulder and headed for her favorite treadmill. Runners flanked her on both sides, sparing her from making more small talk with Griff. After stretching for a few moments, Jamie started up the machine. She glanced around as she slid in her ear buds. Griff wasn't anywhere in sight. Guess she had nothing to worry about.

*****

Griff shook his head at his cowardice, but he didn't leave the sanctuary of his office. That painful, awkward small talk with Jamie in the parking lot sucked. What happened to their camaraderie? He should have never taken her out last night. He most certainly should never have kissed her.

But as soon as those thoughts formed, he dismissed them. Watching the joy on her face when she creamed him in goofy golf had been worth any price. And the kiss? One for the record books. He didn't focus on the fact it would be the first and last one. Relationships didn't always work out the way you think they will. And if this one didn't, where would it leave them? And everybody knew mixing work with pleasure wasn't a good idea. But then, everyone hadn't kissed Jamie Lawler.

He tossed the pen in his hand to the desk. Why was he hiding in here when he wanted to be out there, with her? Because he wanted to be out there, with her. And he'd already gone out of his way to convince himself, and Jamie, this relationship wasn't going to happen. Best to stick with the plan.

He turned on his laptop and waited for it to start. Might as well get some of the dreaded 'paperwork' completed while he was here. While the machine hummed to life, he thought about last night. He thought about all the things he shouldn't. Like Jamie jumping up and down at yet another hole in one. Or the way she charmed everyone she met without even trying. Or the way her lips felt under his. Nope, definitely not thinking about that one.

He loved that he witnessed what looked like a pep talk in her car. She took the whole getting healthier thing very seriously. Some of his other clients could use that kind of enthusiasm.

He opened his scheduling program. Glancing over the next few weeks, everything seemed in order. When business started to take off, he and Jack had hired some part timers to come in during the evenings and weekends, giving them both a much-needed break from the place.

Then why are you here on a Sunday? He hated to admit it, but he'd come in hoping to see her. Hoping he could spend some more time with her, even though it wouldn't be a date. Yep, he was that pathetic. Even worse, instead of actually spending time with her, he sat in his office. Hiding from the one interesting woman he'd met in over a year. *Great!*

Happy with the schedule, Griff closed out that program and opened his work email. There was always a ton of those to go through. He perused the list. No, he didn't need a business loan, thankfully, or solar panels. He deleted more than half of the emails unread.

He opened one from their realtor, Carla Bruno. Carla had been scoping out potential locations for another Getting it Done in nearby towns. He and Jack had talked about opening a second location for over a year now, but it hadn't gone any further than that, just talk. He looked over the listings she attached, intrigued by the idea. Closing the email, he starred it and then forwarded it to Jack for his consideration. Now might be the time to get serious about expansion.

He glanced through the rest, deleting most, and answering the others. He opened one from Darla, dreading its contents. Sure enough, yet another invitation to dinner, at her house of course, loomed. He sent off a brief reply, thanking her but gently reminding her he didn't date clients.

Unless of course they happened to be Jamie.

Disgusted, Griff shut down his laptop. He stood and stretched out his back, staring at his closed office door. He should go out there. See how Jamie fared. Maybe he could offer some tips on other machines she hadn't tried yet. Before he could talk himself out of it, he left the office, pulling the door closed behind him.

Griff spotted her immediately. Jamie ran slowly but still faster than she'd managed yet on the treadmill he'd come to think of as hers. He asked her once why she always used the same one. She grinned and said, "because it hasn't tried to kill me yet." He liked her goofy sense of humor, often self-directed. A man on the next machine got off and cleaned it. If Griff believed in signs, which he didn't, this would be one. Shaking his head at his own foolishness, he crossed the gym and took his place next to her.

While he warmed up, he watched her glance at him from the corner of his eye. She never broke stride, keeping her eyes down on the machine panel. She felt it to, he mused. She must. There was a connection between them, a pull of sorts. He couldn't be the only one who felt it.

He caught her glancing his way a few more times while he ran. She did feel it! She could ignore him no more than he could her. Even though he couldn't act upon it, the knowledge settled over him like an old flannel shirt, keeping him warm.

"I didn't eat all the ice cream," Jamie blurted in his general direction.

Of course, with music blasting in her ears, she had no idea how loudly that had come out. The woman on the other side of her startled before laughing.

"I wanted to, mind you, but I didn't. I consider that a moral victory. Goodness knows you gave me reason to want to eat the whole pint of ice cream."

The other woman didn't even try to pretend she hadn't heard, instead glancing at him with one brow raised.

Griff swallowed a laugh and waved to Jamie in the mirror. When she glanced his way, he pointed to his own ears, hoping she'd get the message.

Instead she tilted her head, all but shouting, "What?"

Griff chewed the inside of his mouth to keep from laughing. Being a smart man, he didn't think she would appreciate the humor in this.

He pointed to his own ears and then to hers. And saw the second she got it.

Jamie took out her earbuds and slowed her treadmill to a fast walk. "What?"

"You spoke a little loudly, since you had your ear buds in."

"Oh, sorry," she mumbled at a lower volume.

"No worries. Congratulations on not eating the whole pint. And I am sorry I caused you any stress."

"I'd love to know what he did to make you want to drown yourself in ice cream," added the woman on Jamie's other side.

Jamie whirled to face her. "Excuse me?"

Griff noted the exact moment it all dawned on her. Her face grew red, and a hand flew over her mouth.

"I was talking very loudly, wasn't I?"

This time, the laugh burst from him. "Well, if by talking you mean shouting, then yes."

Jamie glanced at the woman, who nodded.

"He kissed me. That's what he did. You know one of those great movie kisses where the heroine swoons and time stops? That kind of kiss. After telling me he doesn't date clients, mind you."

"Really? I say eat the damn pint. Was it chocolate?" the blonde asked.

"Ben and Jerry's New York Super Fudge Chunks," Jamie confirmed.

The other woman, whose name escaped Griff, looked around Jamie to fix him in place with a stare. One of those scorned-woman type of stares. "Next time go for the ice cream sister," she advised before turning away.

"Good idea," Jamie answered before turning back to face him. "For the record, I dumped it down the sink."

Griff took in her red face and over bright eyes. She'd never looked more beautiful to him. "I'm sorry about that. All of it."

"I know you are, Griff. I know because you're a good man who wants to do the right thing. I just wish you weren't so cute. And funny." She sighed. Turning off the treadmill, Jamie stood with her feet on either side of the center until it slowed to a stop.

She thinks I'm cute? Yes, that's the first thought that entered his head.

"Maybe we can be friends," she offered. "You know, no more un-dates. But we can still do stuff."

That seemed like the worst idea ever to Griff, but the

alternative left a hole in his chest. "Sure," he heard himself answer knowing he was a true glutton for punishment. "We can be friends. I'd like that."

"Okay great," she answered through somewhat clenched jaws.

Jamie cleaned her machine and wandered off. As much as he wanted to follow, Griff had just started his run. Besides, he wasn't that pathetic. Yet.

He did manage to keep her in view, thanks to the wall of mirrors. He got to watch as one of the regulars, a guy with more muscles than brains in his opinion, stopped to talk with her. But hey, they were friends and he didn't date clients. Jamie could talk to anyone she chose.

So what if he felt the beginnings of an ulcer?

Chapter Twenty

"I can't control my frustration."

-Hassno Plattner

A few days later, Jamie sat in the conference room, once again trying to curb the urge to scream. She had no idea what the dragon droned on about this time. Nor did she care. Now that she and Sam had given the green light to Operation Phoenix, she hated her job that much more. And cared about what the dragon thought that much less. She drew various versions of their new logo while she listened, hoping no one noticed she was about a million miles away.

She only stopped doodling when she noticed those around her getting up to leave. Jamie flipped her small notebook closed and joined them in their exodus. As she reached the doorway, a voice stopped her in her tracks.

"Miss Lawler, may I talk with you for a second?"

His tone of voice told her it wasn't a request. Jamie turned back toward him. "Of course, Mr. Smith."

Fifteen minutes later, with her blood pressure approaching stroke range, Jamie marched down the hallway to

Sam's office, barging in without even knocking. Luckily, she wasn't with a client. She slammed the door behind her.

"Is steam pouring from my ears?"

Sam, used to her rambling, played along. "Not that I can see. Should there be?"

Jamie paced back and forth in the office. "Yes! I feel like one of those cartoon characters. You know how steam pours from their ears when they're angry? That's how I feel right now."

"Okay, what did the dragon do now? I noticed you didn't leave that awful meeting when everyone else ran for the safety of their offices."

"I would have, but he wanted to talk to me." Jamie took a moment to calm herself. Or at least try. Then thought better of having this conversation within the walls of Smith and Smith. "I have a better idea. How about dinner tonight? I'll tell you all about it, and believe me, you're going to want a Margarita in your hand when I do."

Sam raised one perfect brow. "That bad, huh?"

"Worse," Jamie muttered.

"Well, then the first round is on me. For a fee. You also have to tell me about your dinner with Griff."

Jamie groaned but agreed. After all, Sam would get it out of her with or without alcohol. "Fine," she muttered. She waved, backing to the door. "See you later."

Jamie stopped in the kitchen for a quick shot of caffeine before heading on to her own office. She shut her door, the universal sign at the firm for 'do not disturb' and allowed herself to dream for a moment. One day soon, she wouldn't have to deal with that man anymore. She and Sam would open their own firm and be happy. And if they grew enough to add other employees, they would treat them right. And let them bring their dog to work. And if her dream also included a dark-haired man, oh well.

Happy with those thoughts, she buried herself in her accounts.

Many hours later, Jamie and Sam finally made it to La Hacienda. They grabbed their favorite booth in the back, and Sam ordered their round of Margaritas.

"Only one because we're driving," Jamie reminded Sam.

"Yes, Mom," Sam said with a smirk before pulling some warm chips from the basket in front of her. "Happiness is a warmed tortilla chip."

"Agreed," Jamie shouted over the music and grabbed one of her own. "What a day!"

"Okay, let's get the bad stuff out of the way. Tell me what the dragon said to piss you off this much." Sam sat back, waiting for Jamie to begin.

"Well. I'm glad you're sitting down. You won't believe this."

Jamie launched into her tale of their boss questioning her loyalty and commitment to the firm because he had caught her 'drifting' during the staff meeting.

Sam leaned forward, her eyes bugging out of her face. "Are you kidding me?"

"Oh, wait. You haven't even heard the worst past yet. After several minutes of badgering me about productivity and commitment, he said, 'If I didn't know better, I'd say there was a new man in your life.' Can you believe?"

"What? How dare he?" Sam's green eyes spit fire.

Jamie's eyes darted around the crowded restaurant. Sam could be very loud when angry. "That's what I want to know. Stupid, misogynist pig. I ought to sue him."

"Hell, yeah!" Sam yelled in response.

Jamie shook her head. "No. I have a better idea. After all, as someone once said, 'The best revenge is a life well lived.' I just can't remember who."

"Doesn't matter, I'll Google it later. You're right. Leaving there, setting up our own firm, and finally being happy will be the best revenge."

"Hallelujah," agreed Jamie before grabbing some chips.

"Now that you've gotten that out of your system, tell me about your date with Griff. And don't leave out any of the spicy bits." She wagged her eyebrows.

"Well, first of all, it was an un-date."

"Huh? What does that even mean? I haven't had any alcohol yet and you're already not making sense."

"Don't worry, it gets more confusing." Jamie took a bite of her chip before telling Sam all about how Griff 'doesn't date clients.'

"Wait. He owns the gym with Jack? Why didn't one of them mention it?" Sam asked.

Jamie shrugged her shoulders. "Who knows?"

"Okay, next question. If Griff doesn't fool around with his clients, and I can agree with him on that." She pointed at Jamie. "In fact, make that rule number two for Phoenix Accounting. Right after bring your dog to work."

Jamie pretended to write it on the tabletop. "Got it."

"Anyway, as I was saying, why did he even bother to ask you out if that's one of his rules?"

"Good question. Wish I had an answer."

Neither woman spoke as the waiter brought their drinks and took their orders. He left the table but not before giving Sam a long, lingering look.

Jamie laughed. "See? We can't even order dinner without

someone falling under your spell. I finally meet one guy I like, who seems to like me, too, and now I can't date him."

"Let's break this down. He obviously has feelings for you, or he wouldn't have asked you out to dinner. Jack mentioned that women hit on him all the time at work. He always says no. Must have the same rule."

"Was this when you and he had dinner? As *friends*?"

Sam sat straighter then looked away. "There's nothing wrong with Jack and I being friends. And friends do have dinner." She waved her hand back and forth between them as if to prove her point.

"But you like him, Sam. I mean you like him like him. What's the problem?"

"I do like him. That's the problem."

Her strained tone gave Jamie pause.

"I know your parents had a terrible marriage," she started. "At least, I know what you've told me."

Sam didn't discuss her family often. Jamie had met her parents a few times, when one of them came to town Sam dragged her along to dinner as a buffer.

A harsh laugh erupted from Sam. "That's like saying Hitler was a little crazy."

"I get not wanting to be like your family. Look at mine. But Jack isn't them. Isn't he worth the risk?"

"No. No one is worth the risk. That's why I go on a lot of first dates only. And you're not like your family, Jamie, which is the point. I'm not going to be either. And we were talking about your love life. Or lack of one. His rule is stupid, at least in this case."

Jamie barely resisted banging her head on the table. "I get it. I do. Things could get messy for him, for either of them, if they dated clients. And they've probably put everything into

Getting It Done. No need to risk all their hard work. Then why ask me out?"

"Why indeed?"

Jamie grabbed another chip, knowing it meant empty carbs and not caring. "I have no idea."

"I know I haven't spent much time with him, but between the things I've heard from you and Jack, Griff sounds like an all right guy. I don't see him doing this to mess with you. Or to be a dick."

"Agreed." She rested her chin in her hand. "If only he hadn't kissed me."

Sam's eyes bugged

"Way to bury the lead. Why am I only now hearing about a kiss? Come on, fess up."

Jamie sighed. "You know that one kiss that's perfect? Not too wet, not too dry. Has the right amount of pressure. That kiss?"

"Oh," breathed Sam before taking a gulp of her drink.

"Yes, oh. It was perfect, and then he ended it and left. And now, I told him we could still be friends. What was I thinking?"

"I have no idea."

"Oh, and did I tell you he's agreed to be my plus one for my reunion?"

"You mean the one in which you finally show what's his face what he missed out on?"

"The very one. And his name is Chad, as you know."

"Chad, shmad, who cares about him? You have a real flesh and blood man in front of you. Why think about Chad?"

Good question!

Jamie sipped her drink for fortitude. "Thinking about Chad is what brought me to Griff. Or at least to Getting It Done. In a way, I wouldn't have met him without this hair-brained scheme to finally show Chad."

"And Griff is still planning on going with you?"

"I guess. That was a bit ago and before the kiss. And before his announcement about not dating clients"

"Hmmm…"

Jamie took another sip, enjoying the frosty bite of the margarita as it slid down her throat.

"What does 'hmmm' mean? You're never short on words, my friend."

Sam laughed and took another sip of her drink. "You know me too well. I wonder if the kiss changes his plan to go to Pennsylvania with you, that's all."

"Why would it change anything between us?"

"You're asking him to go home with you. Meet your family. Be your 'fake boyfriend,' for all intents and purpose. If he's already conflicted about keeping his hands off you, that might be asking a lot. Just saying."

"Oh. I didn't think of that."

"Exactly! Which is why you have me."

Jamie held a hand to her head. "Can we talk about something else? Anything? How about the alarming trend of man buns?"

Sam laughed as Jamie had hoped. "Sure. Let's talk about what we have to do to take Phoenix Accounting to the next step."

"What a great idea," Jamie agreed.

Their dinners arrived and both women enjoyed their meals while discussing the next steps. By the end of the meal, they'd divided up duties. Sam would research establishing an LLC and finding an attorney to help them with that. Jamie would research necessary local and state permits for their business. And she was in charge of settling on a bank to use for their business accounts.

Although both women had saved for this day, they weren't 'swimming in dough' as Sam pointed out. Jamie did have the trust fund from her family but didn't want to use it unless necessary. They decided on utilizing Sam's home, a big old Victorian she'd inherited from her grandmother last year.

"What all do you think we need to do to the first floor of your home to get it ready?" she asked her friend.

Sam grinned. "I'm glad you asked. Jack, and Griff by extension, happens to have a contractor friend, Gavin."

"Oh they do, huh?"

"At dinner the other night, I mentioned we were moving forward with our plan and the house. Jack and I talked about maybe sectioning off one side of the first floor to hold our offices. That way, the living quarters would be off limits to the general public. Can't have some perv rummaging through my panty drawer."

"True." Jamie bit her lip.

"Come on, out with it."

"What?" asked Jamie.

"Whatever it is that has you gnawing on your bottom lip. It's your tell, you know."

Jamie sighed. "I know we've hashed this out already, but we may have been a bit tipsy at the time. And you know how everything seems like a good idea then. Like the time you cut your own bangs."

Sam winced. "That *was* a terrible idea. Whatever this is can't be as bad." She leaned forward, all attention on Jamie.

"Okay. I feel badly that you're going to destroy your beautiful home. I know we don't have a ton of capital, but maybe…" She stopped at Sam's upheld hand.

"You're right. We have 'hashed this out,' and we made our

decision. Together like we're going to make all the business decisions. We'd be lucky to afford something in that half empty strip mall out on the highway. And that's not what we want. And why throw away money when we don't have to?"

"No, it's not, but I can't help feeling badly about it." Jamie wrung her napkin in her hands.

"Do you remember when we saw *Little Women*? Aunt March left that big old house to Jo. Well, Grandmother Hardy left me my home. Of course, it doesn't have a fancy name, but it does have a purpose now. And besides, I'm one person rattling around in that big old house."

"You might not always be one person, Sam."

"And we won't always be starting out, watching every penny. Which is why this is the time to do it. Now, before both of us aren't alone anymore." Sam reached across the table and squeezed both of Jamie's hands. "This is the right thing to do. Repeat after me."

"This is the right thing to do." She squeezed Sam's hands back. "As long as you're sure."

Sam grimaced. "I can't be any surer than I am. I'm also sure I don't want to have this conversation again."

"Okay, okay. I get it. I promise."

"Well, there is one more thing."

"You're pregnant?" Jamie quipped.

Sam swallowed hard and set down her drink. "You almost wore that. And no, I'm not pregnant. I am, however, paying for the necessary renovations."

Tears welled in Jamie's eyes. She was a crier, which she hated.

"Ugh, no one mentioned puppies in a shelter or veterans coming home to their loved ones. Those are your weak points."

"All true. I can't deny it. But thank you, Sam, really. This is way above and beyond."

"Grandmother Hardy also left me money to care for the house. A lot of money. My family may be dysfunctional, but they're also rich."

"True," murmured Jamie. "However, you don't want to use family money as much as I don't."

"Agreed, except this money came from my grandmother, whom I adored, and who believed in me. She would want this." She shook a finger at Jamie. "No more tears."

"It's the salsa," Jamie fibbed on a laugh.

"Good. Now that we have that settled, let's get you a man."

Chapter Twenty-One

"My mother always told me, 'Don't get married. Make your own life. You don't need a man.'"

-Sandra Bullock

Sam's words, more truth than joke, accompanied Jamie as she walked into Getting It Done the next morning. At least Sam thought they might be true. For several years now, Sam had hinted, and not subtly, that Jamie should 'settle down.' Of course, Sam didn't have any intention of doing so. But then she never wanted kids. Jamie did. Someday. And now, staring down the barrel of thirty-three, she couldn't help wondering if Sam might be right. Not that there was a line of single men at her door or anything.

Jamie continued to mull this over as she went inside and headed for her treadmill. She'd come early, even earlier than usual for her. And not to avoid Griff. Of course not. That would be foolish. So what if they'd shared her best first kiss? Ever. So what if he saw her as a client first and woman second? She was fine with the notion. More lies, she told herself. She came in before the butt crack of dawn because every week from now until D-Day, or April fifteenth, grew busier. Her hours lengthened. Even Fiona might start missing her. Well, if she forgot to feed her. Maybe.

"Focus, Jamie," she told herself aloud. No one here this early to see her talking to herself. Or hear her. "Work on yourself for once and let everything else go."

"Great advice," commented Griff.

"What is wrong with you?" she shrieked while clutching her chest. "Are you trying to kill me? I have pepper spray, you know."

"Do you?" He made a show of looking over her as if checking for it.

"Well, not with me," she grumbled and climbed up on her treadmill.

"I'm sorry," Griff offered from the adjoining one. "I really thought you saw me in the mirrors."

"You move like a ninja, Griff. One minute you're not here and then you are."

She settled into her routine, trying hard to not notice him next to her. She didn't notice the subtle scent of cotton and man. She didn't notice he'd gotten his hair cut. She certainly didn't notice the musculature of his thighs. Or his tight butt. Nope, she'd just try running a bit faster today. Goodness knew she'd need all her concentration for that.

"I can hear you thinking over here. Might have to call the fire department soon."

"Good. Sam thinks I need a man. Maybe I need a fireman."

She also didn't notice when he barely missed falling off his treadmill.

"Really? What brought that on?"

"Her biological clock is ticking," grunted Jamie. She had chosen a faster speed than ever. And she'd be proud of herself if she survived it.

"I know I'm a guy and all, and the female mind is a bit, uh, tricky…"

"We prefer complex."

"That works. But how is her ticking biological clock causing your need for a man?"

"Sam wants to be an Auntie more than she wants to be a mother. At least that's what she tells herself. And since she's an only child, it's up to me." She gulped air into her burning lungs and wondered if anyone had ever required a transplant secondary to running. "See? Not 'tricky' at all."

"Jury's out on that one. And how do you feel about all this? Do you need a man?"

She turned and gave him the look she gave clients who couldn't keep up with her accounting explanations.

"No one 'needs' a man, Griff. Least of all me. But I would like to have children someday. I'm a bit old-fashioned in that I'd like to be married first. And I'm not getting any younger."

He barked out a laugh. "Sorry. What are you, maybe thirty tops?"

She shook her head. "I am *in* my thirties now, Griff, which means that with each passing moment, my eggs are petrifying. At least that's how it feels." She stabbed at the speed button, taking it down to a fast walk. "Whew, that's better."

"Still, Jamie, I don't think you're quite ready for the nursing home."

"Joke all you want. You're a man. You can have babies forever." She hit the stop button and grabbed her towel to mop up the river of sweat pouring down her face and neck. "Is it hot in here?"

"No," he answered, not gasping for air or even yet breaking a sweat.

Bastard!

"My point is this. The whole time I was growing up, everyone said how much better things are for women now. We can have careers and families. We can have it all. But you know what? No one tells you how to do that. I've been building my career since I graduated. And suddenly a decade has passed. How did that happen? When did it happen?"

Griff merely shook his head, probably afraid to answer. Smart man.

"And do you know the worst part, Griff? The dragon, as we call our boss, has it all. He has a wife, although I don't know how, and several lovely children. He doesn't have to juggle things. That's for 'the little woman' to do, as he calls his wife.

And now Sam and I are on the brink of launching our own firm. Finally. And that's great. And I am wildly excited for us. But guess what? Now I'll have even less time to find a man." She dragged in a much-needed breath. "Chad better be as hot as I remember him."

The words flew from her mouth before she could stop herself. *Where had that thought come from?* Jamie busied herself wiping down her machine. Screw the thirty-minute workout. Before the poor man could say anything, she finished up and marched to the furthest point away from him. Which brought her face to machine with some vicious looking thing she hadn't yet tackled. Great!

She felt a tap on her shoulder, and she turned to see Griff.

"I know what you need, and it's not a man."

He led the way to the group room, a place she hadn't ventured into yet. No way she was going to embarrass herself like that. She followed him, having no idea what he meant.

Griff opened the door and flicked on the lights. He pointed to a huge tire sitting on the floor at the opposite end. "Flip that," he commanded.

*****

Griff held his breath while he waited for Jamie to react. He thought about covering his junk while he waited. He didn't usually talk to women like that, and never Jamie.

She stood in the doorway looking like a rabbit about to bolt for cover.

"That?" she squeaked.

"That," he confirmed.

He saw the second she made her mind up to do it. She stood a bit taller, squared her shoulders.

"Fine."

Jamie marched across the floor, her tiny feet making barely any noise. He watched as she circled the massive tire as if trying to figure her best approach.

"Remember to lift with your legs," he called out.

She muttered something under her breath, and Griff was happy to be too far away to hear the actual words. Then she squatted on the far side of the tire, placing her hands under it, and lifting. Nothing budged.

As much as he wanted to help her, Griff stood his ground and let her figure it out.

"You're a sadist," she accused.

Watching her, sweaty in her workout clothes, Griff shook his head. *More like masochist.*

"You've got this, Jamie. Pretend the tire is the dragon's face," he encouraged.

"Right now, I'd prefer it was yours," she grunted.

"Understood." Griff watched as she grabbed the bottom of the truck tire once more, this time raising it off the floor. Her face, already red from running, gleamed with sweat and exertion. She looked beautiful. But he kept that fact to himself to avoid castration.

Jamie growled as she lifted the mammoth tire and flipped it over to the other side. A huge smile wreathed her face. "I did it!"

"Yes, you did. Now, do it again." He grinned at the look on her face. "All the way across the room, then take a breather and all the way back."

Jamie sent him a look but stayed silent. Then she flipped the tire again. And again, until she crossed the room with it. On Griff's end of the room, she stopped, leaning her hands on her knees, and breathed heavily.

"I did it," she exclaimed.

"Yes, you did. Knew you could."

She smirked. "Glad someone did."

Without another word, she turned and flipped the tire all the way back across the floor. When it crashed to the floor the final time, Jamie laid down next to it, flat on her back.

Griff tried to not notice her chest heaving with the effort to breathe. Because that would make him a perv, right? And she was a client. *Remember that.*

"I'm letting you off the hook, by the way," she said, still lying on the floor with her eyes closed.

"Hook? What hook?"

She had him 'hooked,' but Griff didn't think that was her meaning.

Jamie sat up then got to her feet. Already Griff could see she moved with more coordination, even if she couldn't.

"You agreeing to be my plus one for the reunion. I release you from it." She laughed. "Sounded a bit like a royal decree."

He felt the corners of his mouth droop. "Oh. That."

Jamie looked at her sneakers. "Yeah, that. Don't worry, I won't hold you to it. Especially since…"

"Since?"

She blew the hair from her eyes. "Are you really going to make me say it?" When he didn't answer right away, she continued. "Since the un-date we shared, Griff. I don't want things to be any more awkward than they are right now. I would never ask you to go all the way to Pennsylvania with me now."

"You never asked," he said in a soft voice.

Her eyes rounded. Griff could see the whiskey-colored flecks from where he stood.

"What?"

"You never asked me, Jamie. You didn't have to because I wanted to. Want to. Still want to." He dragged a hand through his hair. "Unless that's a problem for you."

He gave her an out while hoping she wouldn't take it. Even though going all that way and spending days with the woman he wanted but couldn't have would be tough. *Please don't give me the out.*

"If you're sure?" she asked.

The feeling of a great weight being lifted spread through him. He could breathe again. "I'm sure."

Jamie shuffled her feet and looked anywhere but at him. "I don't want to impose."

"I think you know by now I'm pretty much a straight shooter. If I didn't want to go, I wouldn't have offered. Besides, who else is going to give Tad a run for his money?"

A grin brightened her face.

"His name is Chad. And thank you."

"I know. And you're welcome."

Griff watched her walk out of the room, a small ache blooming in his chest.

Jack said something to her, making Jamie laugh, as he

entered the room. "You're an idiot, Griff."

Jack hit the nail on the head, not that he'd admit it to his friend.

"Okay, I'll bite. Why now?"

"Hmmm where should I start? Letting her walk away when you clearly have feelings for her? Or maybe it's the agreeing to go to Pennsylvania with her when you clearly have feelings for her but won't act on them. Either way, you're an idiot."

"Gee, thanks," Griff grunted. Jack raised some valid points, not that he'd be telling him that either.

"Bro, I have your back. Always. And part of that is telling you when you're being an idiot."

"Sort of like me calling you out on spending time with Sam as 'friends' when we both know you want more," Griff pointed out.

"True," Jack muttered while the light in his blue eyes dimmed.

"Sorry," Griff mumbled.

"Don't wait too long. A woman like Jamie won't be single forever." Jack offered that nugget of wisdom over his shoulder as he left the room.

"Like I didn't know that already," Griff muttered to the empty room.

Chapter Twenty-Two

"Wait long enough, and people will surprise and impress you."
-Randy Pausch

Jamie dragged herself out of her car and into her house. "I'm home, Fiona," she called to her cat. She dropped her laptop bag and purse on the couch and headed to the kitchen. Opening the fridge, she groaned at the lack of food and grabbed a Greek yogurt. *Good for you!* A few short weeks ago, she would have reached for chocolate. Or ice cream. Or maybe chocolate ice cream. The long, crazy days leading up to April fifteenth were not for the faint of heart.

She glanced at the calendar hanging on the side of the fridge. Taking a red Sharpie, Jamie crossed out today. Hers was a ritual she developed the first year working at Smith & Smith. She felt good making the dramatic red X, even though each day brought her closed to "D Day."

Then the bottom dropped out of her stomach. Only one more week until April fifteenth. Which meant only three more weeks until she and Griff flew to Pennsylvania. They hadn't talked about the trip at all, except to confirm he was still planning to go with her a few weeks ago.

Ever since their un-date, a new, and unwelcome, tension grew between them. They both acted as though nothing was wrong, but it wasn't the same. Jamie had only seen him at the gym and one time when she stopped for takeout at her favorite Thai place on the way home from yet another too long day at the office. It made her wonder how many times they had run into each other, so to speak, before they met. Palm Harbor was a small beach town that shrank to a few thousand in the off season.

Had she stood behind him in line at the grocery store? Maybe pumped gas at the next pump over? The possibilities in their small town were endless. But wouldn't she have noticed him? With that chiseled jaw and his bright green eyes, surely, she would have looked twice? Or Sam would have noticed him. Sam had an eye for these things.

But when she saw him that first morning in the gym, Jamie had not recognized him. Been drawn to him? Heck, yeah. But she had never seen him before.

When she'd asked Griff if he was still coming to her reunion with her, she'd almost hoped he'd say no. Almost. The thought of spending those days with him, pretty much twenty-four seven, made her both anxious and happy. Even now, butterflies swarmed in her belly.

A loud, and very disgruntled, meow sounded from the floor near her feet. She looked down to see Fiona staring at her with her usual impassive glare.

"Sorry, Fiona. Did I forget to feed you the second I walked in the door?"

A twitch of the large cat's tail was the only answer Jamie received.

"What do we feel like tonight, hmm?" She reached into the pantry and grabbed a can of wet cat food. "Tuna it is."

After scraping the food into her bowl, Jamie sat the meal down for Fiona on the mat, next to her water bowl. "Enjoy. I wish choosing my dinner was that easy."

She opened the freezer, peering at the assortment of frozen dinners. She waffled between ravioli and beef stew, saved from deciding by her doorbell.

"Coming!" she yelled as she headed to the door. Thinking it was Sam, she added "What would the dragon think to find you not working?"

She opened the door and froze. Not Sam but Griff, holding a bag of delicious smelling food.

"You're not Sam," she said then immediately wished she could kick herself.

"I get that a lot," Griff joked. "May I come in?" He held the bag aloft as though offering a bribe.

"Of course."

Jamie stepped aside and let him in. And watched as Fiona, the traitor, greeted Griff with a low chirping noise she'd never heard the cat make.

"Remember who feeds you," she groused in the feline's direction.

"Speaking of which, you're probably wondering why I'm here. I brought dinner."

"That smells like Thai."

"That's because it is," Griff announced. He looked around her kitchen. "Where are your plates?"

Still stunned by the fact that he stood in her kitchen, holding Thai takeout, Jamie pointed at the correct cabinet.

"Sit," he suggested. "I've got this. I had to guess, since I have no idea what you like to eat and they don't have pasta," he joked.

"I do enjoy pasta," she answered. She wouldn't think

about how much of it she ate that night. On their un-date.

Griff turned back, placing dishes on the table. "You aren't allergic to shrimp, are you?"

"Ah, shrimp? No. No food allergies. At least not yet."

"That probably seemed random, but I had no idea." He took several food containers out of the bag.

"How would you? I mean what do you really know about me other than I talk to machines?"

Griff's hands stilled. He turned to face her. "I know a few things, Jamie."

He crossed the kitchen until he stood less than a foot from her. The heat in his eyes doubled her heart rate faster than the treadmill ever had. She swallowed hard.

"I know that you prefer to drink beer instead of wine. I know that you care enough about yourself to want to be healthier but not so much that you glance in every mirror you pass. I know that you inspire loyalty in your friends, which makes you a good person. I know you have a great sense of humor." His upper body leaned in a bit more, almost cancelling the space left between them. "And I know that Brad better deserve you."

"His name is Chad," she whispered, barely able to breathe.

Griff grinned and walked to the sink to wash his hands. The tension in the air evaporated with the distance between them.

"Now I also know you're not allergic to shrimp. But do you like it? Because I love it, and I may have bought a lot of it."

Jamie exhaled a whoosh of breath she didn't know she'd been holding. "And now you know another fascinating tidbit about me. I happen to love shrimp also."

"Great! There's shrimp and vegetarian spring rolls

because I didn't know." He pulled out a small waxed bag, setting it on the table. "Then you have your Tom Kha soup." He pulled a plastic container out and set that next to the spring rolls. "And I chose two different entrees, not knowing which you'd like." He started to reach back into the bag again.

"Is this a magic trick, where the bag holds an endless supply of Thai food?"

"Nope. Just two more things. Pad Thai with shrimp, of course." He looked up at her and grinned. "And some Panang with chicken, in case you were one of those odd ducks who doesn't like shrimp."

"Who are those weirdos?" she asked, laughing at his dramatic presentation of dinner. "Wow, Griff, you thought of everything." Jamie glanced at her phone to see the time.

"Hey, I know you're in the middle of your busy season. I won't keep you. Figured I'd save you from wasting time cooking."

"You saved me time from heating a frozen meal, and this looks much better."

"Since you like shrimp as much as I do, why don't we split both entrees?" Griff suggested.

"That's beginning to become our thing."

Silence reigned as both split the food between them and dug in. Jamie enjoyed the fact that he didn't feel the need to fill the silence with chatter. While she loved talking with him, she also liked a companionable silence. Another check in his favor, even though it didn't matter in the end since he wouldn't date a client.

"You seem sad. What's wrong?" Griff asked.

She looked at him, sitting across from her, fork in mid-air to his mouth, waiting for an answer. What could she say? *The nicest guy to show any interest in me since, well, the beginning of time, can't date me because I'm a client.* Nope.

"Just tired, I guess. These last few weeks kill me every year."

The delicious smelling food suddenly held the appeal of eating cardboard. She took another bite to throw him off the scent.

"Oh. That's understandable, I guess. I don't have the same kind of pressure you do."

"But you have all that pressure to succeed, owning your own business." She grinned. "Of course, by next year, I'll have that, too."

He raised one brow. "And that makes you smile?"

"Absolutely! I mean, don't get me wrong. I'll still have the crazy volume in the Spring." She held up one hand, fingers crossed. "At least I hope to. But, somehow, it's different."

"Because you'll be your own boss. I mean you and Sam anyway."

A warmth spread inside her. *He got her.*

"Yes," she murmured, before taking another bite of her dinner before it got cold. She'd be burning the midnight oil. She needed to eat.

"Does Chip have a certain type?"

The piece of spring roll she'd just swallowed threatened to stick. Jamie coughed a few times and grabbed her glass, taking a big swallow.

"Sorry. Did I say the wrong thing?" Griff asked.

"No, of course not. I didn't expect it, that's all. Why do you want to know?"

Griff shrugged before taking another bite. "Curious, I guess," he answered after swallowing. "Trying to understand what we're getting into."

"You really don't have to go. It's okay. I'm a big girl. I can handle it."

"Do you not want me to go anymore? I thought we covered this."

She sat a moment, not sure how to answer him. She *wanted* him to go. But she wasn't quite sure how to handle this new awkwardness between them. Showing up at her high school reunion, with him on her arm, sounded amazing. How many times had she dreamed of going back there a success? And by success she meant with a handsome boyfriend to show Chad, and others, that she'd wasn't invisible.

"Jamie, are you in there?" Griff joked and waved a hand in front of her face.

"What? Oh, sorry." She barely resisted the urge to hold the cool water bottle to her heated face. "I was lost in thought for a moment. I do that sometimes."

"Do you still want me? To go with you, I mean."

So much for cooling her face.

"I do. If you still want to."

He grinned at her. "Of course. That's why I brought it up. Good."

"Good," Jamie echoed, unable to put any other thought together in her addled brain.

"We should probably make up a back story then. You know, to convince people we're in love."

Jamie stared across the table at him. *In love?* She swallowed hard. "Yes, we should. We should keep it simple. Stick to the truth as much as possible. That way our cover story sticks, and we're less likely to make mistakes."

Griff burst out laughing. "Are you a spy by any chance?"

"No, nor have I ever played one on TV. But I may have read that in a book somewhere," she replied, tongue firmly in cheek.

"Okay, Madam Spy, tell me our story."

"Well, in keeping as close to the truth as possible, we met at the gym. You saw me struggling- trust me, everyone will believe that- and came over to help. I was captivated by your muscles. And kind eyes."

Griff laid down his fork.

"Why do you do that, Jamie?"

She blinked once then again, not sure what he meant.

"Why do I do what?"

"Why do you put yourself down like that?"

"I don't do that." *Did she?* Growing up as the ugly duckling, so to speak, in her family had affected how Jamie saw herself. She never realized it until moving away from them and that world. But she believed she'd grown beyond the bad habit.

Griff reached across the table and placed a hand on one of hers. "I'm not saying that to be critical; just pointing it out."

Warmth travelled up her arm from the contact. She moved her hand out from under his. No point in torturing herself. Something flashed in his eyes. It almost looked like disappointment.

"Anyway, we met at the gym. How long ago should we say?"

"Like you said, we should stick close to the truth. Let's leave it at earlier this year." He stood, taking his plate to the sink. "I should go. I'm sure you have hours ahead of you."

Jamie stood, too, perplexed at the change in his demeanor.

"Of course. And I'm sure you have something better to do." She walked him to her front door. "Thanks again for bringing me food." She opened the door. "And thinking of me," she added in a small voice.

"I think of you often, Jamie. Don't stay up too late working."

Griff left before she could say anything else.

Jamie peeked through the sheer panel next to her door to watch him drive away. And even though she did have hours of work ahead of her, she stood there long after he was out of sight.

Chapter Twenty-Three

"There are lots of things that frustrate me. I get frustrated when I have to wait at a red light."

-Kevin Garnett

Griff glanced in the rearview mirror as he drove away. He thought he could see Jamie looking out her window at him. He returned his gaze to the road and made the short drive home. Flipping on a local country station, he tried one of the breathing exercises his sister taught him before leaving for Iraq. Something about breathing in through the nose and out through the mouth. And maybe holding each breath in for a bit. *Probably should have listened better.*

Giving up, he settled for blowing out a long breath that came out more as a sigh. He knew as soon as he'd asked that question, he'd wrecked the nice conversation they'd been enjoying. And that was not the intention. But Jamie did put herself down, and even if she did it jokingly, it bothered him.

Griff shook his head as he pulled into his own driveway. Today sucked. No way around it. First there were stupid things to deal with at the gym. Then Darla made another, less subtle than usual, play for him. How many ways could he say he didn't date clients? *Hypocrite!* In his defense, that had always been the rule. The rule seemed stupid now since meeting Jamie.

The rule had been made for people like Darla. He didn't know anything about her outside of the gym, like whether she worked, etc. What he did know didn't thrill him. Her advances over the last year had grown increasingly aggressive, as though it was a game for her. It wasn't for him.

Griff made sure his comments to her remained neutral. While Miss Harriett flirted outrageously with him, and anything male for that matter, they both knew it didn't mean anything. Flirting came as easily as breathing for her. Darla was a different matter altogether. Griff took care to never be alone with her, never to return any of her teasing comments or outlandish actions. In fact, lately, he'd been maintaining a decent physical space from her. Better safe than sorry.

Letting himself into his empty house, Griff wished for a dog. At least he would have company. Instead, he grabbed a beer from the fridge and plopped down on the couch. He channel-surfed before settling on an all sports channel. Unfortunately, the baseball game didn't keep thoughts of Jamie at bay.

What was he thinking? Travelling to Pennsylvania with her? Meeting her family? Pretending to be her boyfriend? She had already given him an out. Twice! But a promise was a promise. And from the little she had shared about her family, and what's his name, Jamie would need reinforcements. And that meant him.

He took another swallow of his beer and thought about what them posing as 'involved' might entail. Griff had more than a few thoughts of his own on the subject. Thoughts better left in the scary recesses of his mind. But still, if they were going to make people believe their rouse, there had to be some physicality between them. Not that they lacked chemistry.

The one kiss they'd shared almost knocked him off his feet. Just imagine what would happen if they... No, he wasn't going there. They weren't going there. Not now, not ever. But that didn't stop the flow of blood south. Griff shook his head. Why was he making life so hard, pardon the pun, for himself?

*****

Across town, Jamie grumbled to herself, trying to concentrate on work. After watching Griff drive away, she'd stored the leftovers in the fridge and tried to make headway into the seemingly insurmountable pile of things to complete before April fifteenth.

After their planning meeting, she and Sam had agreed to shelve everything related to Operation Phoenix until after the looming tax deadline. Then, and only then, could they proceed full steam ahead. And they planned to do exactly that. Having that plan in mind made the days at Smith & Smith bearable.

Of course, first she had to survive travelling to Pennsylvania. With Griff. Each time she'd given him an out, Jamie had held her breath, unsure what to hope for. Of course, she wanted him to go. Sort of. Attending her high school reunion on his arm, so to speak, would show those people a thing or two. On the other hand, spending that much time with a man who made her pulse race, but wouldn't do anything about it, seemed futile. And painful. And frustrating.

She gave up any pretense of working and leaned back in her home office chair. When she started this plan, the whip herself into shape and make Chad see what he missed plan, things were clear in her mind. Now, not so much.

Did she really care what a bunch of people who had no

time for her in high school thought about her now? And if so, didn't that drag her down to their level? And what about Chad? She'd been madly in love with him back then, spending her nights, alone, mooning over him. And for what? Did he defy all social norms-like in every teenage romantic comedy she'd ever watched-and ask her to prom? No, he had not. Instead, he had taken Mandy Simpkins, head cheerleader and love of his life. And then, after college, he had married the cheerleader. After that, Jamie had stopped looking on social media for updates. They probably had their perfect two-point-five kids like her sister.

And Jamie had a good life here in her adopted home. No, make that a great life. She had Sam, who was really family more than friend. She had money in the bank and a roof over her head. And soon, she and Sam would realize their dream.

Feeling better about herself but no clearer about things with Griff, Jamie gave up the deep thinking and buried herself back in her work.

Late the next evening, Jamie walked into Getting It Done. She loved coming early morning but staying up with work until after one in the morning ruled that out. Especially since her work start time grew earlier with each passing day. Even now, she should be home, working of course, but she'd given in and ducked out to the gym. She missed it when she didn't get to work out every day. Jamie laughed to herself at the thought. Who would have predicted that?

Amused, Jamie headed to her treadmill. She tucked in her earbuds and hit her playlist, stepping up to begin her workout.

A voice reached her over the music in her ears, and Jamie turned to see a woman standing on the adjoining machine, frowning at her. She paused the treadmill and slid out her ear buds.

"Sorry, I couldn't hear you over the music. Can I help you?" Jamie asked.

She didn't know the woman and had no idea what she wanted. Or what might have caused the look on her face. The petite blonde looked as though she'd bitten into a lemon.

The other woman raised one hand, pointing a finger sporting a brightly colored nail toward Jamie's face. "Yes, you can 'help me.' You can stay away from my man."

Jamie's jaw dropped. Literally. She'd always heard the expression but never knew it happened in real life. But there she was, mouth open, staring at the other woman.

"Excuse me?" she countered.

The other woman sneered, twisting her otherwise pretty face. "You know what I'm talking about. Don't play dumb!"

The urge to laugh overwhelmed Jamie, and a small snicker escaped her. She'd never been accused of stealing anyone's man.

"You think this is funny?" The other woman, whose name Jamie still didn't know, pressed forward. Her man-made, overly-endowed cleavage heaved with her anger.

"I kinda do, since I have no idea what you're talking about. Is it possible you have me confused with someone?" Her voice had taken on an edge. The situation no longer seemed funny to her when venom had dripped from the blonde's voice.

The other woman shook her head, overly-processed hair whipping around. Jamie wondered to herself how the hair hadn't fallen out, having been bleached to within an inch of its life.

"Oh, I know who you are, Jamie Lawler." A nasty smirk marred her face. Her gaze raked up Jamie and back down again. "Although, for the life of me, I can't imagine what someone like Griffin would see in someone like you."

Something snapped inside Jamie. Her entire life, she'd been looked down upon by women like this. She stood taller, straightening her spine.

"What Griff and I are doing, or not doing, is none of your business. Now why don't you take your bleached, plastic surgeon-sculptured self out of my space?"

Jamie turned back to her machine and unpaused it. She thought she heard a gasp as she slid the ear buds back in and turned up the volume. She started off at a brisk walk, mentally congratulating herself. The old Jamie would never had stood up to the other woman like that. And if her heart pounded like that of a terrified animal? She had stood up for herself.

Jamie didn't bother looking over where the woman had stood. She didn't care if she still stood there or had huffed off. After a few minutes, Jamie increased the speed, starting her run. Every week, she managed a higher speed and longer time. While she wouldn't be running a marathon anytime soon, she'd take it. She'd also stopped stepping on the scale. The numbers didn't matter. Her looser clothes and general feeling of wellbeing did.

When the timer showed thirty minutes and the speed dropped to her cool down phase, Jamie took a big gulp of water and wiped her sweaty face with a towel. She grabbed her phone from the holding space on the machine and tapped out a brief message to Griff.

"Met your GF today. She 'warned' me to keep my hands off you. Thought you might want to know."

Not interested in his response, she slid her phone into a pocket in her shorts and went about finishing her work out.

When she got into her car and plugged in her phone, she noticed a reply from him.

"*My girlfriend? Wasn't aware I had one...and when did you have your hands on me? I would have remembered that.*"

Jamie laughed in her car. Griff's sense of humor was one of the things she loved, uh, liked, the most about him.

"*About five three, overly bleached blonde with an attitude, and breasts the size of Kansas. Ring a bell?*"

She started her car and clipped her phone into its holder on her dash. Bubbles flickered as he typed a response. Then they stopped, and her phone rang.

"Well, hello," she laughed, answering.

She heard a sigh first.

"Darla is not my girlfriend, in case you were wondering." He sighed again. "And hello to you, too."

"You're free to date whomever you wish. Although Darla might not care for our upcoming trip to Pennsylvania."

The words were true, but pierced her heart, nonetheless. She held no claims on him. Never would.

There was a prolonged silence from the other end. Jamie's stomach flipped around while she waited for Griff to speak.

"I'm sorry that Darla approached you. She had no right. And as for our trip up north, that's none of her business." Another moment of silence prevailed. "Now you understand why I don't date clients."

And she did. But that didn't ease the ache in her chest.

"Message received. Well, I'm almost home and a mountain of work awaits. See you soon."

Jamie ended the call, the sound of his deep voice too much to bear. She turned off the ringer and headed home.

*****

Griff stared at the phone long after Jamie disconnected.

Then he slammed both hands against the leather steering wheel of his truck. What was he going to do about Darla? The woman was a viper, slinking around in overpriced "workout" clothes that had never seen a drop of sweat. He'd never considered her over the top, desperate bids for attention disguised as flirting a compliment. Instead, her obvious and trite ways turned him off, the exact opposite of their desired effect.

He would have to do something about her. Jack would know what to do, having always been the smoother of the two of them. Jack had become the face of Getting It Done from the day they opened the doors. His best friend had a way of letting people down easily without even realizing that's what he was doing. Griff, on the other hand, preferred the direct approach. Like ripping off a bandage.

He drove the rest of the way home trying hard to not think of Jamie. Or the way her face lit up the room when she smiled. Or the taste of her lips against his. Or how she made him feel, like he wanted to spend time with a woman for the first time in a long while.

He shook his head. *So much for not thinking of Jamie.* In a few short days, he'd be spending more time than he ever had with Jamie. Griff wasn't sure if that was a good thing or not.

Chapter Twenty-Four

"The thing that would most improve my life is 27 hours in a day. I could meet all my deadlines."

-Yoko Ono

Jamie covered a yawn with her hand. And then yawned again. When that didn't work, she cracked a can of Diet Mt. Dew. This might not be much better, but one more cup of coffee and they'd have to scrape her off the ceiling of her office. April fifteenth had finally arrived, as it did every year, bringing sheer exhaustion with it. Just a few more hours before most of the madness ended.

The past week had passed in a blur. But even though it meant less sleep, Jamie made it to the gym. Every. Day. Some days, that meant after eleven in the evening. She loved that Getting It Done remained open twenty-four seven.

Jamie grinned at the thought. She had willingly gone to the gym every day. She who had depended on junk food to get her through this season last year. Not only had she gone, but she enjoyed and looked forward to it. Working out made her feel good about herself. Good about the choices she was making. Might be a new concept for her, but she'd take it.

"I see you went for the hard stuff," Sam joked from Jamie's open doorway. She moved into the room and dropped into the visitor chair. Her shoulders drooped, as did her smile.

Even Sam's natural bubbliness was no match for their marathon hours. Jamie glanced at her friend, seeing the fatigue in the lines of her body.

"Homestretch, Sam. We made it. I could sleep for a week." Jamie resisted laying her head on the desk.

Sam slumped further into her chair.

"And not a moment too soon." She covered a yawn with her hand.

Jamie noticed her friend's usually perfect manicure looked less than perfect. The past few weeks had taken their toll.

Sam had leaned back her head and closed her eyes. Jamie wondered if she'd fallen asleep.

"What exactly are you doing with Griff? I know he refuses to get involved with a client, but I don't see how travelling to Pennsylvania with you isn't 'getting involved'."

If only she had an answer… She had no idea what they were doing. Other than about to spend a few days away together in Pennsylvania, pretending to be something they weren't. Her eyes burned with unshed tears. She'd blame it on being overworked.

"It'll be fine. I'll be fine," Jamie answered with more bravado than she felt.

But she wasn't fooling Sam. The other woman leaned forward across Jamie's desk, concern etched in her face.

"I know you're a grown woman. I know you know your own mind. But do you really think this is the best idea, travelling up there with Griff?"

A laugh burst from Jamie, but it didn't hold any humor.

"Of course, I don't. This is a terrible idea. In the beginning, when he first offered, it seemed great! I mean who wouldn't want to show up with that hunk of a man on their arm?"

"True."

"But now that I've gotten to know him better? And after finding out he has no intention of getting involved with a client, like me for instance? Not so much." She sighed. "But I'm going through with it. I've given him an out. Several in fact. And he hasn't taken them. I'll put on my big girl panties and do this thing." *Even if it kills me.*

Sam's brow furrowed, a sure sign she had some plan cooking. "Maybe spending time with you will make Griff realize he should bend his rule."

"Trust me, he won't. Not after what happened." She told Sam about her 'confrontation' with Darla at the gym.

"Oh no she didn't!" Sam exclaimed.

"Oh yes she did. It was, uh, interesting. And then I told Griff what happened in case she went to him with some sort of story. He didn't sound amused. And it only reinforced his not dating a client rule."

"Still, maybe things will be different when you're away."

"No, I can't allow myself to think that way. He's made his decision. Besides, there's plenty of fish in the sea. Or so they say."

"Trust me, most need to be tossed back in," Sam grumbled.

Jamie sipped her soda. And strengthened her resolve.

"Griff and I are going. We're going to have fun. And I'm going to show my family, and all those doubters I graduated with, that I have a great life. And when we get home, nothing will have changed. Griff and I will be friends and that's all."

And if the words didn't exactly resonate within her soul, there wasn't much she could do about it.

The rest of the days flew, and before Jamie knew it, she found herself staring at an empty suitcase on her bed. She and Griff had seen each other at the gym, almost every day. And once, she'd run into him at Mama's Cucina, when she'd stopped in to pick up takeout. At least, that had been her plan. But once Mama herself realized Jamie's intention, she'd planted both fists on her ample hips and shook her head.

Griff, who'd already been seated at a table just inside the door with Jack, laughed at the confusion written on her face. He'd explained that Mama wasn't going to take no for an answer. Before she could reply, Jack had whipped out his phone and invited Sam to join them. As friends, of course. And while dinner took longer than if she had eaten at home as planned, the two women enjoyed a nice break. Even though the sadness on Sam's face when she thought no one was looking broke Jamie's heart. But that was an issue for another day.

She glanced at her phone. In less than twelve hours, Griff would be picking her up to drive to the airport. She's offered to meet him there, but he said it made more sense instead of taking two cars. Funny how the thought of being in a car with him had sent the butterflies into flight. If that had sent her into a tailspin, what would days together do?

Jamie hadn't told Griff about their arrangements yet. Normally, when she went to visit, she stayed with her parents or her sister. Usually the latter. Even though she and Melissa didn't exactly get along, never had, Jamie adored her nephew and niece. She spent as much time as she could with them when she visited her family. But this trip, she'd opted for staying at a hotel. She'd booked a suite with two bedrooms. Even that seemed a bit close quarters but would have to do. This way, she and Griff could enjoy some down time, both from her family and each other.

Knowing she was wool gathering, and avoiding packing which she loathed, Jamie shook her head and got back to the task at hand. *What to pack?* Most of her clothing fit loosely at best these days. And while that was a fabulous thing, it didn't make packing any easier. The last few weeks hadn't allowed for time to shop.

The ringing of her doorbell dragged Jamie from her musing. She ran down the stairs, sure Sam had arrived to collect Fiona.

"Hey!" She hugged her friend before standing back to let her in. "Thanks again for doing this for me. Fiona is not a fan of boarding."

Sam eyed the cat, who eyed her right back. "Anything for you, as you know. She and I will find a truce."

Jamie laughed at the expression on both her friend and cat. Neither was a fan of the other for sure, which made this favor that much more wonderful.

Jamie picked up Fiona, ignoring the cat's grumbling. "Now, young lady, I expect you to be on your best behavior." She maneuvered the unhappy feline into her carrier. Fiona rewarded her with a prolonged hiss. Fiona hated the carrier, usually only subjected to it for a trip to the vet, which she also hated.

"I'll carry her to your car," Jamie offered. She pointed at a tote bag by the door. "That has her food and everything else you'll need."

Sam hoisted the large bag. "What's in here? This thing weighs a ton."

"Oh, just a few essentials. I wanted Fiona to feel at home while staying with you. Besides, most of the weight is kitty litter."

"Ugh." Sam groaned. "Don't ever doubt my love for you. Cat litter boxes are the worst." She wrinkled her nose as though anticipating that task.

"I know you do. I tried to teach Fiona to use the human toilet. She wasn't buying it."

Jamie opened the back door of Sam's car, placing the carrier on the seat. Fiona continued to protest, alternately spitting and hissing.

"No wonder she's still single," Sam quipped. She enfolded Jamie in a huge hug. "Have a great time. And don't do anything I wouldn't do."

"Doesn't rule out much," Jamie bantered in return. She waved as Sam pulled out of her driveway.

Returning inside, Jamie got serious about packing as she stifled a huge yawn. The last few weeks had taken their toll, as they did every year. She needed to finish packing and get to bed early to be up for their eight am flight. Driving to the airport and getting through security in time for their flight meant getting up at the butt crack of dawn. Or earlier. Oh well, that wouldn't be any different from the last few weeks.

*****

Across town, Griff zipped up his suitcase and carried it down the stairs to his front door. He hadn't been quite sure what to pack and ended up throwing in a bit of everything. He included the one suit he owned. Just in case. Griff had no idea what to expect from Jamie's family. She rarely mentioned them. He also wasn't sure how he felt about staying with them, but then this trip was about Jamie, not him.

Walking into the kitchen, he grabbed a cold beer from the fridge and headed back into the living room. Plopping down onto his leather couch, Griff flipped through channels before settling on a spy thriller. He took a long swallow of his beer. His cell phone buzzed, indicating an incoming text message. He grabbed the phone and smiled when he saw Jamie's name on the screen. He couldn't help it.

"All packed and heading to bed. Thanks again for picking me up."

She included a smiling emoji wearing sunglasses. Griff smiled also before typing out a reply.

"No worries. No point in both of us driving. But you owe me…"

He deliberately left the ending open, wondering what she'd say. He didn't have to wait long. Griff stared at his phone while the little bubbles appeared.

"That'll be one large coffee, black, right? If you hit a drive-through on the way I'm happy to spring for a donut as well. Unless of course you're not the donut type, being healthy and all that."

"I never met a donut I didn't like. All things in moderation."

He added a winking emoji.

"Good to know. And I'm going to apologize for my family in advance."

Griff stared at the phone, wondering what that meant. She hadn't talked about them much but how bad could they be?

"I handle Darla on a regular basis. I can take your family. Sweet dreams."

He waited for a reply. A laughing emoji appeared, followed by one with zzz coming from its mouth. Yep, she laughed. And for some reason, the idea pleased him.

Chapter Twenty-Five

"Into the valley of death rode the 600."
-Lord Albert Tennyson

Griff's soft knock came as Jamie perched on the arm of her sofa, staring at the front door. Even though she expected it, she jumped, her nerves not any better after a night of tossing and turning. She leapt up and ran to the door, unlocking it and throwing it open.

"Good morning," she blared a bit louder than expected, and almost forgot to breathe. He stood there, dressed casually in an old, faded pair of jeans and a light sweater. A white crewneck t-shirt peeked out from the vee of it. The dark green of his sweater made his eyes pop.

Griff grinned at her. Then he glanced at her suitcase sitting next to him. "Didn't you have anything bigger?"

She swung her head from the suitcase in question back to him. And then she noticed the silent laughter shaking his shoulders.

"Very funny. There's a method to my madness," she replied. "Go ahead, pick it up.

He grabbed the handle and lifted, the light case throwing

him off balance. "Didn't expect that," he replied.

"Not much still fits, so that's mostly empty."

He tilted his head. "You're bringing an empty suitcase?"

She nodded. "Well mostly, empty. I have shoes and other essentials in there."

"Okay," he agreed in a tone that stated otherwise. "I won't ask what 'other essentials' might be."

"You know, woman stuff. I thought you had sisters." She glanced at the wall clock. "We have to go. I just need to set the alarm."

Jamie grabbed a small backpack while Griff took her suitcase outside. By the time she set the alarm and locked the door behind her, he was shutting the back door of his truck. She followed him to the passenger side and waited while he opened her door. His hand on the small of her back burned, despite the layers of shirt and light jacket. She tamped down the shiver she felt as he helped her up into his truck.

Jamie used the few seconds he took getting into the driver's side to breathe and fix a smile on her face. She hadn't managed to leave her house without feeling affected by his closeness. How would she survive the next few days? *She was screwed!*

Griff started the truck, glancing at her. "Are you a bad flier?"

"What? No, not at all. Why?"

He shrugged. "You seem nervous."

So much for the smile fooling him. "I need caffeine," she grumbled.

"Okay then. Let's see to that first."

Griff drove down her street and then headed out of her neighborhood. He turned on the satellite radio to the Margaritaville station, his fingers tapping along to

"Cheeseburger in Paradise."

"Are you a parrot head by any chance?" she asked him.

He turned to glance at her quickly. His shades hid his eyes, but he was smiling.

"Would you hold it against me if I said yes?" he asked.

"'One Particular Harbor' is my favorite song," she informed him.

"Really? Mine is 'Changes in Latitude, Changes in Attitude'."

"That suits you."

He stopped at a red light. "How so?" Griff pushed his shades to the top of his head, staring at her as he awaited her answer.

She hoped he hadn't taken it the wrong way.

"You seem very chill, like the kind of person who would like Jimmy Buffett's music." *Stop talking!*

He grinned and nodded, pulling forward as the light changed. "I'll take that as a compliment. Now, what can I get for you?"

She noticed they had already arrived at A Hole in One Donuts. She tried not to drool.

"I, uh, haven't been here since I started at the gym. I have, used to have, a little thing for donuts." *That was putting it lightly.*

"Ah. I, too, have 'a thing' for donuts." He pulled up to the drive-through speaker. "What'll you have?"

She glanced at the menu as if she hadn't ordered here a thousand times. "Black coffee, please."

He raised one eyebrow.

"Okay, maybe a caramel macchiato then. Small, please, and thank you."

"And to eat? Unless you want to grab something at the airport."

"I'm okay for now." Her stomach rumbled, making her a liar.

Griff shook his head, not saying anything. He lowered his window instead.

"Good morning and welcome to A Hole in One Donuts! What may I get for you this lovely day?" came a tinny, disembodied voice.

"Good morning to you, too," he replied. "Can I have one large, black coffee, one small caramel macchiato and two chocolate donuts, please?" He glanced at her as if checking for approval.

Jamie nodded. *Calories on vacation didn't count, right?*

"Does that complete your order?"

"Yes, ma'am," answered Griff.

"Pull around for your total and food."

"The two donuts are for me; in case you were wondering."

"Very funny," Jamie replied before punching him lightly in the shoulder. "But for the record, I'm trying to be good."

"Don't on my account."

Griff pulled around the side of the restaurant, leaving Jamie to wonder at his meaning. They were just friends, right? Was he teasing her? Flirting? Who knew?

"It's not about you," she muttered and then wished she hadn't. "Sorry."

Griff said nothing, instead grabbing their order and handing over some money. She waited until they had their stuff situated and he drove out of the parking lot.

"I am sorry. Not sure what's wrong with me." *Might have something to do with the hot, fake boyfriend sitting next to her.* "That's not true. It's my family," she only partially lied. They always were a source of stress for her.

"I know you said they're different from you. Or maybe

you're different from them. Are you nervous about seeing them? Or is it bringing me that has you in knots?"

Always perceptive, Griff had hit the nail on the head. Her stomach knotted. She thought about her words for a bit before speaking.

"Both. They aren't like me. Or maybe you said it better. I'm not like them is more accurate." She sipped her drink, seeking courage in the carbs. "They're perfect."

"What does that even mean? No one is perfect," Griff answered as he pulled onto the highway.

Jamie turned to study the scenery floating by her. How to explain without making them seem horrible?

"My parents both come from old Philadelphia families. Their respective parents were best friends since infancy and on and on. Their marriage might as well have been arranged. My mother attended Swarthmore College, more interested in an Mrs. degree than a bachelors. My father graduated from the University of Pennsylvania, both undergraduate and law school. They married the month after she graduated. He's a managing partner in a prestigious law firm in the city. My sister, Melissa, is my mother's mini me. They even look similar, tall, blonde, skinny, and stunning. She married well and pushed out the requisite two-point-five perfect kids with her perfect husband, who by the way is about to make partner at my father's firm." She blew out a large breath. "And then there's me."

He glanced at her before returning his eyes to the road. "They sound boring, to be honest. Not at all like you. You're funny. You make me laugh. You're hard working and honest. I haven't even met them, and I'm already glad you're 'different'."

His words sent a warmth spreading throughout her body.

"That may have been the nicest thing anyone has ever said to me," she replied.

"Maybe you've been hanging around the wrong people then."

"Maybe."

Neither spoke again until Griff pulled into economy lot B at the airport. Being this close to the next leg of their trip sent a shiver through her. *What had she been thinking?* Far from the first time she'd asked herself that.

"I'll grab the luggage," Griff said as he got out of his truck.

Jamie nodded before grabbing their breakfast trash. She stepped out of his truck and tossed it in a nearby can. She took a moment, with her back to him, to gather herself. She had started this. She would finish it. Being a Lawler wasn't always the worst thing. She'd had manners and class impressed upon her from infancy. She could do this. Straightening her spine, Jamie turned back to Griff.

"This is your last chance to back out." She grinned at him to soften her words.

He walked toward her until he stood mere inches away. And then he tucked a stray hair behind one ear. "I'm in this till the bitter end." A huge smile bloomed on his face. "Hopefully, it won't actually be bitter."

All the breath she'd held rushed out at his humor. "Thank you. I promise to make this as painless as possible for you."

"I can't imagine anything painful about being with you," he added before turning back to gather their suitcases.

*****

A few hours later, Griff rethought his words to her. Watching Jamie as she napped, head lying on his shoulder, an ache spread through his chest. Her face had lost the tension of the last few weeks, making her look even younger than normal. He glanced out the window at the puffy, white clouds. He'd never been to Pennsylvania and wondered what Jamie's home state would look like. His only image of Philadelphia was from the movies, *Rocky* in particular. The thought of Jamie running up the front steps of the art museum brought a smile to his lips.

He wondered how such a lovely, kind, intelligent woman could come from the family she described. He'd find out soon enough.

The rumbling of landing gear lowering woke her. He watched as she blinked twice then jerked her head off his shoulder. "Sorry, I must have fallen asleep."

I'm not. But he kept that thought to himself. This trip would challenge them already, no use making matters worse.

"You didn't miss much. Only an air marshal wrestling an unruly passenger to the floor," he joked.

"Darn, I always miss the good stuff."

Jamie stretched her arms over her head and twisted this way and that as if to get the kinks out from sleeping slumped over on him. He tried to not stare at the sliver of smooth skin exposed when her shirt raised up. Tried.

She glanced out the window. "Oh look! There's the Delaware River. It won't be long now."

Griff leaned across her, certainly not inhaling the light citrus scent of her hair, to look out the window.

"You seem excited. I thought you were sort of dreading this trip."

She looked at him a few moments before answering. He could almost hear the gears turning in her mind.

"I'm excited to show you where I grew up. As for seeing my family, that's a mixed bag. Of course, I'll be pleased to see them. They're my family." She sighed. "I know I should be happier, but they're not the easiest people in the world."

Without thinking, he covered her hand with his. The gesture was meant to give comfort. There wasn't anything comfortable about the zaps of energy streaking up his arm from where their hands touched. He pulled his hand back and placed it in his lap.

"They don't sound easy from what you've described. But I doubt they're monsters. Tell me the best part about your family."

She turned to face him, a huge grin lighting her face.

"That's easy." She flicked open her phone and scrolled through her pictures. When she turned it toward him, the face of a cute little girl of maybe six took up the screen. "This is Lara, my niece. She's the best thing of us all."

He took the outstretched phone from her hand to take a closer look, careful to not brush her fingers with his. The girl was very pretty, with dirty blonde hair and huge eyes the color of the summer sky. The impishness in them drew his gaze. He handed the phone back to Jamie.

"She looks like she might be a bit of trouble," he joked.

"You'd be right. Lara turns six at the end this summer. She's wickedly excited about starting kindergarten. If I ever have a daughter, I'd want her to be just like Lara."

"Tell me more," he asked.

"My sister, Melissa, and her husband, Derek, have two children. Chase, a near carbon copy of my brother-in-law, is the more serious one of the two. He's eight going on forty and prefers khaki shorts and pressed polo shirts to more casual play clothes. He already takes golf lessons at the club. I love him. He's adorable." She swiped to another picture and tilted the phone toward him again.

"I see what you mean. He looks very mature."

Griff couldn't help but notice the stunning differences between the two children. While they looked similar in bone structure and coloring, that's where the similarities ended. The young boy stared into the camera without even a trace of a smile. His close-cropped blonde hair looked perfect without a bit of it out of place.

She swiped through her pictures again, showing him another of Lara. "Melissa will never get over it, but Lara acts more like me than her." She laughed at her own statement. "You have no idea how much that ticks her off."

"I can imagine, since you're the black sheep," he joked.

"Lara is the light of my life. Despite living in that home, surrounded by expensive art and formal, don't-touch furniture, she's a true tomboy, rebelling at every turn, preferring to make mud pies than host tea parties."

"Do you want to have children, Jamie?" *Where had that question come from?*

Her brown eyes widened at his question. He hoped she didn't feel put on the spot.

"Yes, I do. I've always wanted children." She dipped her head as color splashed her cheeks. "The only thing bad about living so far away is not getting to see my niece and nephew very often."

That statement told him all he needed to know about her relationship with the rest of her family.

"What are they going to think of me?"

"Oh, they won't like you at all. But they'll be very polite. After all, appearances are everything."

He'd had no idea what she'd say, but that wasn't it. Laughter poured out of him.

Her hand flew over her mouth. "You did ask," she

reminded him.

"That I did. And I'm glad you were honest with me. My family is, well, not like yours."

The captain came on to announce their descent into Philadelphia International. They both put things away and stowed their carry-ons back under the seats in front of them.

"Staying with them should be fun."

She shot a look at him, gnawing on her bottom lip. The gesture drove him crazy.

"Did I not mention that? We're staying in a hotel."

Chapter Twenty-Six

"I enjoy seeing new places."
-Kareem Abdul-Jabbar

Jamie turned her head away from Griff, choosing the sparkling Delaware River far below to the look in his widened eyes. She figured she had a few moments before he'd ask for an explanation. Getting her heart rate under control would take way longer.

"Does staying a hotel have to do with your family or wanting me all to yourself?"

The words and his deep, masculine chuckle brought her gaze back to him. Two could play at this game.

She licked her lips. "Would it matter?" she asked him.

His straight, white teeth flashed in his grin. "Not really."

She resisted fanning herself under the heat of his gaze. Barely…

"The plain truth is that my parents' moral code is straight out of the nineteen fifties. We wouldn't even be allowed to stay in rooms on the same floor, let alone in the same room. But I decided to stay in a hotel because believe me, we'll need a break from them."

"I see." His raised eyebrow didn't match his words.

Jamie sighed. She took a moment to check her seatbelt as they started their final descent. Anything to keep her hands busy.

"I'm not sure that you do. My parents are difficult and best in small doses. I know you offered to come with me for the reunion, but frankly having my family think I'm involved with you is sort of icing on the cake."

"Why?"

"Being a spinster isn't my favorite role to play," she quipped.

His laugh came out more of a snort. "Spinster? You're barely in your thirties. And this isn't nineteen forty-seven."

And then it was her turn to snort.

"Why thank you, kind sir," she parried in her best fake Southern accent. "I will be thirty-three this year, and unmarried. Yet another of my unpardonable sins according to my mother."

"Would they have preferred you married earlier but to the wrong person?"

Jamie shrugged. "Who knows? At Melissa's wedding, everyone took great delight in reminding me I was next. But that didn't happen of course. Now, every time I visit, I have to endure the pitying looks and snide comments."

"All I get is the 'why haven't you given me grandkids' spiel from my mom. As if the pack of rug rats my siblings have provided aren't enough."

"Do you not want kids?"

"I do, someday, when the time is right and with the right person."

She wondered who that might be. Surely not a gym client. Surely not her.

Jamie turned to look out the window, trying to not think about the woman Griff would marry and have children with. Way too depressing.

"Everything okay?" he asked as if sensing her change in mood.

"I guess," she replied on a sigh. "Coming here is never easy for me." She'd rather he think she was bothered by visiting her family than him marrying someone else.

"Since we're sharing a hotel room, does that mean we're sharing a bed also?"

*****

Griff bit the inside of his cheek to keep from laughing at the expression on Jamie's face. She would never be a great poker player. He couldn't wait to hear her reply. He shouldn't say things like that, but it was too tempting.

Before she spoke, a pink flush spread from her neck to her hairline.

"I booked a suite with two bedrooms. Your virtue is safe." She stuck her tongue out at him. "Although you will be forced to share a bathroom with me."

Images of Jamie wearing nothing but steam from the shower crowded his brain and sent blood rushing somewhere else. This may have backfired on him.

"I grew up with sisters. I can manage."

The second he saw her face fall Griff knew he'd said the wrong thing. Way wrong. Especially since sisterly was the furthest thing from how he viewed her. And yet this was for the best.

"I'll try to stay out of your way," she replied, the previous joking tone missing from her voice.

Well, heck.

Before Griff could take back the words, or apologize, they touched down and the captain welcomed them to Philadelphia. Jamie became interested in gathering her few belongings. The uncomfortable silence stretched as they taxied to the gate.

They both started to stand at the same time, crashing heads into one another.

"Sorry," Jamie muttered as he said the same.

Griff sat back down in his seat.

"Is your head okay?" he asked her.

She nodded. "Luckily, I have a hard one."

How had they come to this? The stilted conversation bothered him. He and Jamie had always enjoyed an easy-going banter between them. Maybe the closer she got to 'home,' the more tense she felt. He certainly wasn't looking forward to spending time with her family. Nor meeting the almighty Chad.

"What do think Brad will think of the new you? After all, it's been a long time."

"I have no idea what *Chad*, as you know is his name, will say or think. I didn't know back then. I won't know now."

Why do you care? That's what he wanted to ask her. What he really wanted to know. But he didn't ask. Because he might not like the answer.

Griff heard a throat being cleared from behind him. An older gentleman waited behind their row. Griff stood and stepped out into the aisle, gesturing for Jamie to step ahead of him. When she brushed against him on the way out of the row, he caught another whiff of her light citrus scent. Griff inhaled deeply before following her off the plane. He hurried to catch up with her as she stepped off the plane and into the tunnel connecting them to the airport.

She walked quicker here than she did back in South Carolina. Exiting into the terminal, the noise accosted him. And then the speed of things. Everyone seemed to be in a hurry. By the time he stopped his perusal, Jamie was already fifty feet ahead of him, disappearing into a crowd of strangers. He quickened his step to catch her.

Coming up alongside her, Griff placed a hand in the small of her back. "Almost lost you there for a second."

She turned her head toward him. "Not quite what you're used to, huh?"

Griff barked out a laugh. "Not quite," he agreed.

He watched her glance around the crowded terminal, taking it all in, as if trying to see it through his eyes. Then she nodded.

"I know how you feel. The first time I flew back here after living in South Carolina for a while, the noise almost deafened me. Which is funny because I never noticed it before."

Griff glanced again at the milling crowd. Everyone seemed to have a purpose, a goal. Each person walked quickly, mostly with eyes down or staring off into the distance. A few even jogged or ran.

"Why is everyone in such a hurry?" he asked her.

Jamie laughed. "I couldn't tell you. We don't have to hurry, but we should get going. I don't really want the airport to be your first impression of Pennsylvania."

Griff faked a bow. "Lead the way, milady, since you're the native and all."

He noticed she didn't refer to the state as her home. Even though it wasn't anymore, it had been for the better part of her life. *Was that because of her family?* He tucked the question away for another time.

"Are you going to play tour guide with me?" Griff asked,

tongue firmly in cheek. "I have a list of must-see places. Plus, you probably have some of your own to show me."

They had reached the end of the terminal and passed through the security gate. "There's no turning back now," Griff joked, pointing out the warning sign.

He expected her to laugh, but her eyes looked serious.

"I gave you an out, Griff. More than once if memory serves."

What was it about this woman that always made him open mouth, insert foot up to mid-thigh?

"Okay, you don't get my sense of humor, clearly," he muttered.

"Sorry. I shouldn't have said that. You're very gracious to come with me." She increased her pace, spine ramrod straight. He needed to lighten the moment, or this would be a long couple of days.

"Now, about those tourist sights. Want to hear my top ten?"

She headed down a flight of stairs labeled 'baggage claim.' Although he had the height advantage, he hurried to keep up.

"Let me guess," she threw over her shoulder. "There's the Art Museum so you can run up the stairs like Rocky. Then, there's the Liberty Bell and Independence Hall, both obvious choices for first timers. Am I close? Maybe catch a Phillies game since South Carolina lacks an MLB team."

She stopped talking when she reached the luggage carousel.

"Actually, I'd love to see Boathouse Row lit at night."

She turned her head so fast he feared whip lash. "Really? How do you know about that?"

"I have my sources," he replied with a grin.

"What did you do, Google Philadelphia?"

"Uh, no, of course not," he muttered before pretending interest in a sign pronouncing them welcome to the city of brotherly love.

He felt her small hand on his forearm, burning the skin she touched. Griff turned to face her. Merriment danced in her eyes.

"You did! You Googled Philadelphia."

"Okay, maybe I did. Figured I should know something about your hometown."

"Technically, Brynn Mawr is my 'hometown.' It's less than thirty minutes from here. At least at this time of the day. Bryn Mawr is part of the Main Line. Did you find that on Google?"

"No, I did not. What does that even mean?"

A loud buzzing sound announced the arrival of luggage. Griff watched in fascination as Jamie strode right up to the conveyor belt, securing a spot. She might have elbowed a man twice her size out of the way. He followed her path, stopping beside her.

"That was impressive."

Her eyes never left the belt. "What was?"

He glanced over his shoulder at the man, who resembled a professional wrestler.

"You just pushed your way through like you owned the place."

A flush spread across her cheeks. "I tend to slip back into old habits when I'm here," she explained.

Griff wondered how many other 'old habits' might be displayed this week.

"Did your search results include Wawa?"

"Wa what?" Griff asked.

"Wawa is a small town southeast of here, but more importantly, it's a chain of convenience stores and home to the best hot chocolate and coffee ever."

The first of their flight's luggage spilled out onto the conveyor belt, saving him from commenting.

"I've got them," he assured her. "Yours will be the ridiculously large but light one."

Her light laugh filled the air, wrapping him in its warmth. Maybe this week wouldn't be so bad. If he could keep her laughing.

Chapter Twenty-Seven

"When in Rome, live as the Romans do; when elsewhere, live as they do elsewhere."

-Saint Ambrose

A few minutes before noon, Jamie took an exit off the Blue Route and headed toward Bryn Mawr. With each passing mile, her grip on the steering wheel tightened. This happened every time she came to visit. Conversation between them flowed easily on the ride, but she grew quieter as they reached their destination. She wondered if Griff noticed or even cared.

"Are you up for lunch? It's a little early, but then we ate breakfast pretty early. If you're not hungry, that's fine, I can wait. There are some great restaurants in town. Or at least there were last year. I imagine they're still there."

Oh, for the love of all things holy, shut up! This visit made her anxious every year. But somehow having Griff with her made it much worse. She wiped one palm at a time on her capris. Maybe he won't notice. She sneaked a peek at him from the corner of her eye.

"I can always eat," Griff murmured. He reached across the SUV's center console and took one of her hands in his.

"Whatever you want is fine with me. Sustenance might be a good idea before facing the firing squad."

Was holding her hand supposed to calm her? Her racing heart mocked her. Nothing about being this close to Griff calmed her. A short, harsh laugh escaped her.

"That's a great analogy."

"I need details about your family, Jamie, to make this thing work. Tell me about them; the details I would know since we're 'dating'."

"Why don't we do that over lunch? I have a great idea."

Without another word, she drove to a local deli. They went in and ordered lunch. When she told the young man behind the counter it was to go, Griff raised a brow but didn't question her. Back in the car, they chatted about little things while she drove to a nearby park.

Griff glanced at a sign as they entered the park. "Who was Clem Macrone, and why did they name a park after him?"

"*She* was a woman who lived adjacent to the park. History has it that she allowed neighbor kids to access this end of the park through her own back yard. Apparently, she was also known for throwing huge, neighborhood parties. They dedicated the park to her in the early nineties."

Jamie pulled into a parking lot next to picnic tables. Griff grabbed their takeout, and they walked to the nearest table. They ate in silence for a few moments. From the sounds Griff made, he enjoyed his lunch.

"Let me give you the basic rundown of the Lawler clan. My parents are Patricia Andrews Lawler and Stewart Lawler. I told you about them for the most part."

"I know your father is an attorney. What else should I know?"

"That pretty much sums him up. My father is a

workaholic. His career always took precedence over every other aspect of his life. He golfs when he has time. He was a distant figure in my childhood. He left for work before I awoke and returned after I had gone to bed. I don't remember him going to parent teacher-conferences or school events. He'd ask to see my report card, ask me why I got an A- in AP Chemistry, science wasn't my thing, then retreat to his office."

"Sounds, uh, I'm not really sure. Sad, maybe? Lonely?"

She stared at Griff, pondering his words. That had never occurred to her.

"I don't know. He was always driven."

Griff took another bite of his BLT, chewing and swallowing. She most definitely did not focus on his neck muscles. That would be wrong. *Chad.* That's who she should be thinking about. Not a guy who's made it clear they didn't have a future. And even though Chad had married the Barbiesque Mandy Simpkins, grabbing his attention after all these years would be the confidence booster she needed. Combined with her new diet and attitude, Jamie could move on with her life and find someone.

"And Patricia Andrews Lawler? What's she like? Does she go by Patty or Patsy?" he joked.

Jamie snorted, covering her mouth with her hand quickly. But not quite quickly enough. Griff smiled.

"Good lord, no. Patricia is Patricia and nothing else. Which is funny because many of Mother's friends have cutesy nicknames like Bootsy or Muffy."

"Father and Mother, huh? Is that how you refer to them?"

Jamie shrugged. "What else would I call them? Stewart and Patricia?"

She took a bite of her sandwich, groaning at the thick sourdough bread. In her effort to eat healthier, carbs had become the enemy. Lost in her bread ecstasy, it took her a moment to realize Griff had stopped eating. He sat there, sandwich in mid-air, staring at her.

"What?" Jamie put down her turkey sandwich and grabbed a paper napkin. "Do I have mustard on my face?" She wiped her mouth just in case.

Griff shook his head. "Sorry. I was just enjoying that noise you made."

"Noise? What noise?" Had she chewed with her mouth open? Jamie hated that in others. "Oh, do you suffer from misophonia, too? Sam and I bonded over that our first day at S&S."

"Misowhat? Since I have no idea what you're talking about, I probably don't have it."

More confused than ever, Jamie grimaced. "Misophonia is the hatred of sounds, often those associated with chewing," she explained.

"Oh, you mean like when people chew like cows."

"Yes, that. Sam and I were the only interns at S&S that summer. We grabbed lunch the first day in the office kitchen, and this man at the next table had no idea how to chew with his mouth closed."

"Scoundrel!" Griff joked.

"Hey, we were young and in a new place. But if that's not it, then why were you staring at me?"

"That noise you made while you were eating. Quite entertaining."

She stared at him for a long moment. And then his meaning dawned on her. She'd sounded like she... OMG! Jamie ducked her face, feeling the tide of red sweep across it. She busied herself with eating her lunch. Without any soundtrack.

Griff reached across the table to touch her hand. "I'm

sorry. I didn't mean to embarrass you."

"You didn't," she protested, despite the heat she felt in her face.

"Really? You're probably one of those people who denies you were sleeping when someone calls and wakes them up."

He took another sip from his water bottle, peering at her over it.

"I don't. Oh, well actually I have. But I didn't want the person to feel badly," she protested. "This conversation is ridiculous." She focused on finishing her lunch.

"I'm sorry."

The timbre of his voice, more than the actual words, caught her attention.

"Never mind, Griff. It was a stupid thing to get upset over. Now, what were you asking me about my parents? What I call them?"

"Oh, right. You always refer to them as 'Father' and 'Mother', which is fine of course but kind of formal."

"Huh. I never thought about it. What do you call yours? Jim and Nancy?"

"Well, no, as their names are Tim and Cheryl, but I call them Dad and Mom."

"That makes sense. Tell me about Tim and Cheryl. What do they do? What are they like? Oh and siblings. I remember you've mentioned a pack of nieces and nephews."

"I have two brothers and two sisters. I fall exactly in the middle. Three of my four siblings are married with kids. Riley Jane, the baby of the family, and I are the only hold outs. She's finishing her residency, which gives her an excuse. For now, at least according to Mom."

"I would think years in the military and now starting your own business would have bought you some time."

"You'd think, right? Not to mention having seven grandchildren already. But no. Although she did cut me some slack when Jack and I opened the gym. Now that it's been over a year..."

"Mine has given up on me, as I told you." She sighed before gathering her trash and getting up to toss it. "You're lucky. Maybe if I had more than one sibling, I would have had a chance. Are you guys close?"

"We sure are. Sometimes maybe a bit too close. Sarah is the only one who doesn't live in Palm Harbor. But despite all living in the same town, you'd be amazed how little we see of each other. Everyone is busy, especially with the kids. Mom insists on a family dinner on the last Sunday of the month. Only serious illness or overseas duty gets you a pass. And by illness, I mean you'd better be hospitalized."

"Sounds amazing," she murmured. "I'd love that."

"Yeah, you're right. It is. I may grumble about them being in my business too much, but I wouldn't trade them."

"Someday," Jamie whispered to herself.

Chapter Twenty-Eight

"It seems to me we can never give up longing and wishing while we are thoroughly alive."

-George Eliot

If Griff hadn't been sitting right across from Jamie, he wouldn't have heard her comment. The word, barely audible, came off her lips on a sigh, a caress. One word, two syllables, but a world of longing. He wondered if she even knew she spoke aloud. *Someday, she would meet that perfect man.* And she would have her family; a warm one that laughed together. And a funny, little pain stabbed his heart.

"Where to next?" he asked, injecting a light tone into his voice.

Jamie stood and gathered their trash. She walked it to a garbage can before answering.

"We're expected for dinner at six, so I thought we could check into the hotel and then take it from there."

"Sounds good," he agreed and got into the rental.

After driving for a few minutes, Griff felt her eyes upon him.

"Uh, I have to do some shopping since, well, you know.

Feel free to stay back, maybe take a nap or hit the hotel gym."

"You don't want my expert opinion? Or to recreate that scene from Pretty Woman?"

"How do you know about Pretty Woman?"

"Sisters, remember?" he joked.

"Does that make me the prostitute in this scenario?" Jamie asked.

Griff laughed, glad that he had taken her mind off things. "No more than I'm the millionaire business tycoon. Can you imagine me in a suit and behind a desk all day?"

"I really can't. But who knows? Maybe Getting It Done will become a national franchise. You can fly around on your private jet, visiting your thousands of locations and counting your stacks of money."

"You forgot about my fabulous vacation homes around the globe. A private jet would come in handy for that."

"True! How could I forget about those? And then there's the trophy wife and string of inappropriately young girlfriends."

Jamie turned down the drive of a several story building. Griff didn't spot the sign for any hotel brand he'd ever heard of and figured it must be a local one. They hadn't discussed paying for this trip, but he wasn't going to let her heft the bill.

Jamie pulled under the covered driveway, parking the vehicle just beyond the front door.

"Ready?" she asked.

"We have to talk about paying for this, Jamie," he answered.

"Nonsense, I invited you. And you're doing me a huge favor by coming."

"And yet, I will still be paying for half, at the very least."

A bell hop appeared at the driver door, preventing any

further discussion. Jamie slid out of the SUV, murmuring a few words to the older gentleman. Griff got out and met her at the trunk.

"This conversation isn't over yet," he reminded her.

"Whatever you say." She smiled at him and breezed in through the automatic doors.

Griff had the feeling he may have just been played.

*****

Jamie smiled at the young woman who greeted her at the reservation desk. While the other woman looked up their reservation, Jamie thought about the brief conversation. The last few weeks had been such a whirlwind at work, she and Griff hadn't had a real chance to discuss the logistics of the trip. Like who's paying for what. She should have known Griff wouldn't be comfortable with her paying for everything. But then again, he hadn't known about staying in a hotel. She didn't know his financial situation, but as she was finding out, starting your own business cost. They'd have to figure it out, maybe split the costs down the middle.

She felt rather than heard him join her at the desk. The air changed when he stood near her. It was the oddest thing. There was a heaviness, a texture to it that had been lacking a moment before.

"Okay, Ms. Lawler, I just need to see the credit card you used to reserve the suite, please," stated the employee, whose name tag read Jill.

She felt Griff stiffen next to her as she handed over her AmEx. Yep, the conversation had been tabled, not finished.

Jill swiped her card before handing it back. "Have you stayed with us before, Ms. Lawler?"

Jamie shook her head. "I'm actually from here. But the hotel looked gorgeous online." She glanced around the spacious, tastefully decorated lobby. "The pictures really didn't do it justice."

"Thank you. The Hotel Bryn Mawr underwent an extensive renovation last fall. We're pleased with the outcome. Now here are your keys. Your suite is on the top floor. Elevators are down to the right. Gerald will bring your bags. Please let me know if you need anything else."

"We will, thanks."

Jamie led the way to the elevator, thanking her lucky stars Gerald accompanied them. The man chatted with Griff, delighted to discover he was a first timer to the area. By the time they reached the top floor, the two men had swapped service stories.

And then, before she felt ready, Griff tipped the bell hop, the door closed behind him, and they were alone in a hotel suite. She wiped her suddenly damp palms on her capris. Walking to the floor-to-ceiling windows in the living area, Jamie opened the curtains.

"This isn't at all what I expected," drawled Griff from way too close.

She turned her head, stealing a glance at him right behind her shoulder. Luckily, the scene below captured his attention.

"What were you expecting then?"

He shrugged his shoulders. "A big city, I guess."

"Well, Philadelphia isn't big by most people's standards. And Bryn Mawr is tiny. But I loved growing up here. There's so many things to do plus plenty of open space."

"Do you miss it?"

"Not until I'm here."

One of his brows raised.

"I really did love growing up here. But the longer I've lived in South Carolina, the more it's home for me. Snow is fun when you're a child, days off from school and all that." She wrinkled her nose. "But as an adult, not so much."

"Sam said that you have travelled quite a bit. Never found another place to call home?"

"You're having conversations with Sam?"

Griff laughed. "Well, it's more like Jack said that Sam said you've travelled quite a bit." He shook his head. "What's with those two?"

"Not my business to discuss." She grinned to soften her words. "I do love to travel, though. Every year since I've been with S&S, I've taken a few weeks off to travel after the crush of tax season. But as much as I love to visit, I love coming home more. There's a lot to be said for having your own safe space in the world."

Jamie gestured to his suitcase. "Why don't you unpack? I'll do the same then run out to buy some clothing." She glanced down at her colorful capris and T-shirt. "Goodness knows Mother would have a heart attack if I showed up for dinner dressed like this."

"What's wrong with how you look?" Griff asked.

She felt the weight of his gaze as it travelled up and down the length of her. Jamie stood her ground, willing herself to not blush.

"I don't have a problem with how I'm dressed. But Mother would. I've learned to compromise to keep the peace. I'll buy some new work clothes. That should keep me from being kicked out."

Griff glanced down at himself.

"I'm guessing this won't fly, then."

Jamie returned his gesture, taking in his jeans and short

sleeved T. She most definitely did not notice the way said jeans outlined his tight butt. She bit her lower lip. The last thing she imagined he would want to do is go shopping.

"I'm sorry, I should have said something earlier. Maybe a pair of khakis and a collared shirt?"

"I'm in luck then. After hearing about your family a few weeks ago, I packed some less casual clothing. Plus, with the reunion, I figured I might need something other than shorts or track pants."

"Oh, good. I'm going to head out." She pulled her phone from her back pocket to glance at the time. "I'll probably only be two hours. Do you need anything?"

"No, I'm fine. I'll take your advice and unpack. And maybe I'll hit the gym."

Jamie picked up her keys from the table. "See you in a bit."

*****

The hotel room door closed with a soft snick. Griff finally turned away. Jamie had all but run from the room. *Suite*, he corrected himself, glancing around. Beyond the living area sat a small kitchen complete with refrigerator and microwave. A coffee maker sat on the counter. Partially opened bedroom doors lay on either side of the living area. He had no idea which was meant for him and chose the closer of the two, bringing his suitcase in with him.

Ten minutes later, everything put away, he changed into workout clothes and sat on the couch to lace his sneakers. Jamie was right. Hitting the gym would do him good. The thought of staying here, with Jamie, made him as tense as she had looked on the way up in the elevator. Thankfully, the bell hop had filled any awkward silence with his questions and chatter.

Griff made his way down to the lowest level and entered the gym. He glanced around, pleased that it contained more than the normal hotel workout room. After stretching for a few moments, Griff started his workout with a run. Maybe the endless pounding of his sneakered feet would take his mind off sharing a hotel suite with Jamie. *Doubtful.*

Even though the room was really a suite, complete with separate bedrooms, Griff had been very aware of her in the space. Not noticing someone you shouldn't be noticing wasn't the easiest thing to pull off.

To not pursue that line of thinking further, Griff went over everything Jamie had told him about her family. It wasn't much, but it explained why she only came to visit once a year. The thought of meeting them didn't faze him. Griff had never much cared for others' opinions. But unease gathered in the pit of his stomach when he wondered how they would treat Jamie.

In the short time they'd known each other, she'd impressed him. Jamie was bright and funny. And way sexier than she gave herself credit for being. Not that he noticed. She was fiercely loyal to her friends, Sam in particular. Her smile could light a room. His fists clenched as he ran. No one better try to snuff that out.

*****

Jamie switched some shopping bags from one hand to the other in order to press the elevator button. She sank against the back wall while it lumbered up to the top floor. She hadn't meant to buy quite so much, especially when she still had weight to lose, but they *would* be here for a few days. And she had planned several different events. As the floors ticked by, the butterflies came out to dance in her belly. Ridiculous, really.

It's not like she didn't know she'd be sharing a room with him. Well, a suite. She wondered what he wore to bed then shook her head to dispel that image.

Leaving the safety of the elevator, Jamie crossed to her, their, door. Her heart pounded. She started to put everything down and leaned one hip into the door as she searched for the key in her purse when the door swung open.

"Hey," Griff greeted her.

"Oh," Jamie yelped. Strong hands caught her when she would have fallen through the open doorway. "I wasn't expecting you."

"But this is where you left me," Griff joked.

She straightened up and away from him, trying to not inhale his scent. He'd showered recently, skin smelling like clean male and hair still damp. Best to keep some distance between them.

"Right! I meant I didn't expect you to open the door just then. Sorry."

They both leaned down at the same time to grab shopping bags. Their heads bumped with an audible thump.

"Oh, sorry again," Jamie muttered. She stepped back and rubbed the side of her head.

Griff's shoulders shook but he remained quiet. Then he grabbed all of the bags in both hands.

"No worries. Let me put these in your room before one of us ends up with a concussion."

She followed behind as he strode to one of the two bedrooms. He must have already claimed the other one.

"I hope you don't mind me already taking the other room. I needed to put my things away." He turned and smiled at her, dimples flashing. "In my defense, I did give you the one closer to the bathroom."

"That's fine."

Griff hip-checked the door open and strode in the bedroom. He placed the bags on the king-sized bed.

"Did you leave anything behind?" he asked.

"What?" Thinking around him, especially when he smelled delicious, became difficult. She ignored the bed.

He tilted his head before pointing to the small mountain of bags. "I asked if you left anything in the stores."

"Oh!" She glanced at the bags, cringing at what he must be thinking of her shopping spree. "I need everything I bought."

Griff held up both hands in the air. "Hey, I'm just joking."

"I actually hate shopping. I do, however, love summer clothing; all the bright colors."

Griff backed toward the open bedroom door.

"I'll give you a chance to get ready for tonight. If you need me, I'll be watching TV."

"Okay, thanks," she called to his retreating back.

Glancing at the time, Jamie realized she'd been gone a lot longer than she had originally planned. But since she really did hate shopping, she had chosen the nearby King of Prussia Mall. The mammoth shopping center held over four hundred stores, offering everything from sporting goods to the high-end boutique shops her mother and sister preferred. One-stop-shopping, so to speak. One good thing had come from her shopping spree. Everything she bought was in a smaller size than she'd worn before starting at the gym. Small step but she'd take it.

She rushed around the room, ripping off tags and putting away her new clothing. If she hurried, she would have just enough time to grab a shower before heading to her parents' home for dinner. The thought of subjecting Griff to that chipped away at her good mood. She brushed aside the thought and stripped out of her clothes.

Then she remembered the bathroom was outside her door. As in where Griff sat watching TV. Hmmm… Jamie grabbed an old shirt, left over from a former boyfriend, she slept in some nights and slipped it over her head. The hem caught her mid-thigh and would have to do.

Holding her shampoo and body wash to her chest like a shield, she cracked her bedroom door, glancing toward the sound of the TV. Griff sat on the loveseat, his profile facing her. Before she lost her nerve, she dashed into the bathroom, locking the door behind her.

*****

Griff caught a flash of something red and a length of lightly tanned leg before Jamie disappeared into the bathroom. He turned back to watch the recap from last night's MLB games. But the broadcaster may as well have been speaking in a Russian for all the attention he paid. It's not like he hadn't seen her legs before. With the warmer weather at home, Jamie had started wearing shorts to the gym, much to his enjoyment. And consternation. Like he really needed another reason to stare at her.

Remember what's his name. That's why he was here in Pennsylvania anyway. His role was to make sure Jamie had moral support at her reunion. Yes, remember that. Focus on showing her off to her old classmates. Not on how much he was falling for her.

Chapter Twenty-Nine

"There is no such thing as getting rid of nervousness."
-Itzhak Perlman

Jamie tapped her fingers on the steering wheel. They had arrived at her parents' home a few minutes ago, but she made no move to leave the shelter of the rental. Of course she would go in. Once the wave of nausea ended. She watched Griff crane his neck to get a better view of the imposing façade.

"I wonder what's on the menu for dinner," Griff joked.

She flashed him a wobbly smile, grateful for his presence.

"Knowing Mother, she'll have had her latest personal chef whip up something meant to impress."

"Latest?" he asked.

"My mother is not exactly employer of the year. When I lived here, I didn't bother learning their names unless they made it more than a few months."

"I have nothing."

She turned in her seat to face him. "We don't have to do this. We can leave. We can go to a diner."

Griff covered one of her hands with his. "We've got this. How bad can it be?"

Jamie rolled her eyes. *How to answer that one?* She took a deep breath, letting it out slowly. "Fine. But don't say I didn't warn you."

They both stepped out of the car. Jamie clutched at her purse strap, desperate to keep her hands occupied.

"Auntie Jamie!"

Her head swung up, and she smiled at her niece's enthusiastic greeting.

Lara ran down the front steps and across the driveway, flinging herself into Jamie's arms. Jamie scooped her up in a hug.

"I missed you so much, Auntie Jamie. Do you like my dress? Mother made me wear it." She pulled at the stiff looking collar. Jamie had also hated being forced to wear such clothing as a small child. "I'm glad you came to visit." She turned her head as if just now spying Griff standing next to her. Her small blue eyes widened. "Is he your boyfriend?" she asked in a stage whisper.

Before Jamie could answer, Griff stepped up and shook Lara's hand.

"Well, hello there. You must be Jamie's sister, Melissa. Nice to meet you."

The little girl giggled. "No, I'm not," she answered.

Griff made a show of scratching his head. "Oh, my mistake. Are you Jamie's mother then?"

This time the little girl doubled over laughing. She shook her head.

Jamie watched the two, a warmth overtaking her heart. He should have children of his own.

"Well I give up. Are you a princess?"

"I'm Lara!" she yelled loud enough to announce it to all of Bryn Mawr.

"Lara, whatever is all that racquet?"

Both adults turned toward the front of the house.

"Grandmother Patricia, look who came." Lara pulled Jamie by the hand. "And she bringed her boyfriend. too."

Jamie was now close enough to see one perfectly-shaped, blonde brow raise. The same look that she'd seen thousands of time as a child.

"She brought her boyfriend, Lara, not bringed."

Jamie watched her niece's mouth droop at the corners, and she wrapped an arm around her. Then she stiffened her spine.

"Mother, I'd like you to meet Griff Layne, my boyfriend." She turned to Griff. "Honey, this is my mother, Patricia Andrews Lawler."

"Mrs. Lawler, I am pleased to meet you. Jamie has told me so much about you."

Her mother looked at him and then Jamie before speaking.

"How very interesting considering this is the first I am hearing of you." She turned to her daughter. "Jamie, were you planning on bringing your guest into the house or maybe eating dinner here in the driveway?" Then Mrs. Lawler looked Jamie up and down. Her expression said she found something lacking. "Do you really think that's your color?"

With that, her mother turned on her heel and walked back inside.

Lara grabbed one of her hands and one of Griff's. "Come on, guys. You don't want Grandmother Patricia to start without us. She might not let us have dessert then."

Jamie laughed. "We certainly don't want that. Let's go."

She mouthed 'sorry' over Lara's head to Griff. He grinned and shrugged.

Jamie wished she could shrug it off so easily. But the worst, she knew, was yet to come.

*****

While waiting for a uniformed servant to bring out dessert, he could only imagine what it might be after the fancy food they'd eaten, Griff decided Lara was the only other of Jamie's family he liked. Even her nephew, Chase, had already developed the stiff upper lip of his parents and grandparents. He tried to remember what he'd been like at the boy's age. Different for sure.

He glanced at Jamie. She smiled at something Melissa said, but he was close enough, and knew her well enough, to notice it didn't reach her eyes. Griff squeezed her hand under the table and tried to not count the remaining time in his head.

"Tell me, Jamie, have you given any more thought to giving up this ridiculous rebellion of yours and moving home?" Mr. Lawler queried from the head of the table.

Griff stared at her father. *Was he serious? Did it not matter that he, her boyfriend, sat right here?* Okay, he was a fake boyfriend. But her father didn't know that.

Jamie squeezed his hand, hard, under the table.

"Father, my home, as you put it, is in South Carolina. I'd have thought you realized that after a decade of my living there."

Griff bounced his gaze back and forth between the two. Her father's face looked as though it was carved of granite. He had yet to see the man smile at anything, even when Lara had told him a series of silly jokes. Jamie had laughed enough for both.

And Jamie. She still looked like the woman he knew, but her voice was different here. Cooler. Losing the soft southern accent she had when she said certain words.

"Why you'd ever choose a place like Palm Harbor when

you grew up here is beyond me," added Jamie's mother.

"I can't imagine how you feel comfortable judging where I live when you've never visited, Mother."

Patricia's steely blue eyes grew even colder if possible.

"If this is how you speak to your mother, then I don't need to visit." She pushed her chair back and stood. "I can't imagine where dessert is. Surely, it doesn't take this long to whip up a Crème Brûlé."

She swept out of the room.

"Nice going," sniped Melissa from across the table.

Mr. Lawler and Derek, Melissa's husband, seemed embroiled in some debate about work, which was the only thing the two had talked about the whole evening. Neither had bothered to speak to him, other than to say hello. Only Lara, seated to Jamie's left, seemed happy, a bright smile on her cute face.

He felt the tension coming off Jamie in waves. The normally free-spirited, outgoing woman had disappeared the moment she pulled into the driveway earlier. In her place sat a pale, subdued version. Her love of reading as a child made sense now. It had been her escape.

"Mr. Lawler, you must be proud of Jamie's plans to open her own accounting firm with Sam this year," he offered by way of starting a conversation with the otherwise silent room.

Jamie dropped his hand under the table and sat up straighter. He feared her spine might snap.

"Must I? Maybe, if I had any idea what you're talking about."

Next to him, Jamie turned to stone before his eyes. *What had he done?*

Patricia breezed back into the formal dining room. Glancing at the shocked, still faces, she paused before her chair.

"What did I miss?"

"Apparently your daughter has gotten it into her head to open her own business," muttered Stewart.

Griff glanced at Jamie, trying to convey an apology in a glance. He wished he could take back the words.

"Jamie is this true?" asked Patricia, her voice devoid of any emotion.

"Sam and I are opening our own accounting firm, hopefully this summer."

The fact that she spoke without making eye contact was not lost on Griff.

"Hopefully? What does that mean?" asked her father. "Do you even have a business plan?"

Griff watched the older man shake his head and he clenched his hands into fists under the table. When Jamie had described her family to him, he'd really thought she might be exaggerating a bit. But, no, she had not. If anything, she'd been conservative. How could they talk to her as if she had a brain injury?

"Of course we have a business plan, Father. 'Fail to plan, plan to fail.' Isn't that what you always say?" she countered.

By the tightness of his mouth, Griff made a wild guess that he wasn't used to having someone, especially his daughter, challenge him. Griff wanted to jump in. Say something. Anything. But he already caused enough damage by starting this conversation. He placed one hand on her knee and waited for the rest to unfold.

"We will finish this discussion another time." He shifted his gaze to Griff. "When it's more appropriate."

The muscles beneath Griff's hand tightened further, although he didn't know how that was possible. And then she stood.

"No, Father, we won't. I didn't come here seeking approval nor support. Obviously, that would have amounted to a fool's errand." She glanced around the table, her brown eyes shining with rage. "And as for the rest of you, could you been any less gracious or welcoming to Griff? Don't get up. We can see ourselves out."

Jamie bent down, whispering something in Lara's ear that made the little girl giggle. Then she turned to Griff.

"Shall we?"

He stood next to her, taking her hand in his. And then he turned to her mother.

"Thank you, Mrs. Lawler, for dinner."

He had been raised right, after all.

*****

Jamie slammed the rental car door much harder than intended. Then banged her fists against the steering wheel for good measure. She glanced at Griff, silent in the passenger seat. He must be sorry he came now.

She drove away from her parents' home without saying a word. The night had ended so badly, even she couldn't believe it. And she was used to her family. Her father's complete lack of faith in her didn't come as a shock. Sadly, his approval would have. But the way they had all but dismissed him was unacceptable. She drove along in silence until pulling into a parking space at the hotel. Then she turned to him in the darkened interior. But before she could say anything, he held up one hand.

"I'm very sorry, Jamie."

She shook her head, not believing what she had just heard.

"What?"

He reached over and tucked a stray hair behind her ear. She shivered at his touch.

"I never meant to start that back there. That debacle. I had no idea they didn't know. Honestly."

"Are you kidding right now? My goodness, Griff, *you* didn't do anything wrong."

He took both of her hands in his, rubbing one thumb across her bounding pulse.

"I couldn't sit there any longer without saying something, Jamie. My God, what's wrong with your family?"

A short laugh, bitter and lacking humor, erupted from her.

"It took me years to ask that question, and you did in one night."

He tilted his head, peering into her eyes.

"What do you mean by that?" he asked in a soft voice that did something to her insides.

Jamie sighed. "Can we talk inside? I'm exhausted."

"Sure," he agreed.

They left the car and walked, side by side, into the hotel. She didn't say a word until they were inside the suite. Jamie walked to the balcony, opening the curtains to see the lights of Philadelphia glowing in the distance. She felt him come to a halt next to and slightly behind her. The warmth of his body offered comfort.

"It's funny being back here. I loved Philadelphia growing up. My grandmother took me to the art museum on the first Saturday of every month for years. We would have lunch in the city first and then wander the halls of the museum for hours." She turned and smiled at him. "You would have loved her. She was the only person in this whole family who ever understood me. I miss her every day."

"I only have one grandmother left, my mom's mother." A

chuckle escaped him. "You're going to love her. She's quite the character."

The thought of meeting his family warmed her heart. More than it should. But she didn't see it happening.

He cleared his throat, dragging her thoughts back to him.

"What did you mean earlier, in the car, about my knowing to ask that question?"

She stood, staring into the darkness, unsure how to answer him without sounding pathetic. In the end, she decided to just tell him the truth.

"It took until I was well into my twenties, and living hundreds of miles from my family, to understand one fundamental truth. It took you one night. What's wrong with them?" She let out a shaky breath and continued in a subdued voice. "Because all that time, I thought I was the problem."

Chapter Thirty

"When angry, count to four; when very angry, swear."
- Mark Twain

"Why on earth would you have ever thought that?" Griff asked her.

He clenched and unclenched his hands, trying to gain control over his anger. Despite trying, she hadn't been able to prepare him for them. No one could have. He laid one hand on her shoulder, but she stayed as she was, staring out into the night sky.

"Who knows? Maybe because that was all I knew growing up."

She stopped talking, took a breath, and then laughed. Long and hard. Until tears ran down her face and she gulped in air. Her whole body shook with the effort until Griff wasn't sure if she laughed or cried. Just when he was about to intervene, she stopped and turned to him.

"Can you believe my mother? She actually believes I'm coming back here someday."

He watched, mouth agape, as laughter shook her body all over again. Having sisters, he wasn't all that concerned, merely waited out the storm.

"I'm s-s-sorry. I can't seem to get control of myself. But honestly, like I'd ever come back. You'd think the fact that I only visit once a year would clue her in."

Jamie kicked off her shoes and walked over to the sofa, curling into one corner of it. He followed suit, taking the other end.

"So that would be a no, then. You're not planning on moving back here?"

For some reason, Griff held his breath as he waited for her answer.

"Ah, that would be a hell to the no. Moving to South Carolina, although anywhere would have worked, saved me. Freed me. I didn't have to apologize for being me anymore."

Jamie uncurled from the couch and disappeared into the small kitchenette before returning with two bottles of cold water. She passed one to Griff before drinking half of hers in a gulp.

"I worry for Lara. She's too much like me, poor girl, always trying to break the mold her parents try to force her into." She took another sip. "Actually, Lara is braver than I ever was. I tried for so many years to be what they wanted. But somehow, I always came up short. She doesn't let them change her like I did."

"Maybe that's because you didn't need to be anything but yourself," Griff suggested.

He took a long drink from his water bottle. Jamie didn't even bother to pretend she didn't watch the muscles of his neck working.

"Thank goodness for books and school. I disappeared into both." She wrinkled her nose. "Well, more books than school. I never fit in there either."

"Let me guess, private school filled with clones of your parents and sister," commented Griff.

"Winner, winner, chicken dinner," Jamie said by way of an answer.

"And that brings us to Chuck."

Jamie grinned at him over her water bottle.

"*Chad* was everything I wasn't, athletic, popular, outgoing. And I worshipped him. From afar, of course."

"He was another thing you aren't. Stupid. Otherwise he wouldn't have needed a tutor and would have certainly noticed you."

"Ah, you're too sweet. Let's just say that he wasn't the sharpest tool in the shed. And I wasn't even a blip on his radar screen."

"Sounds like a tool all right," Griff joked.

"In his defense, I was painfully shy and had braces through most of high school. I never wore any makeup nor dressed the way the other girls did. I also wasn't a cheerleader."

Griff shook his head.

"What?" she asked him.

"I guess I can't understand your need to defend him, even after all these years."

"Chad was my first real crush. He was that golden boy that everyone loved. Guys wanted to be him. Girls wanted to be with him. Even teachers loved him, despite always being in danger of failing. He could charm the birds from the trees. And when he smiled at you, well, you felt like you were the only person in the world."

That last bit sounded familiar. He kept that thought to himself.

"Sounds a bit like Superman," he stated instead.

"Ha ha. Mock me if you must. But he set my teenage heart

on fire."

"And your adult heart?" Griff asked, not sure that he wanted to hear her answer.

"I have no idea. I haven't seen him since graduation."

"All those years have passed without seeing him? Talking to him?"

"Yes."

"Then what's the point to this? What are you hoping to gain?"

"Not sure," she replied, but her eyes didn't meet his.

Griff leaned forward a bit on the couch.

"Is he the one that got away, Jamie?"

She looked at him this time, gazed into his eyes. His heart did a strange little flutter. Stupid heart.

"What if he is?" she replied.

"What if he isn't?" he countered.

She looked away, leaping off the couch and pacing the room. Griff watched her agitated movements. She dragged a hand through her hair. Then she stopped and turned to face him, the back of the couch separating them.

"Why do you care?"

Good question. And the flutter became an ache. He didn't have an answer. At least not one he could tell her. He shrugged instead.

"It's been a long and, uh, complicated day." She rubbed absently at her temples as though she might have a headache. "I'm going to bed."

She turned on her heel and disappeared down the hall.

"Good night," Griff whispered to the now empty room. He stalked into his own room, grabbed something from his suitcase and went into their shared bathroom. He placed the bottle on the sink. Returning to the living area, Griff knew he was too restless to go to bed. Maybe a drink would help. He left the suite and headed down to the hotel lounge.

*****

Jamie paced in her room, way too restless to sleep. She tried to put her finger on what bothered her. It wasn't her family or even the scene with them tonight. Par for the course in her visits north. She didn't live hundreds of miles away by accident.

She padded to the window, pulling back the curtain. The distant lights of the city caught her eye again. And as much as she loved Philadelphia, she longed to hear the gentle lapping of the waves on the beach at home.

Home. Funny how such a small word held so much meaning. Nowhere had ever felt like home until she moved south. Palm Harbor, with its interesting assortment of characters and beautiful beaches, had called to her from the moment she set foot there for her internship. Meeting Sam and gaining the sister she'd always longed for but never had in her own flesh and blood one changed her life.

She had returned to Philadelphia and her senior year of college knowing where her future lay. And it wasn't here. Then what was she doing here? Chasing the dream of 'the one that got away' as Griff put it?

Jamie flopped back on her bed, staring at the ceiling. She had avoided reunions for fifteen years. Why start now? Sure, Chad had starred in all her teenage dreams, fantasies really. Night after night she lay in her bed, dreaming about him. About going to prom with him. About marrying him and having his children. About Chad looking at her like he looked at Mandy Simpkins. But outside the confines of their high school library,

Jamie Lawler didn't exist in Chad Davis's world.

She got up again, resuming her pacing. *So why was she determined to show Chad what she'd become? Why now?* Did she really care about what Chad, and others who hadn't shown her an ounce of attention all those years ago, thought about her now? The question had rolled around her head for the past few weeks. Jamie had taken steps to improve herself, eating better and working out, based on the idea of seeing Chad again. And now that the event loomed less than two days away, she began to doubt the reasoning behind attending. She had nothing to prove to those people, just as she had nothing to prove to her family.

A peace she hadn't felt since stepping off the plane this morning came over her. And she knew Griff played a big part in it. She had worried about bringing him. Worried about spending so much time with him. Worried about how her family would treat him. And she had been right about that. They had pretty much dismissed him the moment she introduced him. And Griff had let it roll right off his back, as he seemingly did everything. Jamie could learn a thing or two from him.

She changed into the new pajamas she bought earlier and headed for the bathroom to get her nightly routine done. A good night's sleep would be nice. She hadn't had that in quite a few weeks. Gathering her stuff, Jamie crossed to the door. She opened it and stuck her head out. No sign of Griff. Maybe he'd turned in already. She headed into the bathroom, shutting and locking the door behind her. Just in case.

An ibuprofen bottle sitting on the sink stopped her in her tracks. She hadn't mentioned a headache to him earlier. But she had rubbed her temples. His thoughtfulness warmed her heart. She brushed her teeth and removed her makeup. Then she did something she usually avoided. She stood there, looking at her reflection in the mirror. Without makeup. And was pleased with what she saw.

Despite the bags that remained under her eyes from weeks of too much work and too little sleep, she smiled at her reflection. Turning this way and that, she admired the new definition her cheeks had taken on. They weren't rounded anymore, resembling a chipmunk storing for the winter.

Her head still ached somewhat, so she popped two of the tablets and finished getting ready for bed. Back in her room, Jamie closed the curtains in order to block out the light. She pulled back the comforter when she remembered she had meant to grab a bottle of water from the kitchen. As she closed the fridge door, she heard the outer door to the suite open and close. Jamie stood, frozen in place, with just the dim light of the room highlighting her.

"Oh, I didn't think you'd still be awake," Griff said as he walked toward her. He stopped a few feet away from her.

"Couldn't sleep." She held up the bottle water. "Thought I'd get a drink."

Great, Jamie! Brilliant conversation…

"I had a drink. Or maybe two," Griff stated.

Jamie moved closer to him, about to pass him on the way to bed, when she smelled the alcohol on his breath.

"Did dinner with my family drive you to drink?"

"No, of course not. They were much harder on you than on me. I just had a few beers in the lounge. Figured I would give you some space."

"Oh." Jamie stood there, inches from him, suddenly aware of how little clothing she wore. And though it was more than most women wore to the beach, she wasn't most women. She clutched the water bottle in her hand to keep from reaching out to touch him. His strong shoulders beckoned to her. She longed to trace the outline of his muscles.

She turned to search his face in the dim light. Griff stared at her, his gaze enough to send goosebumps across her flesh. She tried to think of something other than the two king-sized beds in the suite.

Griff took one step, really only a half-step, closer. Jamie swore she could hear the pounding of his heart. Or maybe hers. When he reached a hand toward her, she turned and bolted.

"Good night," she called over her shoulder and didn't stop until she stood behind the closed door of her room.

*****

Griff slowly lowered his hand to his side. He silently thanked the universe that Jamie had more willpower than he did. Seeing her there, wearing what he assumed were her pajamas, had almost shattered his good intentions. The barely there shorts and tank top left little to the imagination. He wondered if they had been amongst the purchases from earlier today. Used to seeing Jamie fully dressed, he hadn't been ready for the sight of her. Her toned arms and legs spoke of the hard work she'd put in at Getting It Done. *Did she have any idea how smoking hot she was?*

Griff shook his head and grabbed a water bottle from the fridge. Best to keep his mind off that track. He and Jamie were friends. Not friends with benefits. Not more than friends. He'd do well to remember that.

Retreating into his room, Griff was glad their rooms were across the suite from each other and not sharing a wall. He didn't think he could handle hearing her move around in there. It was bad enough he now knew what she slept in.

He pulled the curtains closed, stripped down to his boxers, and slid between the cool sheets. *Think of something other than her skimpy PJs!* Griff replayed the evening and wondered again how she had escaped with such a grounded personality. Not for the first time, Griff was thankful for the wonderful family he had been given. Their childhoods could not have been more different.

An hour later, Griff groaned aloud and flopped over onto his back while he kicked the covers to the bottom of the bed. Sleep eluded him as images of Jamie swirled through his brain. He had no idea what she had planned for tomorrow. They had the whole day and most of Saturday before attending her high school reunion that night. Sunday morning, they'd head back home.

As sleep finally overtook him, Griff smiled at the thought of having a few more days with her. Even if that meant torture for him.

Chapter Thirty-One

"Embarrassment and awkward situations are not foreign to me."
-Paul Rudd

Sunlight streamed around the edges of the heavy curtains. Jamie rolled over, giving her back to it. She reached for her phone, charging on the bedside table, and sighed. She'd already been awake for over an hour, lying in bed and staring at the ceiling. In truth, she was avoiding Griff. Standing out in the suite last night, in her not-so-modest pajamas, played again and again in her head. Worse, she remembered how she had longed to reach out to him. To close the small gap and place her hands on his chest. Her mouth on his. She'd done neither, instead bolting to the safety of her room like a frightened schoolgirl. *Nice going!*

Knowing she couldn't hide in here forever, Jamie threw back the covers and got out of bed. She peeked around the curtain, happy to see bright sunshine. Today, if she ever left this room, she meant to show Griff why she loved Philadelphia and the region. She had today and part of tomorrow to play tourist with him.

Shoring up her resolve, Jamie grabbed her travel bag and

headed to the bathroom. Hopefully, Griff had already showered. If there was a god, maybe he was downstairs having breakfast. She opened her door and stuck out only her head. Looking up and down the short hallway, and not finding evidence of Griff, she dashed into the bathroom. The lack of steam made her think he'd either showered really early or not yet. Either way, she was safe to proceed.

Twenty minutes later, wrapped in one of the thick, plush towels provided by the hotel, Jamie walked out into the hall. And straight into Griff's hard chest.

"Oh," she exclaimed while she clutched the towel to her.

Griff smiled, damn him, popping out those dimples she could never resist.

"Good morning, Jamie."

She took a moment to notice the dark sweat stains on his grey shirt. Instead of repelling her, the smell of him drew her in. It was all male. She stifled the urge to touch him once again.

"Good morning. I've just finished. The bathroom is all yours." *As if he couldn't tell…*

Griff chuckled, the deep sound of it doing funny things to her stomach. He pointed to the towel she still wore and clutched.

"The towel sort of gave it away. If you haven't had breakfast, I'm starving. Give me a few minutes."

"Sure. I'll go get dressed."

Which is what she meant to do, yet she stood there, staring at him. She couldn't help herself. He was handsome, not to mention built. And the damp shirt clinging to his chest did nothing to help her resolve.

Griff tilted his head toward the open bathroom door.

And still she stood there. Until it dawned on her.

"Oh, sorry," she mumbled and stepped aside.

The light in his eyes and grin on his face were pure male.

"I'm not," he said before stepping around her and walking into the bathroom.

The sound of the door closing finally moved her. Waving a hand in front of her heated face, Jamie bolted into her room and closed the door.

*****

Griff couldn't shake the grin on his face, even if he wanted to. Nice to know he wasn't the only one affected by this thing between them. Maybe her being a gym client wasn't such a big deal. Even if he did use the rule to keep Darla at arm's length, or further. Maybe he was creating a barrier where there didn't need to be one. It had been a long time since he met a woman who captured his interest the way she did. It had been a long time since there was a woman in his life period. His time with Sheila was a distant, unpleasant memory. But it was more than that.

Jamie had a lightness to her he found refreshing. While she was very bright and hard-working, she didn't seem to take herself too seriously. After the things he'd seen, and done, in the military, Griff needed that in his life. Needed to learn to enjoy each day for what it was. Starting with today.

He rushed through shaving and showering, eager to start his day with her. He knew he'd been sending her a lot of mixed signals. That ended now. Let's see where the day took them.

Griff dressed in khaki shorts and a T-shirt, hoping that would suit whatever lay ahead. He found Jamie seated on the patio, soaking in the morning sunshine. With her eyes closed and head tilted back to catch the rays, she looked younger and carefree. Not at all how she had looked seated in her parents' formal dining room. He stood there for a moment, drinking in the sight of her. Although loathe to disturb her, he was eager to start their day.

And then his stomach rumbled, taking the decision from him.

Jamie turned her head, a smile on her full lips.

"Someone's hungry," she said.

"I am. What's on the menu? Did you want to grab something here or stop somewhere on the way to, well, wherever we're going?"

She stood up and stretched, her cotton shirt revealing a small strip of exposed flesh. *Speaking of hunger...*

"I know just the place. Let's go."

Twenty minutes later, Jamie pulled into the parking lot of a small store. She turned to Griff.

"Uncle Abe makes the best bagels ever. That's one thing missing from the South, real bagels. Oh, and real pizza too."

"Don't let Mama hear you say that!" He glanced at the sign above the store. "Uncle Abe?" Griff asked.

"Not my uncle, of course. And maybe he's no one's actual uncle. But he'll always be Uncle Abe to me."

She moved her hands as though to hurry him along before dashing into the small store. Once inside, Jamie turned in a tight circle, taking in the interior. A hugs smile spread across her face.

"Nothing's changed," she cried, glee ringing in her voice.

Griff glanced around, taking in the few, small tables in the front. A counter divided the eating area from the back. Several glass-fronted coolers offered a choice of drinks and other wares. All in all, what the place lacked in size it made up in charm.

"Jamie, Neshama, you have returned to me!"

She whirled at the sound of her name.

"Uncle Abe!"

Griff watched as a wizened, little old man came from behind the counter. He could have been sixty or ninety. Not much taller than her, he gathered Jamie in his arms, hugging her. She hugged him just as tightly. Finally, they broke apart, and Jamie turned to Griff.

"Uncle Abe, this is my friend, Griff. Griff, Uncle Abe is the reason I made it through college."

The man grinned and shook his head.

"Hog wash! My Jamie is the brightest young lady to ever grace my humble establishment." He stepped toward Griff, wiping his hands on the apron he wore. "Any friend of Jamie's is a friend of mine. Welcome!"

Griff shook the outstretched hand. The older man stared him down for a moment before grinning. Griff got the impression he'd just passed some sort of test.

Pink flushed her cheeks, and her eyes shone with delight at the compliment.

"I spent my weekends studying here. I always found the library too crowded." She turned and pointed to a table tucked into the corner. "In fact, that's the very table I claimed as my own."

"And yours it shall be again today. I assume you've come for food and not just the company of an old man."

"You're not old," she protested, letting him lead them to 'her' table. "But we did also come for breakfast. You know I couldn't pass up the opportunity to visit while I'm here."

"Ah, how is your family?"

The way he said the last word gave Griff the impression he'd heard all about her family over the years. It made Griff happy knowing she had an ally.

Jamie's smile faltered for the slightest moment. Griff

might have missed it if he hadn't been looking at her.

"Oh, you know them, Uncle Abe. Some things never change."

The older man made a sound that conveyed general disapproval. Griff found himself liking him even more.

"I know the tales you've told me over the years." He turned to Griff. "And you? What did the high and mighty Main Line Lawlers think of the first man my Jamie brought home?"

Jamie squirmed in her seat and then rushed to speak before Griff had the chance.

"Oh, it's not like that, Uncle Abe. Griff and I are just friends."

Her emphasis on the word 'friends' caused a funny little pain in his chest.

"Although her family doesn't know that," Griff added.

Uncle Abe's bushy, white eyebrows nearly reached his hairline. "Ah, good going, my wise girl. You brought him to throw them off the scent, so to speak."

His round belly jiggled with his laughter.

"I'm also her plus one for her high school reunion tomorrow night," added Griff.

Uncle Abe's head swiveled from Jamie to Griff and back. A frown marred his elfin features.

"Are you gay?" he asked Griff.

Jamie burst out laughing, covering her mouth with her hand. A look of mischief danced in her eyes.

Griff cleared his throat. "Ah, no, sir, I am not gay," he clarified.

The old man's frown deepened.

"This I do not understand. Why 'friends' when my Jamie is so gorgeous?"

Griff glanced across at the woman in question, whose face

bordered on the color of a summer tomato.

Because I'm an idiot...

"Uncle Abe, maybe we could order. We're both famished."

"Of course, my little sweet potato. I already know your order." He turned to Griff. "Young man, what may I get for you? Everything on the menu is pure perfection."

Jamie nodded. "He's not kidding."

"I'll have whatever she's having then."

Uncle Abe beamed at him.

"Very good. Jamie, your young man is smart as a whip. I will be back with your meals. Help yourself to drinks."

He shuffled away, leaving the two of them alone.

"I'm sorry," Jamie whispered to him. "He seems stuck on the idea of your being my 'young man'."

"I've been called much worse," he assured her. "And besides, it's been a very long time since I was referred to as young." Griff stood up. "I'm going to grab some orange juice. What would you like?"

"Cranberry for me, thanks."

Griff thought about being her 'young man' as he fetched their drinks. The older man had given Griff a great opening. He needed to test the waters. To find out how she'd feel about that after the mixed messages he'd been sending these past few months. He whistled a happy tune as he grabbed their drinks.

*****

Jamie's heart did a funny little pitter patter inside her chest at the thought of Griff being her 'young man' as Uncle Abe had put it. Aside from wanting to die of embarrassment when he asked Griff if was gay, the idea held strong appeal, as it had for months. Yet, Griff seemed determined to keep her in the friend/client zone. Not much she could do about that. Better to focus on getting through tomorrow night. But she vowed to give the whole dating thing a whirl when they got home. She wasn't getting any younger, and she did want a family someday.

Strengthening her resolve, she smiled at Griff, trying to not get lost in his bright green eyes, when he handed over her cranberry juice.

"Thank you."

"Of course."

They both started talking at the same time, and Griff motioned for her to continue.

"I wanted to talk about tomorrow night. You know, the reunion? To see how you wanted to play it."

Was it her imagination or had his eyes dimmed a bit.

"Play it?" he parroted as if he wasn't quite sure what she asked.

"Yes. I mean I know you agreed to be my date and act as though we were, uh, together and all. I just don't know how we'll pull that off." She gestured with her hands. "You know because we aren't really an item. I mean it was one thing last night, but my parents would never have expected nor appreciated any type of public display. But tomorrow night may be different. I mean if we want them to think that we're really, uh, boyfriend and girlfriend."

Good lord, woman, shut up already!

Uncle Abe appeared with their breakfasts, interrupting their talk. And saving her from inserting her foot any deeper down her throat.

"Here we are. Two everything bagels with egg, cheese, and bacon. Enjoy!"

He dashed away before either could respond.

The aroma wafting up from her hot breakfast sandwich drove away all thoughts of the ridiculous conversation she had started.

"What exactly is an everything bagel?" Griff asked.

She laughed at his raised eyebrow.

"I probably should have mentioned that beforehand. It's what it sounds like; a bagel with a bit of everything. Don't worry, our next stop involves a lot of cardio. You'll burn off the calories."

"After what I've eaten in the desert, this doesn't scare me." He took a big bite of his, as if to prove his point.

She wondered about his years in the service. He hardly ever referenced them. She waited until he chewed and swallowed.

"Well, what do you think?"

He nodded while wiping his mouth on a napkin. "Very tasty. I approve."

"Of course he does," came a shout from behind the counter. "He's a smart boy. But not too smart if he's only 'friends' with my Jamie."

And Jamie wondered, not for the first time in her life, if it was possible to die of embarrassment. Not waiting to find out, she ate her breakfast.

"Uh, about tomorrow night," Griff started. When she looked up to meet his gaze, he continued. "You really don't think we can convince them? That we don't have chemistry?"

She thought about the amazing kiss they'd shared weeks ago. *No, chemistry would never be their issue.* She shook her head.

"No, it's not that. I just, uh, think I might be asking a bit much of you. I mean you already flew all the way up here. And dealt with my family…"

"This is what I agreed to, Jamie. And believe me, playing the part of a beautiful woman's boyfriend for an evening is no hardship."

Griff went back to finishing his breakfast as if that closed the matter, leaving her sitting across from him, trying to not gawk. This gorgeous man was willing to do that for her? Okay, who was she to argue?

"Fine. Now that we have that settled, how much PDA are we planning?"

Jamie held back her laughter when he appeared to choke on his last bite of sandwich. Griff gulped down some orange juice before answering her. Maybe he wasn't so blasé about this after all.

Chapter Thirty-Two

"I long, as does every human being, to be at home wherever I find myself."

-Maya Angelou

That evening, Jamie drove Griff along Martin Luther King Jr. Drive, across the Schuylkill River from her beloved Boathouse Row. Since there wasn't a place to pull over, she drove as slowly as she could to afford him the best view. The lights outlining the boathouses glowed on the river, warming her heart.

"I get why you love this place," Griff acknowledged.

"Right?" she said on a sigh. "If only I could take this home with me."

"Palm Harbor is really home, huh?"

She risked a quick glance at his face, searching for a clue that he was joking. But his deadpan gave away nothing.

"Was there ever any doubt, Griff?"

"No, not really. Although your family certainly hasn't given up hoping."

"Which is odd when you think about it. I mean they all but ignored me growing up. Except for the time they spent trying to 'improve' me." She winced at the bitterness of her words.

"Sounds rough," Griff commented.

"I know, and I don't mean that. First-world problems really, when you think about it. I had every advantage growing up, good schools, safe neighborhood, travel. I should be more appreciative." She sighed. "And my family isn't all bad, despite how they treated you last night."

"And you," he pointed out.

"They just have a different view of the world. A rather narrow one. They surround themselves with people just like them, who eat the same food, like the same things, visit the same places. I never fit their mold. I wasn't perfect like Melissa, but then I never tried. I'm, I don't know, different."

"And thank goodness for that. Don't they ever find it boring?"

"No. It's what they know."

"How did you turn out so differently, so much better?"

"Why thank, you kind sir. I spent my childhood trying all the things they wanted me to try. But I wasn't graceful and coordinated like Melissa was. I sucked at tennis and golf. Although, I did love riding. Always thought I might get another horse someday."

"You had a horse?" Griff asked.

"I did. Her name was Cricket, and I loved her. On horseback, I'm not as clumsy."

"But wasn't being an equestrian something that would win over your parents?"

"You'd think, right? But it wasn't enough to ride horses. They wanted me to ride competitively. To show at Devon, which is local, but a show of international importance."

"And you didn't want that."

She loved that there wasn't any question in his voice.

"No, I just wanted to ride. Being the center of attention was never my thing. Not sure why they never understood."

"Because they needed you to be a reflection of them," Griff guessed.

"Pretty much. But let's talk about better things. Tell me what you thought of your first, authentic Philadelphia cheesesteak."

After several hours tramping around Valley Forge National Park, she'd taken him on a gastronomic tour of Philly. Determined to get an outsider's opinion, she'd taken him to Passyunk Avenue to try cheesesteaks from both Pat's King of Steaks and Geno's. They'd ordered one from each and split them.

"I do believe 'one whiz wit' edged out 'one Provy wit' out.' I'm not sure which was from which shop though."

Jamie laughed out loud at his imitation of other diners at the steak shops. All traces of his delightful drawl had vanished.

"Although, I might weigh three hundred pounds if I lived here," he added.

"Well, there was the soft pretzel and water ice as well. I wanted you to try all the Philadelphia food staples."

"We still have tomorrow," he reminded her. "We could have saved some for then."

Jamie smacked her head with a palm.

"Now you tell me."

"Very funny."

His mention of tomorrow made her quiet. She was starting to dread the reunion. It would just be more time spent with people who didn't understand or respect her. Like dinner last night.

"About tomorrow night..."

"After all your hard work, the big night is finally almost here. Aren't you excited?"

Not really!

But Griff seemed excited enough for them both, and she didn't want to wreck that for him. After all, she was the one who dragged him all the way up here. What she wanted to say was, *let's skip the reunion. Let's go home right now. Screw those people who never had time for me back then. In fact, screw your rules about not dating clients while we're at it. But she didn't say any of that.*

"Sure, I am."

"Huh," he grunted in return before falling quiet in the passenger seat.

Neither spoke again for the rest of the ride back to the hotel. But it wasn't the comfortable silence they'd shared before. It was more of the stilted, things left unsaid type of silence. The kind that leaves a person feeling edgy.

By the time she parked the rental, Jamie felt like screaming. Instead, she got out and walked inside with Griff. They passed the lounge. Music from a live band spilled out into the lobby.

Griff touched her arm. "Did you want to get a drink and listen to some music?"

"No thanks, but don't let me stop you," she replied and kept walking toward the elevator bank. The last thing she needed was alcohol. She'd be sure to throw herself at him if she had any drinks.

Letting herself into their suite a few minutes later, Jamie cursed herself for being rude to Griff. They'd had a fun day together, but the more time she spent with him, the more she wanted to. And not just as friends. But he seemed determined to stick to his guns, forever mentioning Chad and the reunion.

What did he look like? Did they have anything in common she could use as an opener tomorrow night?

It was all too much. Frustrated, Jamie stripped out of her clothing and pulled on the gym clothes she'd brought from home. After months of watching her diet, today's intake weighed heavily, both physically and mentally. Besides, she may as well burn off some frustration as well as calories.

Jamie headed down to the basement level gym, happy that at least for this moment, she had a plan. The rest of her life, including her growing feelings for Griff, would have to wait.

*****

Griff rolled the cold bottle of beer in his hands while he listened to the band play an assortment of jazz. While it wasn't his favorite, the notes soothed him. His third beer didn't hurt either. He watched the red head he'd turned down stalk her next choice with a sense of detachment. The woman had been very upfront about what she sought. But it hadn't appealed to him. She hadn't appealed to him, which he found as surprising as she had.

But a meaningless one-off night no longer held any appeal. It never really had, although he had taken advantage of similar situations in his twenties. And though the woman had been beautiful, she wasn't sassy with whiskey-colored eyes. Like the one up in their shared suite right now.

I'm an idiot! Not wanting to waste another second, Griff threw some bills down on the bar and left. He stood by the elevator, switching his weight from one foot to the other while he waited for it. Who cared if she was a client? Rules were meant to be broken, right? Jack would certainly agree with him. And besides, he wouldn't be breaking this rule again.

Griff all but ran into the suite the moment the elevator reached their floor. He swiped his card key and burst through the door.

"Jamie!" he called, excited to see her.

But no one answered. Could she be asleep already? He glanced into the kitchen. Empty. Next, he walked to her bedroom door. Closed. He knocked softly. When she didn't answer after a few moments, he opened the door. Moonlight spilling in revealed another empty room. But no trace of her.

Griff backed out the room and closed the door. *Where could she be?* Not knowing but not feeling any alarm, Griff turned on the TV and sat down to wait.

*****

The faint glow of the TV greeted Jamie as she let herself back into their suite. Griff lay stretched out on his side, one hand under his cheek, snoring softly. As much as she wanted to talk about things, about them, he looked too peaceful to disturb.

Padding into her bedroom, Jamie grabbed a spare blanket she'd spied in the closet yesterday when she hung up her new clothes. Returning to his side, she spread the blanket over Griff.

"Goodnight," she whispered before returning to her room.

Thanks to her heavy workout, Jamie needed a second shower. But that was a small price to pay. She stood under the hot water as long as she could, letting the day's stress wash down the drain along with her hard-earned sweat.

The long day caught up with her, and she rushed through the rest of her bedtime routine. With her damp hair tied up in a messy bun and a towel spread across her pillow, Jamie climbed into bed. Grabbing her iPad from the bedside table, she signed into her Netflix app and clicked on an old but favorite episode of *Lucifer*. She watched as the title character cradled his beloved detective within his arms, shielding her from harm at his own cost.

Jamie sighed. *Why couldn't real life be like this?* Of course, the man was the devil. And who needed that? Still, with that five o'clock shadow and delicious accent, she'd take her chances. She chuckled to herself at her fanciful thinking. She couldn't manage a real man in her life…

"Jamie, wake up," came a yummy, male voice interrupting her sleep.

"Not yet," she protested, burrowing under the comforter. She had been in the middle of the most delicious dream. She stood on a darkened balcony, Lucifer whispering naughty nothings in her ear. But he didn't have an accent anymore. Odd.

"I thought you might want some coffee," came an amused male voice inches from her face.

Her eyes sprang open. First, she noticed Griff standing there, clad in workout clothes and holding a steaming cup of coffee. Then she spied the silly grin on his face. Jamie pulled the comforter over her head. But as she did, she caught a whiff of the coffee.

"Is that Dunkin Irish Crème coffee?" she mumbled from under the comforter.

"It is. With one sugar and a Splenda, just how you like it," Griff answered with more than a little amusement in his voice. "But you have to come out here to get it."

"You're cruel," she accused.

"Make you a deal. I'll take it out to the living room. But if you're not out in three minutes, I can't promise I won't drink it."

Before she could agree, she heard the sound of his retreat. Then the door closed. Taking him at his word, Jamie leapt out of bed. She pulled a sweatshirt over her head and left the safety of her room. After a quick pit stop in the bathroom, she joined him.

Griff held out her drink, still grinning.

"Not that I'm questioning this miracle, but how did you know my favorite coffee? And where did you get it?"

"When you didn't get up, I went for a run. There happens to be a DD not far from here. I texted Jack, who then texted Sam for me. Sam spilled the beans." He grinned at her. "Get it? Spilled the beans?"

Jamie groaned before taking a first sip of the brew. Closing her eyes, she sighed around the taste,

"Very punny," she replied, tongue firmly in cheek. She returned his grin. "How's that for early morning humor?"

"Not bad, not bad."

"For being 'just friends' my friend seems to be spending a lot of time with yours. She hasn't said a lot. What do you think is going on?"

"No idea, but I hope she doesn't break his heart."

A knock at the door prevented her from saying anything else. She looked at it and then Griff.

"Who could that be?"

"That would be breakfast. I took the liberty of ordering. Be right back."

She sipped more coffee and did not ogle Griff as he jogged to the door. That would be wrong. He came back a few moments later carrying a silver tray covered by a dome. Her stomach chose that moment to respond, gurgling loudly.

"See, my timing is perfect. I was going to let you sleep in, but this is our last full day here."

Jamie followed him to the small table tucked into the corner. She slid into a chair as he lifted the lid.

"I went for healthy after the day we had yesterday." With a flourish, he handed Jamie a small plate. "We have an assortment of fresh fruit and Greek yogurt for your pleasure."

Other pleasure comes to mind. She banished that thought and scooped some yogurt onto her plate. She added berries, swirling them in. Then she speared a few chunks of pineapple.

The two ate for a few minutes, both apparently lost in their own thoughts. Until Griff wasn't.

"Want to tell me about the dream I interrupted?" he asked.

"What?" Jamie coughed and finished swallowing the bite of pineapple. "What dream?"

He shrugged one muscled shoulder. "Seemed like a good one from the smile on your face. And the little noises you made."

"Noises?" she squeaked. Maybe she'd heard him wrong. Please, let her have heard him wrong.

"It sounded kind of like the noise you make when you eat donuts. Or drink Irish Crème coffee from DD."

OMG! Had she made THOSE noises?

And then she heard him laugh. Long and hard.

"Oh, you!" she cried, balling up her napkin and throwing it at him.

"Sorry, but your face! What did you think I heard?"

"I fell asleep watching *Lucifer*. Anything is possible."

"*Lucifer*, huh? Never pictured you as the type." He offered no further explanation.

"What type? The kind that lusts over hot men with a British accent? Yes, I'm that type."

She ignored the heat seeping into her face. If he was going

to ask such questions, he better be ready for the answers. Instead, she speared another chunk of fruit.

"This is a nice treat for breakfast. Usually, after pounding away at the gym, I grab something on my way to work. And by something, I mean a protein bar," Jamie exclaimed.

"I've rubbed off on you is what you're trying to not say," Griff bragged.

"I guess you could say that. I have been trying to eat better." She sighed and ate another spoonful of her yogurt. "What that means is that a Snickers doesn't live in my desk drawer anymore."

"I never said you can't have a Snickers. Ever again. I'm not cruel," he protested.

Jamie laughed and pointed her empty spoon at him.

"And while I appreciate that, you have no idea how hard I have to fight still. If I kept one in my drawer at work, where stress is a daily thing, then I'd eat one. Every day. And that's not what I want."

"What do you want?"

She stared at him for a moment. The air grew heavy around them. Suddenly they weren't talking about snack choices. She played with the linen napkin in her lap, twisting it this way and that.

"What are you asking exactly?" she parried.

Griff put down his spoon and sat back in his chair. All without breaking eye contact.

"What do you want, Jamie? Out of life."

She laughed then. A curse of hers really. She always laughed when she felt nervous.

"I guess what everyone wants."

He shook his head, a hunk of dark hair falling over his forehead. She continued to twist the napkin to avoid reaching out and brushing it back.

"That's a cop out. It's an easy question."

"Well, I want to be my own boss. I want to be respected at work, not just a number."

"Thus, Phoenix Accounting," he said.

"Yes, exactly."

"You wanted something, and you went after it. I wonder. Does that apply to other areas of your life?"

His green eyes darkened, but she couldn't look away.

"It took me awhile, though. To get to the place where Operation Phoenix becomes a reality."

"Doesn't matter. You're still doing it. That's what matters." He leaned the tiniest bit closer toward her. "And what about the other areas of your life, Jamie? Is tonight about getting what you want? Is Chad what you want?"

She didn't speak right away, not really sure how to answer.

"It wasn't a difficult question, Jamie," Griff prompted with a bit more edge to his voice.

What I want is sitting right in front of me. That's what she wanted to say. But she didn't. "I don't know. Maybe. I haven't seen Chad in fifteen years. I guess I'll see tonight."

The bright green of his eyes dimmed a bit. "Well, it's good to have a plan." Griff stood up and excused himself. "I have to hit the shower."

She watched him go, longing to call him back. To tell him the truth. To ask him to bend his rule. Instead, she sat there, playing with her yogurt. Her appetite had vanished.

*****

Griff stood under the shower spray, letting the hot as he

could stand it water soothe his aching muscles. Sleeping on the couch had not been his best idea ever. Too bad the heat couldn't touch the ache in his heart.

What was he doing? If he was willing to break his own rule and get involved with Jamie, then why hadn't he said something to her yet? Anything? Was he afraid of her answer? Had she moved on? Couldn't blame her really, what with all the mixed messages. But it felt like every time he tried to say something, she brought up what's his name and the reunion. Or was that just a convenient excuse?

He noticed her shampoo sitting alongside his and picked it up. Taking a whiff, it brought up the memory of the slight citrusy scent that followed her everywhere. The scent that stayed with him long after she left the gym. The scent that followed him into his dreams at night. Shaking his head, Griff picked up his own shampoo and got on with his shower. Standing here, ruminating, wasn't getting him anywhere.

After his shower, Griff shaved and brushed his teeth. He stared into the foggy mirror. There was something in her eyes at breakfast. A warmth with a hint of uncertainty, yet she never dropped his gaze. It had to count for something. She wasn't immune. With the towel knotted around his hips, Griff left the bathroom. And crashed right into the center of his thoughts.

"Sorry," she gasped.

He reached out and grabbed her upper arms to steady her.

"No worries. My bad for not watching where I was going."

Griff hid a smile at her widened eyes. And how her gaze dropped from his face and travelled down his chest and abdomen to where the towel lay. Maybe she wasn't so immune after all. This could be fun. He released her and crossed his hands over his bare chest.

"Did you have any plans for this afternoon? We do have a few hours to kill."

He watched her drag her gaze back to his face and smirked.

"Oh, well, I, uh, haven't planned anything. Is there something you'd like to do? We don't have a ton of time. I have to get ready and everything tonight."

He loved that he made her nervous. Had to be a good sign. But being a smart man, Griff kept that information to himself.

Chapter Thirty-Three

"Throw caution to the wind and just do it."
-Carrie Underwood

Pull yourself together! Jamie stood in her bedroom, staring out the window but not really seeing the gorgeous day beyond. Maybe her impromptu pep talk would help. She'd showered and dressed for the day but not yet left the safety of her room. Seeing Griff, more of him than she had ever seen, in that towel had short-circuited her brain. Good Lord, that man was built. She knew he was fit. After all, he owned a gym. But she had no idea he was *fit.*

She'd already wasted most of the morning. And this was their last full day here. Gathering her purse, phone, and her courage, Jamie left her room. The bathroom door stood open, light off. He wasn't there. She walked farther into the living area of the suite. The curtains flapping in the breeze caught her eye. Griff sat on the balcony, back to her, talking on the phone.

Taking a moment, Jamie stood there, staring at his shoulders and neck, all she could really see of him. Her fingers itched to trace the muscles barely hidden by the cotton of his shirt. She took a step to the left and stretched her neck. Now she could see a portion of his tanned, muscular calf. A smattering of dark hair dusted the surface.

The sound of his chair scraping the floor broke her from her daydream, dragging her back to reality. And the reality that she was a perv.

"Hey, are you ready to head out?" Griff asked as he walked in from the balcony.

"Sure, just waiting for you," she answered. Not adding that she wanted him to choose her. To break his rules. She juggled the rental key in her hand, passing it from one to the other.

"Everything okay?"

She looked up, noticing he watched her anxious movements. Jamie shoved the key in her pocket. *Get a grip!* Apparently, she needed another pep talk. She could do this.

Several hours later, Jamie led the way into the Reading Terminal Market. They'd parked the car in the lot on the side street after playing tourist for several hours in Old City.

"Well, what did you think?" She frowned, wondering if she'd dragged him to too many historical sights. "Are you bored yet? The good news is that everything in this building will set your taste buds on fire."

He held the door for her as they walked inside the building.

"Are you kidding? I loved it! You showed me things I've only read about in school. We saw the Liberty Bell and Betsy Ross's house."

Jamie grinned. "I'm glad. I really love showing Philadelphia off to people who've never been before. Have you worked up an appetite?"

His intense gaze made her think of other appetites, but she

shook off the thought.

"Well, we did walk about five miles this morning," he joked. "And that's beside my run. Yeah, I could eat. What's good here?"

"Everything! What are you in the mood for? There's everything from burgers and hot dogs to deli or ribs. Ooh, there's also the Pennsylvania Dutch food. I haven't had that in years."

"I have no idea what that means, but you haven't steered me wrong yet. I'm game."

Jamie rubbed her hands together. "Oh goody, we'll work our way over there."

They wandered around the different stalls with Jamie pointing out ones she knew and other, newer ones. The eclectic mixture of cultures under one roof had always enchanted her. You could find everything from African crafts and jewelry to Caribbean food to Amish baked goods.

"Thank you for showing me Philadelphia. I've never been much of a city person, as you've probably guessed by now, but it's beautiful." He grinned at her and shuffled his feet.

"I'm not either, despite growing up here. Believe me, like any big city, there are areas of Philadelphia a lot less charming." She grinned back at him. "That's why I only showed you the good parts. Have to leave you with a favorable impression."

"Oh, you have," he murmured without elaborating.

Griff stopped walking. She followed his gaze to a rack of gorgeous, handmade Amish quilts. He pointed to one.

"Didn't I see something like this in your house?"

She followed his finger to a red and white one with stars.

"You remember?"

"Yes. The night I brought Thai for dinner. I saw something similar to this hanging on a wall." He stepped closer to the display as if to get a better look. Then he turned to her. "But yours is blue and white, right?"

"It is," she breathed, still not quite believing he had remembered.

"Where's this food you promised me?"

Jamie laughed at the little boy look on his face. He may be older than her and had certainly seen things in war she never had, but he seemed to enjoy the simple things in life. Like good food.

"The great food is all around us in case you hadn't noticed. But since you've decided on Pennsylvania Dutch food, it's all right here in this area." She grabbed his arm, small shocks racing up hers from the contact. "Let's do this."

*****

Griff allowed Jamie to pull him through the crowd, enjoying the heat that came from her small hand on his arm. He felt a sense of loss when she released him to point out the various vendors selling 'stick-to-your-ribs' food as she put it.

"Basically, it comes down to what you're in the mood for. Chicken pot pie? Deli sandwich? Chicken and waffles?"

She grinned at him, and he wondered if he looked a bit lost.

"Oh, and you have to leave room for dessert. There are so many delicious choices like shoe fly pie and fresh apple dumplings. And every variety of pie imaginable. Wow, just thinking about that makes my mouth water."

She turned to peruse a menu, and Griff stared at her. His own mouth watered, but it had nothing to do with the cornucopia of delicious scents wafting through the air.

Jamie turned back to him, still grinning. "Well, do you

know what you want?"

You. Instead he glanced again at the menu overhead. "I have no idea. Why don't you choose?"

Her eyes sparkled, the gold flecks in them shining.

"I have a great idea. Why don't we split two different meals. That way, you don't have to choose." Her smile lit her whole face. "And we can do that with dessert as well."

As soon as he nodded, Jamie turned back to the counter and ordered what seemed like enough food for an army. He drew the line when she reached into her small purse for her wallet. Griff placed a hand on her wrist.

"I've got this."

"You are my guest here, Griff, which means I pay for lunch."

"And yet, you're not." He grinned at her while reaching around and handing the young woman behind the counter some bills. "Keep the change," he told her before turning back to Jamie. "I may be the guest, but I am also a southern gentleman who was raised right. I don't need my mom finding out I let you pay for my lunch, now do I?"

Jamie laughed and accepted defeat as she turned away from the counter.

"Lord knows we can't have that. But out of curiosity, how would your mom ever find out?"

Griff shuddered, making her laugh even harder, as he hoped.

"Trust me, that woman has her ways. She'd find out. She used to tell us she had eyes in the back of her head when we were little. Took me a long time to figure out that was just an expression. My siblings and I never got away with a thing. Of course, growing up in a small town didn't help."

They stood off to the side to allow other customers to

order. Griff watched Jamie as she watched others. Her eyes alight, she took in everything from the crowd to the different vendors, almost as if committing it all to memory.

"It's not like you're never coming back," he said to her.

"What?"

"You're taking it all in as though you'll never see it again. But, you will."

She stared at him, and he bathed in the warmth of her smile. Jamie was like that. When she smiled, she lit the room. And if you were lucky enough to be at the center of that smile, well then you had everything.

The woman behind the counter called their number, and Griff went to grab the tray bearing their lunch. He grinned at the amount of food. Nothing like a woman with a healthy appetite. Turning, he spied Jamie waving from a table off to the side of the stand. She'd managed to grab space for them despite the heavy lunchtime crowd.

"I hope you're hungry," he joked with her as he set down the tray and squeezed in next to her. "Or I hope you've brought some friends."

Jamie tilted up her head and laughed.

"I am hungry. You're right, we walked a ton this morning. And I'm not sure what they'll be serving tonight at the reunion. If it's anything like I imagine, the menu will consist of fancy appetizers that leave you hungry. Best to fill up now."

She slid their food off the tray, placing the tray on the floor next to her. Then she cut each entree in half before handing him a plate. Jamie dug right into her lunch, making those cute noises she made when enjoying her food.

Everything looked and smelled delicious, but it may as well have been cardboard. Her casual mention of the reunion took away his appetite. Even though they had come all this way solely for the event, the idea of taking her to it, to *him*, brought a pang to his chest.

"Aren't you hungry?" Jamie asked.

"I am. Don't worry about me. If you're not careful, I might eat all of the shoe fly pie, whatever that may be."

Knowing he needed to get through today before he could say anything to her, Griff picked up his fork and dug into his half of the chicken pot pie. Jamie had chosen well. The flavors exploded on his tongue. Pushing aside thoughts of tonight, he ate everything she had placed in front of him.

*****

Jamie ate the last bite of her half of the apple dumpling and resisted licking the plate. It had been that delicious. Even with all she'd eaten on this trip, she'd done better than before she started at the gym. She'd always been a grazer, snacking throughout the day at work or at home on the weekends. Those calories added up. Then, like most women she knew, there was her stress eating. Or happy eating. Whatever. She ate when she was happy or sad, depressed, etc. But no more, or at least ninety percent less than she had in the past.

"Penny for your thoughts. I can almost smell your brain burning from whatever it is you're thinking about," Griff joked.

"Save your money. It isn't even worth a penny."

His dark brows pulled together. "Let me be the judge of that."

"It's nothing, really." When she saw he wasn't breaking his gaze from hers, she gave in. "I was thinking about how much I've changed in the last two months. Or how much my habits have changed, at least in terms of eating and exercise." She waved a hand in the air. "Told you it was nothing."

"That's not nothing, Jamie. That's actually a big deal. You saw something in yourself you were less than happy about, and you changed it."

She laughed at that, a sort of high-hitched one. "Changing, not changed. At best, I am a work in progress."

She stood and gathered their garbage, wanting anything to keep her hands busy. But then she felt his hand on her shoulder, his skin burning hers through her thin shirt.

"Please don't do that. You should be proud of this and of everything you're doing. And we are all a work in progress."

She didn't answer, didn't protest, because he was right. She didn't need a shrink to tell her a lifetime of never meeting her family's expectations takes its toll. If she let it. And she had. For too long.

"You're right," she said, grinning at his raised brows.

"I'm sorry, can you say that again?" Griff joked.

Jamie punched him in the shoulder and kept walking.

"For years, way too many, I let what they said, what they thought of me, weigh me down. Dictate how I lived and felt about myself. Well, no more." She let out a big breath and smiled. "I know that this started years ago. But somehow saying it out loud makes a difference."

"Because saying it out loud, whether others can hear the words or not, makes them real. You did this, Jamie. Not your parents or your holier than thou sister. You broke away from them. From that life."

"I did, didn't I?"

They walked out into the bright, spring sunshine, and Jamie stood there for a moment, tilting her face up to the sky.

"It couldn't have been easy," Griff murmured close to her ear, sending chills across her body.

She turned to face him.

"What? Leaving all this and moving away? Much easier than you would think." She felt her smile slip a bit. "To be honest, it was probably too easy. Which says a lot about my family."

"I'm sorry. I can't imagine. Having a bunch of siblings can be rough in its own way, but I wouldn't have it any other way. No matter what, someone always has my back. Like when Jack and I opened Getting It Done. My parents offered me money to help, no strings attached or questions asked. We turned them down, but just knowing they would meant the world to me."

They walked into the shaded parking garage. Jamie took a moment for her eyes to adjust. Then they walked to the rental. When they got in, she didn't start the car right away but turned to him.

"You have no idea how much I envy you for that. I know on some level my parents love me. But they've never understood me. Nor have they ever really tried. At some point, I needed something different."

"When you'd had enough?" he guessed.

"Actually, it was when I went down to Palm Harbor for the internship. I met Sam, and we just clicked. She's more my sister than Melissa ever was. And then it dawned on me. Family is who you choose, not just those you're related to."

"Makes even more sense now after meeting them," Griff added.

"Exactly! In college, I knew what I wanted to do, just not where I wanted to do it. All I knew was it wouldn't be here. And then I got invited to spend six weeks in Palm Grove, SC of all places. And those six weeks changed the course of my life."

A hearty laugh exploded from Griff. Jamie sat there, watching him, before joining in. The sound of his deep, masculine laugh sent shivers up and down her spine.

"Are you going to let me in on the joke?"

"I would have given anything to be a fly on the wall the day you told your parents."

Jamie shook her head, laughter pouring from her.

"You can't even imagine," she choked out, still laughing. "My father's face reached purple by the time he finished. 'Young lady, what exactly do you think you're doing? I forbid it.' Can you imagine? There I was a college graduate, and he thought he could still order me around."

Griff reached across the middle and covered her hands with his.

"I can't imagine, you're right. When I enlisted, my parents had a very sober conversation with me about being careful. My mom cried, but she supported me one hundred percent. Not having that kind of support? Can't imagine."

"Consider yourself lucky."

She started the car and drove out of the garage. They talked about everything and nothing on the way back, which helped to calm her nerves. This night was fifteen years in the making and somehow, she couldn't be less interested.

By the time she pulled into the hotel parking lot, she had almost talked herself out of going at all. She turned off the car but made no move to leave it. She turned to Griff.

"Hey, I have an idea. Instead of getting all dressed up to go to this reunion, why don't we get all dressed up and go grab a pizza?"

Chapter Thirty-Four

"Among mortals, second thoughts are wisest."

-Euripides

If there was a soundtrack for this conversation, there'd be nothing but crickets. Griff stared at her. It took him a moment, or two, to recover.

"But isn't the reunion the reason we're here?"

Ignoring the heat in her face, Jamie squeaked out a laugh. "Of course. I was kidding."

She jumped out of the car before he could say anything else. She had no idea what possessed her to blurt that out. Last-minute nerves? Cold feet? Second thoughts? But she couldn't take it back now. Best to pretend she'd been joking.

She clicked the locks shut as soon as he got out and turned toward the hotel. Griff stopped her with a hand on her arm.

"I'm sorry. You took me by surprise. I thought this was something you wanted, had planned for. Why else are we here?"

"Yes, of course. You're right." She hoped the words sounded stronger to him than they did to her. She walked on, breaking his hold on her. At least physically. Tonight would be fine. She was tired and a little stressed. Maybe a quick nap. She heard him catch up with her.

"Hey, I'm sorry. Of course we can go get pizza if that's what you want to do. I'll even get 'dressed up' as you put it."

"No, I'm sorry. I'm being silly. We'll go, eat fancy appetizers that we have no clue what they are, drink overpriced drinks and chat with people who don't remember me."

"Are you sure you're not in marketing?" he quipped. "Because that sounds like a fun time."

Jamie felt the laughter bubble up from inside. But as she turned to face him in the parking lot, tears burned in her eyes. She threw her hands in the air.

"I give up. I'm such a mess. Why would you even want to be seen in public with me?"

Hot tears rolled down her face. She didn't try to stop them. Instead, she marched into the hotel, past a stunned looking doorman and didn't stop until she got to the elevator bank. One dinged, and she waited for the doors to open. When they did, she slid inside, stabbing their floor with a finger. Jamie didn't realize Griff had stayed with her until he gathered her into his arms as the doors closed.

"Shhh," he whispered in her ear, stroking one large hand up and down her back. "It'll be okay."

She nodded against his chest, unable to form words past the lump in her throat. Her tears continued to soak his shirt, but she couldn't even care. The bell dinged, signaling their floor, and she stepped out of his embrace. And immediately missed the warmth of his body. *No use thinking about that.*

She didn't say a thing, just walked to their door and dug through her small purse for the key.

He brushed up against her side, nudging her out of the way.

"Let me."

When he opened the door and held it for her, she walked inside, intent on heading straight to her room. Coward's way out maybe, but she was okay with that.

"Jamie, wait," he called to her.

She took a deep breath before turning to face him. "I don't know what that was. Not even the right time of the month."

And her hand flew to her mouth.

"I have no idea what's wrong with me," she mumbled through her fingers. "I need a nap."

She started to turn away, but he stepped in front of her. One strong hand reached out and gently tipped her face up to his.

"No reunion is worth this. Seriously, we can bag it and go for pizza."

"It's fine really. I'm fine." She gave a short laugh. "To the contrary of recent behavior. Coming here stresses me. And now this, tonight, added to it. But I think going will be good for me. Laying ghosts to rest and all that."

"And catching up with the one that got away," he suggested.

"He was never mine to lose." She gestured to the door of her room. "I'm going to catch a quick nap then the hottest shower I can stand. I promise to not cry on you again." She made a little X over her heart and walked away.

*****

"I don't mind," Griff stated to the empty space. He watched her door close before heading out to the balcony. He flopped down on the chair then ran a hand through his hair. *How did this get so out control?* No more lying to himself. He cared about Jamie. A lot. He wanted to be with her, see where things went. And the flimsy excuse he'd used as a wall between them didn't seem to matter anymore. And they'd been alone, together, for two days. Why hadn't he said anything?

Griff leaned back, closing his eyes, and soaking up the afternoon sun. After seeing how her family had treated her at dinner the other night, Griff didn't doubt the pressure she felt. He didn't know anything about her high school, but if the people she'd gone to school with were anything like her family, then the stress had doubled. The best thing he could do would be to support her tonight. There'd be plenty of time to talk to her about the possibility of them when they got home.

His phone buzzed from his back pocket. Griff reached around and grabbed it. A new text from Jack flashed on the screen.

"How's Philly? Have you told Jamie yet how you feel?"

He grimaced at the message. His best friend was worse than a girl sometimes. He sent a quick, snarky reply.

"Didn't realize you were channeling Oprah. Back off asshole."

The dots bubbled, signaling Jack was typing a response. Not caring to read it, Griff turned off the ringer on his phone and slid it back in his pocket. He smothered a yawn with his hand. A nap sounded like a great idea.

*****

Jamie put on the finishing touches of her makeup, way more than she normally wore, and sat back on the bed. Her nap, though brief, had done a world of good. And the hot, steamy shower had driven away the last whisper of a headache. She needed to think about installing that type of shower in her own home. The rain shower effect from the overhead shower head had washed away the last of her troubles. At least for a few minutes. She'd stood under it, with the water as hot as she could stand, and sighed as her troubles swirled away down the drain.

Tonight, she would walk into the reunion with her head held high and a hot man on her arm. So what if Griff wasn't hers? They didn't need to know that. She'd show them what she'd made of her life and then walk away without looking back. And she would go home, where things made more sense.

Making Phoenix Accounting a reality would be enough for her. It had to be. And if pining over a man she couldn't have felt a bit lonely, she would get over that, too. She did want to get married and have a family, preferably before she hit forty. But if Griff remained too caught up in his rules, it would be his loss. She would be happy.

Satisfied that her hair and makeup looked right, Jamie padded over to the closet. The dress had been a last-minute purchase on her way out of the upscale mall the other day. A bit more daring than her usual choice and in a smaller size, the dress had called to her from the store window. She pulled it off its hanger and slid the dress over her head. The soft material flowed over her body yet clung in all the right places. The tropical print had caught her eye, fun and reminding her of some of the beaches she had visited in the past ten years. The spaghetti straps left her shoulders bare, while the hemline flirted with her ankles. A deep slit up one side showed a fair amount of lightly tanned skin when she moved.

Jamie reached back in the closet for the light shrug she'd bought to go with the dress. Even though it was May, the nights could be cool. Grabbing her purse and phone, Jamie headed for the door. She stopped for a moment, hand on the doorknob, and concentrated on her breathing. In. Out. So what if Griff had never seen her dressed like this before? No reason to feel butterflies in the pit of her stomach. Right?

Shaking her head at her own foolishness, Jamie opened the door and crossed the suite to where he waited, seated on the couch.

"Sorry it took me so long. I guess I needed that nap more than I thought," she said by way of greeting.

Griff stood. And stared at her. Jamie fingered the clutch in her hands under his scrutiny.

"Wow," he said before taking a few steps toward her.

"Oh, this old thing? I've had this for two days now," she joked. Anything to break the tension.

He closed the distance between them. "You look beautiful," he murmured before kissing her cheek. "Shall we go?"

Griff held out his arm. Not wanting to leave him hanging, Jamie slipped her arm through his.

"You don't look so bad yourself, Mr. Layne." She fingered the material of his suit jacket. "Nice. Although you don't strike me as a suit kind of guy."

"Oh, you know me so well? Are you saying I can't wear a suit?"

His grin told her he hadn't taken offense.

She looked him up and down, from his slightly damp hair to his polished dress shoes.

"I never said you *couldn't* wear a suit, just that you didn't usually. You wear it fine."

And she didn't laugh at the slight red on the tips of his ears. Even though it was really cute.

"Well, shucks, ma'am, maybe I should wear one more often."

She laughed, punching his arm lightly.

"Let's get this over with," she said, tugging him toward the door.

"Don't sound too excited. Wouldn't want you to pull something," he joked and held the door for her.

They kept up the light banter all the way to the venue, a ritzy hotel in center city Philadelphia. She chewed on her lower lip as the valet drove away in their rental.

Griff took one of her hands in his, then led the way inside.

"You've got this, Jamie," he growled in her ear, sending shivers across her body. "And I've got you."

She didn't say anything but squeezed his hand. Signs for the reunion led them around the corner and down a carpeted hallway. Bits of conversation mingled with laughter as music spilled from the opened doors of a ballroom. She started to enter, still holding his hand when he stopped, forcing her to as well.

Before she could say anything, Griff took her in his arms and kissed her. Kissed the stuffing out of her, right there in the doorway. And when she started to relax into the kiss, he released her.

"There. Now let them ask questions," he smirked before leading her inside.

His words felt like a bucket of ice water over her head. The kiss had meant nothing to him. Well, nothing more than proof of their 'relationship.' It had meant a lot more to her. But there wasn't time to examine those feelings since they now stood in front of the registration table.

And manning it was no other than Mandy Simpkins Davis, former head cheerleader and wife of her long-lost crush. *Great!*

Mandy stood, cheerleader smile in place, and welcomed them.

"I'm so sorry, but I can't place your face," she told Jamie.

And why should she? Mandy had run in an entirely different circle than Jamie in school. She doubted the other woman knew her name even back then.

"No problem," Jamie muttered. She went to the Ls and picked up her name tag.

Mandy came out from behind the table, her eyes on Griff. "Now I know you didn't graduate with us. You, I would have remembered." She placed a hand on Griff's arm and actually batted her eyelashes at him.

Wasn't that only done in the movies?

Griff, bless him, addressed Mandy while Jamie fought back the desire to shake her to the roots of her colored hair.

"Hello. I'm Griff Layne, the luckiest guy in the room." He turned to Jamie, tucking her into his side with a strong arm around her waist. "And this is my girlfriend, Jamie Lawler."

Jamie smothered a laugh at his thickened southern accent. He really knew how to lay it on.

"Yes, Mandy, it's been a few years. Now if you'll excuse us, Griff and I are going to find the bar."

Griff flashed a smile at the sputtering Mandy and led Jamie away. Jamie relished the weight of his hand on her lower back. *Might as well enjoy it while I can.* They walked straight to the bar.

"May I have a beer, please? Whatever you have." He turned to Jamie. "What would you like?"

Jamie stepped up and smiled at the bartender who looked like he wasn't even old enough to drink.

"May I have a Diet Coke please?"

Griff raised one brow but didn't comment.

"What?" Jamie needed to keep her wits about her tonight. Once they had their drinks, they circled the room. His hand remained at her back. Jamie marveled at how seriously he took his role. She glanced through the crowd, looking for someone she knew. Everyone seemed vaguely familiar, yet high school felt like a thousand years ago.

Griff pointed to a table off to the side of the small dance floor. He handed his beer to her.

"Why don't you grab us a seat? I'll go score some of those appetizers you teased me with earlier."

He walked away before she could answer. Jamie headed for the table. She had just put down their drinks when a man approached her.

"Jamie Lawler? Wow, I almost didn't recognize you."

The man enveloped her in a hug, giving Jamie a moment to remember his name. She stepped back and grinned up at him.

"Drew Myers, how lovely to see you. How have you been?"

Drew, with whom she'd competed in Math Bowl, grinned down at her. The geeky kid who always seemed uncomfortable in his own skin had grown into his long limbs. Gone were the thick glasses and shy exterior. In their place stood a confident man.

"I'm great, Jamie, thanks. Wow, I haven't seen you since graduation. I'd about given up seeing you at one of these."

Before she could respond, a petite redhead appeared at his side. She was glowingly beautiful in a long dress that did nothing to hide her pregnant stomach.

"Hi there. I'm Tessa, Drew's wife. Nice to meet you."

"Honey, this is Jamie Lawler. She and I were math nerds together."

"Drew!" She turned to Jamie. "Please excuse my husband. Sometimes he fits his entire leg in his mouth."

Jamie laughed, already liking this woman. "He speaks the truth, I'm sorry to say. Drew and I were not exactly part of the in-crowd."

"Maybe, but that big brain of hers saved my skin all four years," came a masculine voice from behind her.

Jamie turned around. And there stood Chad Davis, star of all her teenage dreams.

Chapter Thirty-Five

"Reality is the name we give to our disappointments."
-Mason Cooley

Where was Griff? The thought popped into Jamie's head. The fact that Chad recognized her came a distant second. She glanced around, trying to find her pseudo date, but he was nowhere to be seen.

"Jamie, it's Chad. Don't you remember me?"

She turned back to face Chad and plastered a big smile on her face. "Of course, I do. How are you?"

Oddly enough, she found she didn't really care. But years of good manners being pounded into her head took over.

"Great! I'm living in LA now; just came back east for this. And to see my family, of course. How about you?"

"What?"

She'd tuned him out in her search for Griff in the crowd.

"I asked how you are, what you've been up to all these years."

"Oh, of course. Sorry." She turned back to face him fully. "I'm living in South Carolina near the beach. Have been since I graduated from college. I came in for a few days for this and to visit family also."

She turned to introduce Drew and his wife to Chad. The two men shook hands.

"Of course I remember Drew. How are you, man?"

Jamie stared at Chad, hardly believing the words coming from his mouth. He, and his football buddies, had not been kind to Drew in their high school years. Chad seemed to have forgotten that. Drew had not, if the tightness of his jaw meant anything.

"Excuse me, won't you?"

Jamie slipped away before anyone could answer. She circled the room, seeking Griff but not finding him anywhere. *Where could he be?* She accepted a shrimp puff from a passing waiter before continuing to search for Griff. When she didn't see him, she opened one of the French doors and stepped out onto the terrace for some air.

*****

Griff left the men's room and approached the table where he'd left Jamie. A couple sat there. His beer and Jamie's glass waited on the table.

"Excuse me, have you seen Jamie Lawler anywhere?"

The man stood up, approaching Griff with his hand outstretched.

"Hi. I'm Drew Myers. This is my wife, Tessa."

The pretty redhead stood to shake Griff's hand. The other hand rested on her rounded stomach.

"Nice to meet you both. I'm Griff Layne, and Jamie is my girlfriend. Sorry, but have you seen her anywhere? I went to get hors d'oeuvres, and she disappeared."

"She was here a moment ago. Then Chad came along, and

Jamie excused herself. She should be right back."

Griff's shoulders tensed at the mention of her old crush. He glanced around, but all he knew about Chad was that he was blonde.

"I'm sure she will be. I'll go see if I can find her, thanks."

Not knowing where to look, Griff headed to the edge of the room and circled it, glancing this way and that to find her. After a few frustrating moments and no Jamie in sight, he headed back toward the restrooms. Maybe she had ducked in there. Not wanting to seem like a perv, he waited a fair distance from the door, keeping an eye on the crowd as well.

After ten minutes, Griff gave up on the idea of her being in the restroom still. He circled the room once again. When he didn't spot her, he moved toward the doors leading outside.

And stopped in his tracks.

Jamie stood on the terrace. But she wasn't alone. She was kissing a tall, blond man. Knowing he could only be the infamous Chad Davis, Griff stood rooted to the spot. Jamie wanted this. She talked about Chad, and this reunion, for weeks. Seeing Chad again, and making sure he saw her, motivated her to make changes in her life. Griff held no claim on Jamie. His own stupidity had ensured that.

He took one last look at the couple, wrapped in each other's arms, before turning on his heel. Griff kept walking, not stopping until he rushed through the lobby doors. Knowing he couldn't stay here any longer, he hailed a cab idling at the curb. Once he got in, he gave the driver the name of their hotel in Bryn Mawr and slumped in the back seat. He would not think about the funny, little pain in his heart.

*****

"What are you doing?" Jamie cried as she tore herself out of Chad's arms. She took a few steps back, chest heaving. "Have you lost your mind? Your *wife* is in there!"

Chad took a few steps toward her, trapping her against the wall.

"Wife? Oh, you mean Mandy. Nah, we divorced a few years ago."

He looked her up and down in the dim moonlight. Instead of making her happy, his attention brought nausea.

"Oh. I'm sorry to hear that. Nevertheless, I should get back to my date."

She tried to step around him, but Chad stepped into her path.

"Why don't you stay here with me instead?"

He leaned in, running a hand down her bare arm. She could smell the alcohol on his breath. Cold tendrils of fear trickled through her.

Jamie straightened to full height which, even with her heels, left her far shorter than him. And he outweighed her by at least sixty pounds. Surely, he didn't mean to press the issue. But she knew that alcohol didn't help the situation.

Chad leaned in once more, clearly intent on kissing her. She pulled back and ducked, avoiding his lips.

"Chad, I have to go back inside and find Griff. Please let go of me."

She hoped her fear didn't leach through to her voice. She didn't want to give him any advantage.

"What's the matter, Jamie? I thought this was what you wanted." He leered down at her. "At least you did in high school."

How could she have ever liked this guy?

"Back off right now, if you don't want my knee in your

groin."

That got his attention. He held up both hands as though in surrender.

"Fine, be that way," he grumbled.

Jamie turned and race-walked back inside. When she closed the terrace door behind her, the tightness in her muscles released. She headed over to where Drew and Tessa sat.

She dropped down in the chair where their abandoned drinks sat.

"Hey, we met your boyfriend, Jamie. Didn't he find you?" asked Drew.

"Oh, Griff came back to the table?" She glanced around, not seeing him. "Where did he go?"

Drew shrugged. "He went to find you."

Tessa laughed softly. "Seems like you two may be passing each other in the night."

"My wife, as usual, is right. Please join us. He'll come back, and here you'll be."

"Okay, thanks. I'm sure you're right."

Jamie enjoyed catching up with Drew and getting to know his wife. After getting his medical degree from Northeastern University, the couple married and stayed in the Boston area. Jamie exchanged contact information with them and asked about their pregnancy. The proud father-to-be dragged out his phone and showed Jamie the ultrasound pictures. She oohed and awed as expected but kept one eye on the room, seeking Griff.

When an hour had passed, Jamie gave up on Griff returning. She'd panicked at first, convinced something bad had happened. Various scenarios, one worse than the previous, raced through her head. But he had her phone number. Surely, he would have called her if something happened. *Then, where was he?*

Not sure what to do, Jamie tuned back into the conversation at their table. Along with Drew and Tessa, another couple, Karen and Tim Brady, had joined them. Karen had graduated with them and still lived in the Philadelphia area. Jamie enjoyed a spirited conversation about what had changed in the area and what had not. Currently, Karen and Drew argued over gentrification happening in some areas of the city.

"Jamie help me out here," Drew begged. "Karen believes that cleaning up certain areas will mean losing the original charm. Tell her she's wrong."

"For the record, I am not in favor of stripping away what makes this city great. But you have to admit there are areas that need help. A lot of help," Karen countered.

Tessa ended the debate by standing and turning to Jamie.

"I think it's time for a ladies' room break. Jamie why don't you come with me? And yes, I know I went not long ago, Drew." She smiled down at her husband. eyes soft. "You try growing a human whose favorite sport is jumping on your bladder."

Jamie joined Tessa and the two made their escape. Once inside, both women confessed to not actually having to go and laughed at their joke.

"Sorry about that. I just needed a break. You can tell those two used to debate in high school," Tessa said.

"I know. They always were the ones to beat. And don't apologize. I needed a break, too."

Jamie stepped up to the mirror. She leaned in to fix her lipstick when she caught Tessa's gaze in the mirror.

"Feel free to tell me to mind my own business. Drew always kids with me about being nosy. Well, maybe not kids.

But what's the deal with you and Griff? He seemed, uh, almost frantic when he couldn't find you earlier. Then he just disappears? Doesn't make any sense."

Jamie's shoulders drooped. She turned to face Tessa, leaning back against the counter.

"I wish I knew. I passed confused, moved along to worried, and now I'm sliding into angry. Why would he leave without so much as a word to me? No text. No call. No anything. What am I supposed to think?"

"It does seem odd. How long have you guys been together? Has he ever done anything like this before? And tell me if I'm prying."

Jamie hesitated, not sure how to respond. And then she just blurted it all out.

"We met in March, and we are not a 'couple.' We're, uh, friends? He owns the gym I work out at."

"Oh, you're not together? Really?"

"Not even a little, although not for lack of me trying." She sighed and then filled in Tessa on all the gory details. She folded her hands together and waited for whatever the other woman might have to say about this.

"And you think he doesn't have feelings for you? I think you're wrong," Tessa said.

"Wow. That's not what I expected to hear. But you're wrong. Or if he does, he refuses to act on them, in which case he may as well not have feelings at all."

Exhausted by everything, Jamie flopped down on the couch in the outer room. Tessa came and lowered herself next to Jamie.

"That gets harder with every passing day. Now tell me this. If Griff didn't have any feelings for you, why is he here? Why would he fly hundreds of miles to hang out with you and be dragged to a reunion for people he never met?"

Good questions.

"I don't know. I started going to the gym after getting the reunion save-the-date in the mail. I wanted to, uh, make some changes before coming. And Griff helped me to do that. We sort of became friends. And one day, I blurted out my long ago feelings for Chad and how I hadn't seen him since graduation. Next thing I know, he volunteered to be my plus one. He had dinner with my family, and even I can barely tolerate them." She stood, pacing the length of the small room.

"I'd join you in wearing out the carpeting, but getting up and down isn't easy anymore. Besides, I'm comfortable. But that's exactly my point, Jamie. Why would he do any of those things if he didn't care?"

Jamie threw her hands in the air and groaned.

"I have no idea. Who can figure out men?" She stopped pacing. Her new shoes were meant to look sexy, not actually walk in. "Right before coming here tonight, I suggested skipping the whole thing and going for pizza. But Griff said I had to face my past, move on. So here I am, only without him." She barked out a laugh that held no humor.

Tessa maneuvered her pregnant body up and off the couch. "Now, I really have to pee. After all, it's been thirty minutes. Hold that thought."

Jamie nodded and turned back to the mirror. Despite more makeup than she normally wore, the areas under her eyes appeared dark, bruised. Lack of sleep would do that. Usually, at this time of the year, she'd fly up for a brief visit with her family and then jet off to some fabulous, tropical locale for a week or two. Plenty of time to catch up on sleep.

This year, she'd taken off the same amount of time but would be flying home in the morning. She and Sam had a lot to do before opening their new business. They had already met with Gavin, the contractor friend of Jack's. By now, he was most likely already starting on the necessary renovations.

First thing Monday morning, Jamie would start buying everything they needed for the office. She had decided to start with the bigger ticket items like desks and office machinery. She actually looked forward to this. Bargain hunting was practically an Olympic sport for her.

"Sorry, that took so long," Tessa said as she approached a sink to wash her hands.

"No worries. I was staring at the bags under my eyes. And plotting out my next few days."

The two women headed for the door.

"Does that include having a heart to heart with a certain gorgeous man?' Tessa laughed. "Don't mind me; pregnancy hormones."

"I'm not sure." She told Tessa about her plans for their new business.

"Oh, that sounds exciting. Good for you!"

"I wish I knew what happened with Griff. Why he left without saying anything to me," Jamie said on a sigh.

"It does seem strange. The last time I saw him, Griff was heading toward the French doors. Then he turned and practically ran from the ballroom. Odd."

Everything in Jamie turned to ice. The sounds of the room faded away as a thought took hold in her brain. *No!*

"The French doors? When was that?"

Tessa turned to her, a frown on her face.

"I'm not really sure. He talked to Drew and me for a few moments before setting out to find you. A few minutes after that, he doubled back by the table and headed toward the doors."

And saw Chad kissing me...

"I have to go."

Jamie raced back to their table to grab her purse and keys. She said a quick goodbye to everyone, promising to stay in touch and then turned toward the ballroom exit.

She had to find Griff. Now.

Chapter Thirty-Six

"Desperation is sometimes as powerful an inspirer as genius."
-Benjamin Disraeli

The hotel room door banged back against the wall. Jamie flung her heels down, having removed them in the elevator. Her poor feet felt bruised from a few hours in them. But none of that mattered. She'd driven from the reunion to the hotel in record time, desperate to see him. She had to find Griff and set the record straight. He might know what he thought he saw, but he didn't know the truth.

She was falling for him.

On a half sob, she called his name, but her voice echoed off the walls of the empty suite. No sign of life greeted her in the living area nor in the small kitchen. She continued on to the partially ajar door of his bedroom. Heart racing, Jamie lifted her hand to knock, listening for any sounds from within. Nothing. She knocked and softly called his name.

No answer.

Takin a deep breath, Jamie pushed the door open. Only moonlight seeping in from the window lit the room.

"Griff?"

Nothing.

Jamie flicked on the wall switch, flooding the room with light. The empty room. She crossed to the closet and opened the door. Empty hangers hung on the rail. His suitcase was missing.

She backed out of the closet and sank onto the edge of his bed. He was gone. Griff had left. Why? Where had he gone?

On automatic pilot, Jamie left his room and crossed to hers. She stripped off her new dress, grabbed her pajamas and headed for the bathroom. Seeing the empty spot that had held his shaving stuff brought tears to her eyes. She washed her face, brushed her teeth, and went to bed.

But not to sleep. Hours later, she tossed and turned, trying to find a comfortable position. But nothing worked. She missed Griff. She wanted, needed really, to talk to him. To explain what he had seen. To tell him how she felt.

At seven in the morning, her alarm woke her from a troubled sleep. She'd dreamed of Griff, but in her dreams, she could never reach him. She called out to him over and over again, but her cries fell on deaf ears. When she finally made her way to him, on the crowded dance floor from the reunion, Mandy turned her head, grinning at Jamie. The other woman laughed, saying, "You couldn't have Chad, and now you can't have Griff either."

When Jamie reached out to touch his shoulder, the Griff in her dream turned his head and glanced coldly at her, as though he had no idea who she was. Then he spun Mandy in his arms and away from Jamie. She stood on the dance floor watching them.

Jamie reached over, shutting off her alarm before flopping back in bed. Her eyes burned. Her throat ached. At some point, she must have cried herself to sleep. But she remembered seeing the time after four in the morning, so she couldn't have had much sleep.

Her flight wasn't until early afternoon, but between traffic, turning in the rental, and security, Jamie knew she didn't have a ton of time. She got up and showered, throwing on comfortable clothing for the plane ride home.

After packing and ensuring she hadn't forgotten anything, Jamie headed to the kitchen to grab a bottle of water for the road. Her stomach growled, and she vowed to hit Wawa once again for a breakfast sandwich. *Screw the calories! If ever there was a time for stress eating…*

A piece of the hotel's stationary on the counter next to the fridge caught her eye. She picked it up and forgot to breath.

"Jamie, I'm sorry I didn't get a chance to say goodbye. But you got what you wanted all these years. The one that got away. I'm happy for you. I caught a late flight. See you at the gym. -G"

Tears burned her eyes, making the strong script waver in front of her. She hadn't gotten what she wanted. The 'one that got away' had taken a plane home. Without her. Jamie slid the paper into her purse and gathered her things. She left the suite without looking back, thoughts already hundreds of miles away.

Hours later, Jamie slid out of the back seat of her Uber. After handing the driver a tip, she gathered her luggage and walked to the front door of her house. Once inside, she flipped through mail on the entry way table. Sam had been by.

"Mreow," caught her attention. Fiona waddled over to Jamie, nudging her calf with a head butt. That was her cat's way of showing affection.

"I missed you, too," she told the cantankerous feline as she scooped her up and snuggled her.

After a moment, Fiona protested, and Jamie set her down. The cat walked to her empty dish and looked back over one shoulder as if to remind Jamie of her purpose.

"I'm fairly sure Sam fed you already, but I guess you can have a kitty treat. What'll it be today? Salmon?"

Fiona's ears perked at the name of her favorite flavor treat. She followed Jamie to the cabinet that held them.

"My life should be so easy," Jamie complained to her cat. "When you want something, you meow long enough to annoy me into giving in."

Jamie stopped, box of treats in hand, when inspiration struck.

"That's it!" she told the uninterested cat. Dropping a few treats into her bowl, Jamie took her luggage and unpacked as ideas percolated in her brain. There was no reason she couldn't have what she wanted also. And that was Griff.

*****

That night, Griff sat on Jack's couch sipping a beer and not at all interested in the game on TV. Jamie occupied his thoughts as they had since he left her in Philadelphia last night. If he were honest, she'd wormed her way in a long time ago. Right around the time they'd met. The memory of her talking the machines into not hurting her brought a smile to his face.

"I thought you'd forgotten how to do that," Jack snarked from his seat.

"Huh?" Griff asked, not even pretending to have been listening.

Jack smiled and pointed to his mouth. "You, smiling. First time I've seen it all day."

Griff stared at his best friend. He wasn't wrong, but that

didn't mean he would admit anything. "What's next? A pedicure? Maybe some white wine as we discuss our feelings?" He smirked and took another sip of his beer.

"What crawled up you and died?" Jack asked without any trace of his trademark smirk.

Griff put down his beer and dragged a hand through his hair. *Where to start?* But his friend, who knew him better than almost anyone in the world, beat him to the punch.

"Something happened in Pennsylvania."

As much as he didn't care to talk about it, Griff like that there wasn't a question in there. Jack knew.

"Chad happened. Well, Chad and Jamie happened."

He would have laughed at the widening of Jack's eyes if his heart didn't hurt so much.

"Wow. You're going to have to say more than that, Griff."

With a sigh, Griff poured out the whole story, start to finish, including her difficult family and catching the two of them kissing on the terrace.

"And then what? How did you leave it with Jamie?"

"I didn't."

"Huh? What does that even mean?"

The back of Griff's neck grew warm. He wasn't pleased with how he'd ended things. The more he dwelled on it, the more he felt like a spoiled brat who took his toys and went home. Time to man up. He looked Jack in the eye.

"I flew home early. Well, late last night but earlier than planned."

"Oh."

"Oh? That's all you have to say?"

"I'm not sure what to say. That doesn't seem like you. Running away in the night."

"You didn't see them." Griff tried to not grind his back

molars. "What would you do if you saw Sam kissing another guy?" He knew as soon as the words left his mouth, they had been the wrong ones.

Jack agreed.

"Sam and I are friends. She can kiss whoever she wishes. Just like you and Jamie."

The words sounded right, except for his friend's hands clenched into fists.

"And you wouldn't be pissed if you caught her kissing some other man?"

Jack's shoulders slumped. Griff regretted his words. "I'm sorry, man. That was a low blow."

Jack lifted his gaze to Griff. "Yes, it was. Jamie doesn't answer to you. You've made that abundantly clear to her. You two are 'friends,' right, Griff? Isn't that what you keep telling her? What you keep telling yourself?" He blew out a deep breath. "The difference between you and I is you have a choice. I don't."

Griff dropped his eyes to the floor, unsure how to answer. His friend had a point. He had sent Jamie all kinds of mixed messages. She deserved better. She deserved a man willing to show her how he felt. And if that man was Chad Davis... *NO!*

"No. I won't let it happen." He jumped up, pacing around Jack's living room. "He's not good enough for her."

"The ex-boyfriend, I presume?" Jack asked.

"He's not her ex anything," Griff corrected through gritted teeth. "He had his chance, years ago, and never even noticed her. Never noticed how wonderful she is. Never noticed how smart and funny."

"But you did."

"You're damn right I did."

"Of course, you also threw that away."

"I did that, too." Griff flopped back down on the couch. He reached for his beer and emptied it in one long swallow. "I'm going to need more of these if you have them."

Jack grinned and jumped up. "Coming right up," he joked before heading into the kitchen.

"And then I'm going to need a plan."

*****

The next day, Jamie sat in a booth at La Hacienda, waiting to have lunch with Sam. Knowing they were dining here had meant extra time at the gym this morning. Now she could eat tortilla chips and salsa without worrying about the carbs. Not finding Griff at Getting It Done had spurred her on further. There had been nothing but radio silence since Saturday night. And while she could just as easily reach out to him, she hadn't. What she needed to say should be done in person, not on the phone or worse, via text. She would have to wait. In the meantime, she and Sam would concentrate on their new business. Thinking about it, and telling the dragon they quit, brought a smile to her face.

"Got started without me, I see," joked Sam as she slid in the booth opposite from Jamie. She nodded toward the basket of chips before taking a few.

"I did my time at the gym. I can have as many as I want." Jamie grabbed a few more for herself.

"And how was Griff? Did you give him a piece of your mind? And mine?"

Jamie shook her head. The tortilla chip turned to dust in her mouth. "No, I did not see him. Who knows? Maybe he's still in Pennsylvania."

Sam tilted her head as if trying to study her. And Jamie

knew what was coming. Her friend wasn't going to let her off that easily.

"If only there was a way to contact someone. To talk with them but not in person." Sam, always one for theatrics, rapped her palm against her own forehead. "Oh, that's right, there is. It's called a phone." She grinned before dipping another chip in the hot salsa she preferred.

Jamie was spared from answering by the arrival of their waiter, Miguel, who happened to own the restaurant.

"Ah, my two favorite ladies. What can I get for you today? Wait, let me guess. Sam, you will have the taco salad. And Jamie, you will have my most delicious fish tacos, pico on the side. Am I right?"

"You know us too well, Miguel," Jamie commented. "And as boring as that makes me, I will have the fish tacos, thanks."

"Well, I'm not boring," Sam said. "I'll have the beef empanadas, please."

"Excellent choice, both of you. Your lunches will be out in a minute."

"Wow, spicing it up, huh?" Jamie joked.

"Yes, I am. And nice try, but I'm not letting you off the hook. Why haven't you called him?"

"And say what, exactly? 'Sorry you saw Chad force his tongue down my throat. It's not what you thought'."

"That's a start. Then maybe you could tell him that after years of pining for some guy from childhood, when the chance finally came, you picked Griff instead." Sam smirked at Jamie's expression. "Just a thought."

"This is not about me. This is about Griff and his ridiculous rules. We were alone together for days up north. Not a gym he owned in sight. He had ample opportunity to act on his feelings. If he has any."

And he did, damn him. At least she thought he did. There had been several times when he seemed like he wanted to say something, do something, about their 'friendship,' but he never did. But she wasn't telling Sam that.

"I will explain it to him. When I see him. This is not a conversation for the phone." She blew out a breath. "Now, for the love of all things holy, can we please talk about something else? Oh, I know! How about the business we're about to open together?"

There must have been a hint of desperation in her voice because Sam dropped it. At least for now. Jamie knew her better than that.

"Well, while you were gone, Gavin started on the house. You have to come over after lunch and see it."

"I'd love to. Tell me more."

Chapter Thirty-Seven

"Nothing ventured, nothing gained. And venture belongs to the adventurous."
-Navjot Singh Sidhu

The next morning, Jamie dragged her tired butt out of bed. Not as early as normal since she was still on vacation, but still earlier than she wanted. She'd gone to Sam's after lunch to see the beginning of the construction and stayed for dinner. Dinner had turned into talking well into the evening. By the time she drove home, Jamie had fallen into a dreamless sleep.

The initial work on the house pleased her, as did the plans Gavin shared with her. About her age, the contractor poured over the plans with her and later asked her for coffee. Although he was handsome, not to mention single and owned his own business, she felt nothing other than interest in the project. And there was still the unsettled issue of Griff. She said thank you but no and walked away.

Knowing she was putting off the inevitable, she pulled on a set of the new workout clothes she had bought in Pennsylvania. Pleased that they still fit after her binge-eating comfort food on the way to the airport Sunday, she left the house with a smile.

Maybe Griff would be at the gym today. Maybe not. Palm Harbor was a small town. She'd find him. And when she did, she'd give him a piece of her mind, as Sam had said. Like life is short, and it wasn't every day you met someone with whom you clicked. And whether or not he cared to admit it, they shared a chemistry. And that didn't happen all the time; Gavin being a case in point.

By the time she finished the short drive to the gym, Jamie had worked herself into quite a lather. What was wrong with Griff? She was a catch. She was smart. She was about to own her own business. Hoping her head of steam would translate into a great workout, Jamie bounded from her car and marched to the door. She swiped her access card while all sorts of things to tell Griff danced through her brain.

And then she walked right into the door. *Even I'm not that clumsy.* Jamie looked at the door. No sign stating they were closed. She swiped her card again, this time attempting to open it more carefully. Nothing. She peered in through the glass and saw more than a few people working out. *Hmmm...*

"Excuse me, dear," came a voice from behind her.

Jamie turned to see Miss Harriett dressed in one of her endless matching jogging suits, this one trimmed in leopard print. The fact that she was also wearing bright red lipstick and pearls never failed to delight Jamie.

"Good morning, Miss Harriett," she greeted the old woman.

"Good morning, dear. You're getting a late start this morning, aren't you?"

Jamie smothered her laughter. Griff had warned her about the octogenarian, whom he swore was a spy in a past life. Miss Harriett knew everything about everyone.

"I am indeed. But I'm on vacation this week. I slept in."

"Ah, I remember those days. Well, have a lovely day."

Miss Harriett stepped around Jamie and swiped her card. The door clicked open and in she went. And let the door shut in Jamie's face.

Jamie knocked on the door. "Miss Harriett, can you let me in, please? My card doesn't seem to work today."

The little old woman shook her head. "Sorry, dear, but you have to be a member."

Miss Harriett walked away before Jamie could respond. And even through the glass, she heard a chuckle. *WTH?*

Not sure what to do, Jamie turned around to walk back to her car. And then stopped dead in her tracks. Griff stood ten feet away, looking better than he should, in a pair of shorts and sleeveless workout T.

"Hey," she mumbled because words escaped her. All of her brilliant thoughts from the car vanished.

"Hey," he said in return with a smile on his face.

Damn the man and his irresistible dimples.

"I'm glad you're here." She held up the offending access card. "There's a problem with my card."

"Oh?"

His calmness raised her temper.

Jamie retraced her steps to the door, once again swiping her card. Nothing. She turned back to a grinning Griff.

"See what I mean?"

"I do." Griff closed the distance between them. Then, without warning, he plucked the card from her fingers. "These are only for members," he scolded.

"What?" she sputtered. "I am a member. I paid my dues this month and last month and the month before." She shut her mouth before she said something else.

Griff, damn him, took a big step toward her. He reached out to push a stray hair back behind her ear.

"If you check your bank account, you'll find I have refunded your money for this month. Seeing how you're not a member here anymore."

Words failed her. She stared at Griff, trying to make sense of what he said. Lost in thought, she barely registered the door opening behind her.

"Kiss her already for goodness sake," came Miss Harriett's voice.

And in front of her the tips of Griff's ears grew red. He looked around Jamie at the older woman.

"I'm getting to that part, if you give me a second." Then he glanced down at Jamie. "I am getting to that part, but first I have something to explain."

Jamie nodded, not able to form a reply over the buzzing in her head. *He was going to kiss her?*

Griff took her hands in his and waited until Jamie raised her gaze to his. "I'm an idiot. Let's start there."

Jamie bit her lip to stop her grin. "Seems like a good place to start." She wasn't letting him off easily…

Griff returned her grin, then he blew out a breath.

"I told myself I was doing the right thing, keeping you at a distance. I couldn't have been more wrong."

"Go on," she encouraged.

"You're not going to make this easy for me, are you? Fair enough. I thought I should keep my distance, and then by the time I figured out the depth of my feelings for you…"

"I knew it!" Jamie cried out. "Oh, sorry. Continue."

"As I was saying, before I was interrupted, by the time I figured out my feelings, it was too late." He stopped at the vigorous shaking of her head. "I thought it was too late. We were in Philadelphia, and then you mentioned Chuck."

"Chad," she automatically corrected.

"What's his name," Griff reiterated. "That night, before the reunion when you wanted to ditch and go for pizza, I was an idiot again. I should have said heck yeah. But I believed you needed to see it through. See how you felt about Chaz all these years later."

"I didn't kiss Chad. He kissed me. But you didn't give me the chance to tell you," Jamie pointed out.

His eyes rounded at that bit of information. Encouraged, Jamie rushed on.

"Chad followed me out onto the terrace when I was searching for you." She poked him in the chest with a finger to drive home her point. "He cornered me and kissed me before I figured out his intention. And then he wouldn't let me leave."

Griff's face hardened in a way she had never before seen.

"He what?"

She covered his fisted hands with her own.

"He was drunk. I may have threatened to knee him if he didn't let me pass."

"For the love of all things holy, kiss her already!" came from an agitated Miss Harriett.

"She has a point," commented a very amused Jack, whom Jamie just noticed leaning against the wall of the building, arms folded over his chest. Sam, standing next to him, waved wildly to Jamie.

"You kiss him if he doesn't," her best friend advised.

Griff turned to face the growing crowd.

"You guys are worse than the old men in the balcony from the Muppets," Griff admonished.

"Oh, he means Statler and Waldorf. Those guys crack me up," Miss Harriett cackled.

"Okay, let me cut to the chase, since the peanut gallery won't stop giving me advice. I love that you have no idea how sweet, funny, and sexy you are. I love that you came here, way outside of your comfort zone, to make a positive change in your life. I love that you split your meals with me when you can't decide your favorite. I even love that you kicked my ass in miniature golf. And gloated about it!"

Anything else he would have said was cut off by Jamie's kiss. She was done waiting for things to happen to her. She took control. After a moment of surprise, Griff recovered and slanted his mouth over hers for a better angle. Memories of their first kiss floated through her brain before feeling took over. She pressed into his hard body, reveling in the feel of him against her.

When she finally broke the kiss, they both gulped in air. Griff rested his forehead against hers.

"Did I mention the fact that I love you, Jamie Lawler?"

She grinned as the crowd broke out in a cheer. She specifically made out Sam's raucous whistle.

"It took you long enough, young man," called Miss Harriett.

"I thought you couldn't get involved with a client," Jamie murmured.

"That's why your access card doesn't work anymore. You're no longer a member, which means you're no longer my client."

Jamie tilted back her head in order to see his expression. His green eyes sparkled. She burst out laughing.

"Whoever thought being 'fired' would feel so good?" She stroked a hand along the line of his jaw. "Turns out *you* were the one that, almost, got away."

Griff sealed it with another kiss while the crowd cheered.

The End

Acknowledgments

First and foremost, this book is for all the people who helped to keep me sane in this ridiculous time. The COVID 19 pandemic swept across our planet, bringing with it destruction and change unlike anything we'd ever experienced. This book was meant to be finished and released in March…and clearly that didn't happen. So thank you to the people who kept me going and got me back on track. You know who you are.

Thank you to my lovely niece, Justine Holtz, for answering my idiotic questions about being an accountant. I appreciate your patience.

Thank you to Jeni Burns, my intrepid editor, for saying, "Hey, are you sure this isn't going to be a series? Because I can see…" And my first attempt at writing a standalone is now the first novel in my brand new Palm Harbor series. So thanks for putting words to the ideas swirling in my mind.

Thank you to Margie Greenhow, PA (extraordinaire) for saying other things. Like "When will you finish the book?" "When will editing be done?" "When's release day?" "When will ARCs be ready?"

Thank you to Rebecca Pau of The Final Wrap for this amazing cover. Again! And once again, all I said was, "gym."

Thank you to Chelly Hoyle Peeler, my proofer and formatter. Everyone says to just format your own book. Clearly people who don't actually know me. I always feel badly because by the time Chelly touches the book, I'm over it and just want it out in the world. Thank you for your wicked speed and humor.

What's Next?

Honestly, this book started as a standalone. One book. One story. One couple. But then I fell a little in love with Palm Harbor. And Sam and Jack. Between her sass and his laid-back flirting, how could I just let them go? Well, obviously I could not. And so, here's a sneak peek of Leaving the Friend Zone (tentative title).

Prologue

Brilliant sunlight streamed through a crack in the curtain, temporarily blinding Sam. She squeezed her eyes closed against the onslaught. Although she normally enjoyed the brightness and warmth of the almost summer sunshine (how did people survive in places like Seattle?), today was the exception. It might have had something to do with the marching band performing in her head. Even her eyelashes hurt. Was that a thing?

Pain reliever! That's what she needed. But that meant getting up and traipsing into the bathroom, a feat that seemed Herculean at the moment. Instead, Sam burrowed back into the pillow beneath her aching head. Maybe wrapping it in a cocoon of goose feathers would help. She lay still for a second to test her theory. And while it did take the edge off her pain, the down pillow did nothing for the layers of wool on her tongue.

And her head still hurt…

She drew in a deep breath, drawing the strength to make it to the bathroom and prayed the vague queasiness in her stomach didn't escalate when she moved. Just as she prepared to get up, a horrible thought crawled into her aching brain.

She didn't have curtains in her bedroom…

Where was she? Sam clutched the sheet to her body, almost afraid to look beneath it. Was she naked?

The mattress dipped as a solid wall of warm muscle flanked her back. She squelched a scream when a tanned, muscular arm encircled her waist, drawing her back further.

And then she remembered.

"Tequila Makes Her Clothes Fall Off" by Joe Nichols sprang to mind. Apparently, she had something in common with the fictional subject of the country hit. And flashes of last night exploded in her brain. Memories of *him.*

What had she done?

"Good morning, darlin," rumbled a deep, male voice from behind her, sealing her fate.

"Is it?" Sam asked with a touch of bitch to her tone.

She pulled at the sheet, desperate to cover herself, and rose from the bed. She grasped the headboard for a moment to steady herself before glancing around for her clothing.

"Little late for modest, don't you think?"

Sam whirled, dropping the sheet. He had a point. She breathed a sigh of relief to find she still wore her underwear. And though they didn't cover a whole lot, she'd worn less on the beach.

"You're right. Of course, a gentleman would not have reminded me," she drawled in her best debutante voice.

"Thought you knew me better by now," Jack quipped with laughter in his voice.

Find your clothes and leave!

The advantage at being at his instead of hers. Easier to leave than to kick Jack out.

Sam thumped across his bedroom floor, plucking items of her clothing as she went. And ignoring the throbbing on her head and the eyes glued to her butt.

"If you'll excuse me," she snarled before locking herself in his bathroom.

Safe for the moment, she bought a few minutes by taking care of the necessities of life. And getting dressed. After washing her hands and splashing cold water on her face, Sam stared at her reflection in the mirror.

Blood shot eyes stared back. She wiped away the last remnants of mascara. That had been the last of her makeup. Nothing she could do about it now. Or the rat's nest that her hair had morphed into. Reaching into the pocket of her linen pants, now crumpled beyond salvation, Sam grabbed a ponytail holder. She wrestled her wild curls into a messy bun. It would have to do. Then squaring her shoulders, Sam left the sanctuary of his bathroom.

She wasn't prepared for the sight of a shirtless Jack sitting up against the headboard, navy blue sheet bunched at his waist. Instead of looking 'ridden hard put away wet' as her dead grandmother would say, Jack looked like sex on a stick.

Bastard!

Summoning generations of Hardy women, Sam straightened her spine, pulling herself to her full height. Then she fixed her eyes on Jack's. "I'll be leaving now. This, uh, whatever this was, remains between us. Understood?" She waved a hand between them as if to underscore her words.

"Yes, ma'am," replied Jack with a glint in his eye she didn't trust.

"Good. I'll be going now." Sam turned to leave when Jack cleared his throat. She halted but didn't bother to turn back to face him.

"One question before you leave. Does this mean I've left the friendship zone?"

About the Author

Kimberley O'Malley is a transplant to Charlotte, North Carolina from the frozen North. She is learning to say y'all but draws the line at sweet tea. Sarcasm is an art form in her world. She writes small town Contemporary romances and hilarious Cozy Mysteries. When not writing, she is a full-time nurse and part-time soccer Mom, but not necessarily in that order. She shares her life with an amazing husband of almost 25 years, two teenagers, and two sweet but mischievous Shetland Sheepdogs, Molly & Callie.

To ensure you're up to date with all the shenanigans and news, click the link to follow along with my monthly newsletter: http://eepurl.com/dgonEX

Are you following the Author?

Facebook - https://www.facebook.com/KOMalley67/
Instagram -
   https://www.instagram.com/kimberleyomalley67/
Twitter - https://twitter.com/K_OMalley67
Website - www.kimberleyomalley.com
Amazon Author Bio -
   www.amazon.com/author/kimberleyomalley
Good Reads Profile - http://bit.ly/grKOM
Book Bub Profile - http://bit.ly/bookbubKOM

www.ingramcontent.com/pod-product-compliance
Lightning Source LLC
Chambersburg PA
CBHW071848220626
47052CB00002B/15